The only signs of movement came from one corner, where a small semicircle of stouthearted or ghoulish souls had gathered.

Jenny found herself walking toward them, compelled by some force she couldn't have named if offered a million pounds. People parted easily to let her pass. Being so tall, Jenny could clearly see between the shoulders of two male guests the sight that changed the ballroom from one of gaiety to tragedy.

Justin lay on his back, his eyes wide open, staring at nothing. His hands were clenched into fists, but whether it was pain, rage or fear that had clenched them in those final moments of life, Jenny would never know. His legs were bent, his head thrown right back. His mouth was open, and just a trace of saliva gleamed on his chin. He'd obviously had some kind of convulsion before dying.

It seemed to Jenny, still reeling under the influence of shock, that it was a very inappropriate way for someone of Justin's elegance and beauty to die, and she felt a sudden and overwhelmingly fierce rush of rage wash over her.

★

D0752415

BIRTHDAYS
CAN BE MURDER
JOYCE CATO

W💠RLDWIDE®

TORONTO • NEW YORK • LONDON
AMSTERDAM • PARIS • SYDNEY • HAMBURG
STOCKHOLM • ATHENS • TOKYO • MILAN
MADRID • WARSAW • BUDAPEST • AUCKLAND

Recycling programs
for this product may
not exist in your area.

BIRTHDAYS CAN BE MURDER

A Worldwide Mystery/March 2010

First published by Robert Hale Ltd.

ISBN-13: 978-0-373-26791-0

Copyright © 2010 by Joyce Cato

Printed in U.S.A.

PROLOGUE

I⟨T⟩ W⟨AS⟩ A lovely spring dawn in deepest, rural England.

And in one particular garden, everything was awake and busy. Bees buzzed in the flowering cherry trees, birds patrolled the well-cut lawns for worms and grubs, and in a large, deep pond, ornamental carp checked the surface for flies and other tasty morsels.

The gently floating body of the young man in the water didn't seem to bother them at all. Perhaps because he did nothing to disturb them, but simply floated placidly wherever the slight warm breezes took him. His short fair hair spread around his head like river weed and his wide blue eyes stared serenely at the azure sky above him.

He was, of course, quite dead.

A grey wagtail chinked up and down the bank of the attractive, lily-strewn pond, looking for a nesting site, while in the large, recently modernized country house a hundred yards away, its human inhabitants began to stir.

A little while later, a rather disreputable bicycle creaked its way up the sun-drenched drive as the old gardener arrived from the nearby village. He sighed as he parked the bike beside a brand new garden shed and looked around. There was nobody in sight, which meant that his temporary help was late, yet again.

And as he was soon to discover, 'late' was exactly the right word for him.

ONE

THE HOT MAY sun shone down blithely on the green corn-fields, lush water meadows, grazing cattle and scattered copses of Rousham Green. Jenny Starling turned her ancient cherry-red van onto the main village lane, but even with all the windows rolled down, she still felt uncomfortably flushed.

It was a Friday morning, and nearly everyone had deserted the small village for their daily commute to work. Only up at The Beeches were people still stirring at just gone 9.30 in the morning.

A white-haired man dressed in baggy trousers and a loose-fitting shirt looked up from his task of hoeing the weeds out of some rose beds as the bright little van came through the main gates, and he paused to watch it come towards him. Just beginning to rust in places, he could hear the engine protest as it went down into first gear and he wondered, with a grin, how on earth it had managed to pass its MOT.

As if reading his mind, the van's exhaust gave a jaunty and defiant little backfire as it swept past him, and the gardener could just make out the driver—a woman with a shoulder-length cascade of jet-black hair—give a little grimace in response as it did so.

With a shrug, the man got back to work, wondering what someone driving such a disreputable-looking machine could want with the rich and rather supercilious inhabitants of the big house.

The lime and beech trees forming the avenue that led to The Beeches widened out into a spacious semicircle around the house itself, and as Jenny drove towards it, she spotted a gravelled area that she assumed was used as a car park. She stopped the car for a few moments to study the building, and decided that she rather approved of it. Square and simple in shape, it was almost certainly Georgian in date, with row upon row of large sash windows at the front. It was built of good solid Cotswold stone, glowing at the moment like clotted cream in the hot spring sunshine. There was pretty variegated ivy creeping along the south face, and a splendid Morning Glory was just beginning to bloom over the classical pillared porch.

She was beginning to look forward to catering the big dual birthday party that was to be held here this weekend. But then, cooking always made her feel happy.

She pulled up and parked under the shade of a nearby lime tree, turned off the engine, and stepped out.

Jenny was six feet and one inch tall, with a heavy bone structure that was well padded, and curvaceous in many places. Men tended to be either fascinated by her or terrified—or occasionally both. Jenny had become rather adept at cherry-picking the fascinated ones over the years, but had been careful to remain resolutely single. Marriage and motherhood, as yet, held no appeal for her.

The gardener, who'd followed the van's progress to the house, now leaned on his hoe and whistled appreciatively at the Junoesque vision that emerged from the unpromising-looking vehicle. The day was just getting weirder and weirder, the old man mused silently. First of all finding the poor lad dead like that in the pond. Then the coppers coming. And now the appearance of this eye-catching woman. He shook his head and began his weed-ing again. It just went to show, he thought philosophically, that you never knew what life was going to throw at you.

Jenny Starling habitually marched, rather than walked, and now she moved rapidly towards the big oak doors, her comfortable trainers making rhythmic scrunching noises on the gravel. The noise sent some grey squirrels, searching for beech mast on the grass, scampering for cover into the branches above, and she could hear them chattering at her angrily as she headed for the elegant rounded steps leading to the front door.

Unsure whether or not to go around to the back, she found and pulled the old-fashioned wrought-iron chain and hoped for the best. Employers could be an odd bunch, as she'd discovered during her life as a travelling cook. And she wasn't sure if the inhabitants of this splendid house were old money or new. She herself had no prejudices about that either way, so long as they didn't look down their noses at her. If there was one thing Jenny Starling hated, it was working for snobs. Those, and militant vegetarians.

She seemed to wait a very long time for a response, and was just about to give the bell chain another tug when the door was suddenly opened, and a six-foot-tall, stoop-shouldered individual with a fine crop of silver hair looked back at her, blank-faced. He was dressed in a dark blue suit, discreet tie, and actually wore white gloves.

Ye gods, Jenny thought in utter dismay, a real-life butler! She'd thought the species to be all but extinct in this day and age.

The butler, for his part, was slowly looking her over, his eyes gradually widening in surprise. Today Jenny was wearing a calf-length loose floral skirt that was maybe a little bit creased and a crisp, white blouse and very little make-up. She looked, she knew, perfectly respectable. It was just the fact that there was so much of her that had this paragon of implacability so nonplussed. Since it was a reaction she had become used to over the years, she didn't take offence.

But he was also, Jenny realized with a sharpening of interest in her periwinkle-blue eyes, somewhat distracted.

'Yes?' he said at last, and his voice was not encouraging. He sounded as if he expected her to try and sell him patio sliding doors, or convert him to some weird and wonderful sect of Christianity.

'I'm Jenny Starling,' Jenny said simply, and waited. Despite their rarity, she was not afraid of handling butlers. In fact, there was very little that tended to scare her. Except perhaps militant vegetarians.

At last, in the lengthening silence, the butler was forced to speak. 'Oh, yes. The cook.' He sniffed. 'The tradesman's entrance is around the back. I'm Mr Chase, the Greers' butler.'

Jenny gave an inner sigh. 'I am *not* the cook,' she corrected him, patiently. 'I have merely agreed to cater for the upcoming birthday party of a Miss Alicia Greer and her twin brother. She is in, I take it, Chase? I do have an appointment.' And, she allowed her voice to imply, she didn't like to be kept waiting.

The butler was so surprised by this full-frontal and totally unexpected attack that he forgot himself so far as to actually blink. However, he quickly recovered. 'Certainly, Miss Starling,' he agreed, his voice every whit as neutral as hers but his behaviour shifting just ever so slightly towards dumb insolence. 'Miss Greer is, of course, expecting you. There, er, may be some delay, however,' he added reluctantly, and again Jenny had a sense that something was not quite as it should be at The Beeches.

She'd always been very good at picking up nuances.

Ever since childhood she'd been blessed with a razor-sharp mind but also—thankfully—a much more sympathetic heart to counterbalance it. This unusual combination had allowed her, over the years, to become one of those people who could pick up on the tiniest little clues in people's behaviour and thus read them accurately. And, from her early twenties onwards, friends and family had often turned to her in times of crises. Sometimes, they even actually listened to her advice, which was invariably solid if not always particularly welcome.

Now she crossed the threshold into a hall that was a haven of coolness and tradition, and hoped that whatever the problem was here, she wouldn't be required to mess with it.

Black and white tiles spread across the floor to a large wooden staircase, and a genuinely old grandfather clock ticked ponderously in one corner. On a pedestal table between two doorways stood a freshly arranged vase of irises and sweet Williams. It all looked very staged to her, as if someone had been studying photographs in *Homes & Gardens* to see just how high-class country living should be managed, and she felt herself sigh inwardly.

Although she was a one-woman crusade for real food, Jenny got the distinct feeling that she wasn't going to find many aficionados of it here at The Beeches. She simply knew, without having to ask, that what the Greers would require for their festivities would be all flash and very little content. No doubt based on what the latest 'in' celebrity chef was cooking on the BBC. Or, if they were very daring, Channel 5.

But she would soon work her way around *that!*

'I'll inform Miss Greer of your arrival,' the butler assured her and shuffled off. Jenny waited patiently, glad of the coolness in the hall. Presently there came the sound of footsteps, unmistakably feminine, clacking their way down the long tiled corridor that led into the rest of the house, and Jenny turned to meet her employer.

With soft blond hair cut into a very designer pageboy revival, the woman walking towards her was one of the loveliest Jenny had seen in a long while. As slender as a supermodel, she was dressed in an exorbitantly expensive white sheath that was not quite see-through. Perfectly tanned, she wore white strappy sandals and a delicate single pearl drop on a long silver chain. Her pointed, gamine face was expertly made up, even at ten in the morning.

'Miss Greer? I'm Jenny Starling. Your caterer,' she introduced herself firmly, holding out her hand. 'You live in a wonderful house. I'm not surprised you wanted to hold your party here. I can't imagine there's a hotel or venue for miles around that can match it,' she added pleasantly.

Alicia Greer, who had been staring at her with wide, pale blue eyes, made an obvious effort at politeness, and quickly proffered her own slender white hand. The two women shook hands warily.

'Miss Starling,' Alicia Greer said, absolutely refusing to call her Jenny. 'I'm so glad you could come. I've been in such a damned flap about this party, you wouldn't believe it,' she carried on, trying not to stare at this huge woman in front of her. 'Mum and Dad have insisted on making it such a big thing, and now all this has happened.' She fluttered one hand helplessly in the air.

Jenny raised one dark eyebrow. 'All this?' she repeated gently. All this what? she wondered.

Alicia smiled tremulously. 'I'm sorry, Miss Starling, you've rather caught us at a bad time, I'm afraid. There's been an awful accident here, you see.'

Jenny hoped the kitchen hadn't caught fire. In her time

she'd cooked in some adverse conditions, but that was her worst nightmare. 'Oh? Nothing too serious, I hope?' she asked, with an ingenuous smile. Jenny, so she'd been told, had rather a good line in ingenuous smiles.

But Alicia Greer wasn't about to be bested. 'Someone has drowned,' she said flatly. 'We have the police all over the place, I'm afraid.'

Jenny just about managed to stop her mouth from falling open, but her heart did a nasty downward slide. 'Oh,' she said, somewhat inadequately, and hid a sudden shudder that threatened to overtake her. Holding a party in a house where tragedy has just struck didn't seem to her to be a very good idea.

'How sad,' she said inadequately, once it was obvious that Alicia wasn't about to elucidate. 'Well.' She rubbed her large but shapely hands together and looked at the younger woman questioningly.

'Oh, yes, sorry,' Alicia responded to the hint at once. 'Please, come into the study and I'll go through things with you.' She led Jenny into a library decked out in rich oak panelling that boasted a wonderful, if old, oriental carpet. Jenny was even more pleased to note the generously sized, button leather armchairs. Jenny, being the size she was, had to be very careful of the chairs she sat in.

'Mum's hired a party co-ordinator, of course,' Alicia said, taking a seat and indicating the armchair opposite with a polite smile. 'And Daddy's so old-fashioned, he's insisting on a champagne pyramid, can you believe it? Mind you, I can't resist sticking my oar in occasionally, if only to cause mischief,' she added, so obviously trying to get a handle on her caterer that Jenny almost felt sorry for her.

What she really wanted Jenny to know, of course, was

that her daddy was so rich he could afford party orga-
nizers and the best of everything. And that she wanted a
caterer able to keep up.

What Alicia would say if Jenny was to tell her that
her own father could probably buy out the Greers twenty
times over, Jenny couldn't be bothered to find out.

'It was a friend of a friend who recommended you to
me,' Alicia carried on, watching the Amazonian cook
with a kind of fascinated repulsion. For all her life, Alicia
had had Mrs Wallis Simpson's philosophy drummed
into her that a woman couldn't be too thin or too rich.
Now, here she was, face-to-face with society's worst
nightmare—a size eighteen woman—and she hadn't a
clue how to treat her. For a start, instead of giving out an
apologetic air, this woman seemed to radiate a confidence
and imperviousness that Alicia found utterly disconcerting. Worse, she seemed to exude a kind of powerful sex-
uality that Alicia instinctively guessed men would find
very compelling.

In spite of all the appearances to the contrary, Alicia
sensed that this annoyingly, incongruously attractive
woman could probably snap her fingers and have men
come running. And it made Alicia dislike her intensely.

'Would you like a drink, Miss Starling?' she asked,
smiling brightly.

Jenny's smile widened just slightly. Those who knew
her well would have recognized the glint of battle in her
eye and been forewarned. 'Oh, please, call me Jenny,'
she said silkily. Then, seeing the other woman twitch,
added smoothly, 'Oh, unless of course you prefer to be,
er, more formal?' the subtext plainly being that perhaps
Alicia thought herself too high and mighty to be on a
first-name basis with a mere hireling.

Naturally, Alicia wasn't about to let her get away with

that. 'Oh, no, of course not. Jenny it is. Would you like a cup of tea, Jenny?'

'No thanks, it's far too hot for that,' Jenny said brightly. 'But I'd love some lemonade, if you have any.'

Alicia smiled brightly. 'Of course.' She walked to the drinks cupboard and poured a cloudy liquid from a Tesco's bottle that purported to be 'real' lemonade.

Jenny hid her sigh of resignation and accepted the glass. Well, she'd asked for it! But the first thing she'd do when she hit the kitchen was to make some proper cordial, she promised herself. She took a sip just to be polite and her tastebuds, connoisseurs every little darling one of them, shuddered at the onslaught of artificial flavourings.

'You mentioned in your letter,' Jenny began, getting down to business, 'that you had in mind a six-course meal for twenty guests, to be served at 6.30 in the evening, before the main birthday party is to begin. Is that correct?'

'Hmm?' Alicia, who'd been staring out of the window towards the pond, suddenly jumped. 'Oh, yes, that's right. And then, of course, the usual nibbles for the party itself.' She waved a hand vaguely in the air. 'Something different if possible. It's so hard nowadays to do something original, isn't it?' She smiled blandly but her eyes gleamed with spiteful challenge.

Jenny smiled wolfishly. 'Oh, you can leave that to me,' she promised simply.

'We're expecting up to a hundred guests, since I've invited just about anyone who's anyone,' Alicia warned her uncertainly. 'I want Justin to have a really good time,' she added firmly.

Jenny took about two seconds to figure out that Justin must be her twin brother.

'The invitations are for 8.30, which should give us plenty of time to finish dinner,' the beautiful daughter of the house continued, her blue eyes becoming slightly animated now.

'So, for the nibbles,' Jenny said, keeping her mind firmly on business. 'Something along the line of Bengal eggs, oyster cocktails, that sort of thing?'

'Yes! Exactly,' Alicia said with real enthusiasm now, for the first time beginning to sense the brain and talent behind the Amazonian-like exterior. 'Justin really likes hot food,' she carried on, leaning forward, her stick-like body all bone and poise. 'So plenty of spices, and all that. And he likes Thai food too, so perhaps one of the courses could have lemongrass in it? He loves lemongrass.'

Jenny nodded. Her mind, however, was not for once on food, but on Alicia's sudden and unexpected selfless-ness. While she was sure that the whole world could go to hell if it suited Alicia's books, her twin brother, obvi-ously, was sacrosanct.

'No problem,' Jenny said. 'We can go through all his likes and dislikes and create a menu to suit not only him, but also your guests.'

'Oh, that can wait until tonight,' Alicia broke in quickly, already bored. Jenny took the hint and nodded, and rose with surprising grace to her feet, mentally plot-ting her menu. As always, she was going to earn her astronomical fee.

She took her leave and returned to the hall, where she found Chase waiting. He'd retrieved her very small suit-case from the van, and now led her upstairs.

She nearly always had it written into her contract that she be given bed and board for the duration of her ser-vices, and her room at The Beeches turned out to be very pleasant indeed, with generous windows and a lofty ceiling. And most importantly of all, for a woman of her stature, there was a spacious and sturdily built king-sized bed.

Chase deposited her case on the floor and left silently.

'Well, that's another fine mess you've got me into, Stanley,' Jenny told her rueful reflection in the dressing-table mirror. Then she gave a mental shrug, and set about unpacking her case.

With her few yet elegantly tailored clothes neatly put away, she wandered to the window and looked out over the well-tended gardens. Extravagant herbaceous borders lined lush green lawns, and there looked to be a large walled vegetable garden in the far corner. The vegetable garden made her eyes glitter. Once she'd unpacked her utensils from the van, her very next task would be to check it out and see what goodies were ripe and available.

A stream cut through the main part of the ornamental garden, meandering very picturesquely with twee little wooden bridges crossing it at strategic points. The stream itself terminated in a big pond, and as she looked, a body was just being pulled out of it.

With her heart thumping sickeningly, she opened the big sash windows and half-leaned out. The painted windowsill, warmed by the sun, was hot to her palms, but she ignored the discomfort.

The garden around the pond was host to a small, select gaggle of people and she had no trouble in picking out the head of the group. Tall and with a distinguished crop of short silver hair, he was talking to a dark-haired, squat individual.

She looked away quickly from the sight of the body, but not before she'd caught a fleeting glimpse of wet fair hair. She had the impression of a pale, young, handsome face before the body was zipped unceremoniously into a black bag.

Jenny sighed deeply. She didn't like being in the sort of house where they pulled bodies from ponds right under your bedroom window. She realized her mind was already drifting towards thoughts of murder, and wondered why she was immediately assuming that foul play was involved. After all, accidents *did* happen, and all the time.

Disgruntled, she walked out onto the landing, where the house seemed eerily silent. She quickly made her way downstairs and sought out the kitchen, which was situated down three steep steps. There, one quick glance told her all she needed to know, and she could relax. As well as a big electric oven, there was an Aga and a microwave. There was also a deep double sink, and best of all, plenty of workspace. It would most definitely do.

The room was not empty though. A dumpy middle-aged woman was sitting at the table drinking a mug of tea, and over by the sink and peeling potatoes was a small, wiry, brown-eyed woman, who could have been any age between thirty and sixty.

'You must be this posh cook they've hired then?' the seated woman said, with barely concealed hostility. 'I'm Martha. That over there is Vera.'

Jenny guessed that both women had probably lived locally for all their lives, and didn't think much of travelling cooks. She smiled warmly. 'Yes. Hello. You must be the Greers' proper cook?' she said brightly, bustling into the kitchen and thrusting out her hand.

Martha reluctantly shook hands, her eyes making a quick inventory of the interloper. Late twenties, she guessed, so not the total young know-it-all she'd expected. And at least she *looked* like a cook. Martha had never trusted skinny cooks. Still, the woman had no business being in her kitchen.

Jenny, accurately reading all the signs, gave a mental shrug. Well, she was only here for the weekend, after all, and then she'd be gone.

Just then a sudden movement out of the corner of her eye made her turn sharply. And there, sitting on the floor next to a pile of shoes, was the biggest tabby cat Jenny had ever seen.

It promptly spat at her.

'That's my cat,' Martha said with evident satisfaction, as the feline shot like a bullet into the space underneath the nearest set of cupboards, and commenced to growl awesomely from under cover.

As an example of the welcome she'd come to expect at The Beeches, Jenny thought with grim amusement, the cat's reaction said it all.

TWO

A FEW HOURS LATER, Jenny walked along a grass path, her eyes noting the maturity of the various spring vegetables growing in well-ordered ranks. Along with everything else, the Greers' kitchen garden appeared to be immaculate—and she'd bet her last pay cheque that this was all down to the as yet unseen Mrs Greer. She simply couldn't see the walking fashion statement known as Alicia lifting so much as a well-varnished fingernail—not even to give a set of instructions to an employee.

One of the few good things about global warming, Jenny mused sardonically, was how the mild winters and early warm springs chivvied the veggies along. Not that she'd ever dare suggest that there was *anything* good about global warming to her mother.

She valued her hide too much.

The new potatoes were especially enjoying themselves, Jenny noted, more than happy to cast thoughts of her mother aside. No doubt at some point she'd be getting a call from some police station or other with a message to come and bail her mother, Starstream Starling, out of jail, yet again.

Jenny had no objections at all to her mother's change of name by deed poll. After all, Muriel Agnes didn't have the same cosmic ring to it as Starstream; even a pleb such as herself could see that. But having to bail her out every time she and her fellow protestors succeeded in getting arrested for chaining themselves to some tree or other was getting to be somewhat tedious.

She heaved a sigh as she ran her eye over the south-facing brick wall, where young pear trees had been carefully pruned and trained horizontally against it. Come autumn, she thought wistfully, they'd produce a good crop. She thought longingly of her pear and Camembert tarts, one of her specialities, and shook the thought away.

Although she had given the activity still centred on the pond a very wide berth indeed, she nevertheless managed to nearly bump into a young constable, who was lurking in the shrubbery. He seemed to be guarding a gate in the hedge that led out onto a back lane.

'Oh. Hello,' Jenny mumbled, and began to do a very quick U-turn. She was not, however, quick enough.

'Excuse me, miss, er, madam? Are you supposed to be here?' the young bobby yelped keenly.

No doubt, Jenny thought, he'd been told to keep an eye out for nosy neighbours and reporters. Not, she fervently hoped, that she looked like either one of those!

'I certainly am, Constable. I'm the cook,' she informed him with a helpful smile. She was only a 'chef' or a 'caterer' to butlers and obstreperous employers.

The constable visibly stiffened. 'Mrs Vaughan is the household cook, madam,' he stated, his young eyes glittering in triumph at having caught her out in a lie.

Jenny smiled. 'I'm only temporary, Constable,' she explained patiently. 'I've been hired to cater the Greers' upcoming birthday party.'

'Oh,' he said flatly, looking crestfallen. But he wasn't quite done yet. 'And what time did you arrive, madam? I'm not sure that Inspector Mollineaux has your name on his list.'

Jenny Starling hoped very much indeed that Inspector Mollineaux *didn't* have her name on his list. 'I only arrived a few hours ago, Constable. Around half past nine, in fact.'

'Oh,' he said unhappily. For a moment there, he'd thought he'd found something worthwhile with which to relieve his boredom. Jenny silently commiserated. A young constable on what must be his first big case, and assigned to guard a lowly gate in a hedge, could be forgiven for wanting to cast his net onto wider waters.

'You arrived by car, madam?'

'Sort of,' she hedged. 'I've got a van. I need it to transport all my'—she was about to say specialist knives, and quickly changed it mid-sentence—'er, pots and pans, and the kitchen gadgets I simply can't do without.'

'And its registration number, please?' he asked, taking out his notebook.

Jenny heaved a mighty sigh, which, naturally, set her very impressive breasts rising and falling. The young constable stared at them, gulped once and then determinedly dropped his eyes to his notebook.

'EAT ME1', Jenny said morosely. The personalized number plate had been yet another gift from her father, whose sense of humour, it had to be said, left something to be desired. It wasn't hard for Jenny to understand why her parents had been divorced for years.

Jenny watched the young copper blink, battle with a smirk, then finally write it down. 'And you came from…?' he pressed relentlessly. Now that he had *someone* to question, he was not about to let her go without a struggle, that much was clear.

'I came from Broadway.' She named the Cotswold beauty spot that had been her last place of employment. 'From the Acorn Guest House, to be precise.' However, an unfortunate clash of wills with the owner over the proper recipe for Dundee cake had abruptly ended her stay there. Jenny sighed. It was a pity. It would have been a nice billet for the summer.

But Jenny was fussy about her Dundee cake. And anyone who didn't appreciate a proper cake was a Philistine anyway.

'I see,' the deflated constable said pathetically. Apparently, Broadway wasn't known to be a particular hotbed of crime, Jenny surmised with a smile.

'Is it very bad?' Jenny asked, more because she felt sorry for him than out of any real desire to know. 'The accident, I mean,' she added, when he looked at her blankly.

As she'd guessed, the lad's chest visibly swelled as self-importance set in. 'Well, madam, it is. A young man has died. He was here to help out the regular gardener, see. I knew him too, worse luck. We went to the same local comp together. It looks as if he hit his head on one of them low-lying branches across the bridge and fell in,' he trustingly repeated the knowledge he'd no doubt gleaned from listening to his superiors.

Jenny felt her conscience prick her. If this Mollineaux character heard him giving away such information to a member of the public, he'd probably be severely reprimanded. She could only hope the young constable had enough sense not to let on that he'd been doing it. But before she could warn him, he swept on blithely.

'Either he couldn't swim, or he wasn't awake when he hit the water. Poor sod,' he added, with much more feeling now.

So he must have drowned then, Jenny thought automatically. The M.E. would probably have been able to pick up on the signs, even this early on. Jenny, like a lot of people, was an avid murder-mystery reader, and favoured the same genre on television. Besides, she knew all about murder investigations from first-hand experience. An experience she was not anxious to repeat.

'I'm surprised his partner didn't kick up more of a fuss. When he didn't come home, I mean,' Jenny added as he gave her a blank look. 'Or did he live alone?'

'Oh, it didn't happen last night,' he gushed, his enthusiasm at being in the know again outweighing any sense of discretion. 'No, he arrived at the crack of dawn apparently. He was on the Rousham Green First Team, you see. Football,' he added, as this time he was the one being given the blank look. 'Whenever there was an afternoon match on, the old man who does the gardening used to let him work odd hours so he could get off in time to play. They were playing Marsh Gratings today. They'll have to find another centre forward now, I reckon,' he added sadly.

Jenny reckoned they probably would too. 'Well, I'd better get on with it.' She indicated the kitchen garden. 'I was just seeing what vegetables there are that I can use for the party.'

The constable, not in the least concerned with vegetables, nodded and gave her a final, suspicious look.

Ten minutes later, and satisfied that she had mentally marked down all that was available by way of salad items and early summer fruit, Jenny turned her attention to the greenhouse.

It was a large, long building, and the moment she stepped into it, her heart lifted. Rows of fresh tomatoes were just beginning to ripen. Cucumbers and marrows grew in the curling profusion of their own large orange flowers. Better yet, hanging in strings from the wooden benches, were last year's onions, still good enough for her purposes. Overhead hung clusters of grapes but, alas, as yet much too small and hard to be of much use to her.

Her eyes ran professionally over the shelves, seeking out any hint of trouble. Although she was sure from the evidence she'd seen thus far that the gardener must know what he was doing, Jenny didn't know for a fact that he was totally organic in his approach. And chemical enhancement in her food was something she tried to avoid if at all possible. Fortunately, her nose could detect only good, strong farmhouse manure, mixed with a liberal spreading from the compost heap.

On the dusty shelves just inside the door, however, there was a little collection of pest-control paraphernalia. She reached for what looked like a jar of homemade spray and lifted the lid before sniffing cautiously. Rhubarb leaves, if she wasn't mistaken. There was also a spray of popular branded weedkiller and, much more unusually, a single and very old bottle half full of paraquat. This lethal brew, Jenny knew, had gone out of manufacture at about the same time that Noah had begun to build his ark. Obviously the gardener here was one of those people who never threw anything out.

At the bottom of the shelves, there was a large bucket of ashes set to one side, which was no doubt used to keep the slugs at bay. On the whole, she'd seen far worse inventories than this.

She made copious notes of what fruits and vegetables were ripe, plus a few shorthand reminders for various recipes they could be used for, before walking to the door at the far end of the greenhouse. There she found herself facing a half-hidden little nook of the gardens that she hadn't noticed before.

High box hedges that must have been centuries old surrounded a tiny garden that almost made her melt in ecstasy. A herb garden! She sent up a brief prayer of blessings on the gardener, and set to mentally naming them all. Basil, thyme, rosemary, mint (of course), parsley....

'Oh, damn it, Keith, you've got to come. I won't have you chickening out. Besides, since whatshisname fell into the pond, I need you to be with me more than ever. You know how people talk. They'll be saying next it's Daddy's fault for not having the branches cut down.'

The voice, wailing and insistent and coming from the other side of the high box, was unmistakably that of Alicia Greer. And from the obvious petulance of the tone, Jenny didn't need to be a fortune teller to surmise that she was not in a good mood.

'You know I won't be welcome, Al. Why don't you just face up to it? Your dad will avoid me, as always, and your mum will be so damned excruciatingly polite. And as for Justin!' The voice was deep and definitely pleasant.

Jenny had always thought you could tell a lot about a man from his voice alone.

She glanced at the small arched entrance in the box where she had come in and wondered if she could safely slip out again without being seen. The trouble was, she was not sure of the layout of the garden, and the last thing she wanted to do was blunder into a lovers' quarrel.

'But I *want* you there,' Alicia insisted, and now there was no mistaking the pleading quality in her voice. 'It'll be so dismal and boring without you.'

'And I thought this was going to be the party of the century,' the unknown male voice countered drolly.

'It will be, you rat! I've even ordered birthday crackers from Asprey's, with gold cuff links for the men and earrings for the ladies, all with a lovely enamelled Greer coat-of-arms on them. You know Daddy had that researcher trace the family tree? We've managed to get a band that's big in Soho, and good old Arbie is providing the flowers.'

'Well, then, you won't miss me amongst all that splendour.'

'Don't be so damned working class and superior! You know full well that I can't live without you. Not even for a day. An hour. A minute.'

Much to Jenny's horror, the ardent young couple suddenly appeared in the archway in the box, and she took an instinctive step backwards, out of the parsley and into a shadowy corner. She could see now that Alicia's boyfriend matched his voice. Tall, with dark wavy hair, he had a strong, handsome profile. Bizarrely, he was dressed in dirty overalls, liberally smeared in black grease.

Jenny winced for Alicia's white dress as she pressed herself close to him and sensuously raised her long white arms to encircle his neck.

Love's young dream was all very well and sweet, of course, Jenny mused, but did they have to indulge in it in the herb garden! Couldn't they find a deserted haystack or something?

The handsome young couple began to kiss passionately, and Jenny sighed wearily. Perhaps she could just barge her way through and create her own exit in the thick hedge. She had the build for it, after all.

'Besides…' Alicia finally unglued her mouth from his. 'You're going to be part of this family soon. Mummy and Daddy will just have to get used to you. And so will Justin.'

'They never will, and you know it.' He pulled her arms from around his neck but held on to her hands, as if unable to completely let her go, and Jenny found herself taking a harsh breath. There was an undeniable pathos to be had in the age-old story of star-crossed lovers, even in this modern day and cynical age.

Abruptly, she began to wish herself very far away, knowing instinctively that she shouldn't be seeing this.

'I don't care,' Alicia said, her young voice grim and defiant. 'As soon as your divorce is final, I'm going to marry you. And I'll allow no one to stop me.' She sounded undeniably fierce and determined.

As they at last moved away, Jenny heard a harsh masculine laugh that sent the blackbirds panicking out of the bushes. There was an echo of a painful irony in that laugh, and something almost soul-destroying.

Whoever the poor sap was, he obviously had it bad, Jenny thought, with a pang.

Slowly the garden returned to normal. A breeze stirred softly in the flowers, and the blackbirds returned to their nests. Almost warily, Jenny left the enchanted herb garden and stepped out into a wide expanse of immaculate lawn, bordered in blooming roses. Alicia Greer and her unpopular lover were nowhere to be seen.

Jenny shrugged her wide shoulders and returned to her notebook and the task in hand. She had, after all, a menu to prepare. And yet she felt inexplicably disturbed. It was as if something dark and heavy, something that went far beyond the accidental drowning of a young gardener, hung over the country house, just waiting to gatecrash the party.

Jenny shuddered and told herself not to be such a twit.

THE BEECHES BOASTED its own large lake—as opposed to the small ornamental pond—and where there was a lake, there were usually fish.

It took her only half an hour to find her way to the two-acre expanse of water, and as she carefully negotiated the winding track around it, she felt herself begin to relax once more. The sun sparkled on the silver-topped water and the sounds of moorhens echoed peacefully from the reed beds. There was a lone angler on the far side of the lake and she made her way towards him. It was not until she was almost upon him that the fisherman turned his head, and she realized who he must be. The bright fair hair and pale blue eyes were the same. Only the square jawed face was different from that of his twin sister.

'This is private property,' Justin Greer said shortly, his voice as clipped as only Oxbridge can make it. His eyes, as they looked her over, were wide and wondering. Like most men, he was fascinated, attracted and yet unsettled by Jenny's size and grace. Fat, according to modern society's way of thinking, should mean obese and ugly—not unexpectedly beautiful.

'I know,' Jenny snapped, in no mood to pander to anybody's ego. 'Can you tell me what fish are stocked here, Mr Greer?'

'Why? Thinking of doing a spot of poaching?' he shot back, clearly amused.

'Only in white wine sauce with capers,' she shot back just as briskly, and finally got his attention.

Justin Greer stared at her for a moment, and then burst out laughing. 'You can only be the fancy cook my sister has hired for the party. I hope you realize you're about as popular around here as a flea circus at a dog show?'

Jenny smiled coolly. 'I had noticed,' she agreed dryly. 'Even Martha's cat is against me.'

'Oh, *that* animal,' Justin said archly, winding in his reel and watching the float come bobbing back, 'is against *everyone*. Vera is terrified of it, as is my mother. Even Chase gives it a respectfully wide berth. Martha found it half-wild as a kitten. And it gives the postman merry hell. But besides all that, you've come at a very awkward time. One of our gardeners has managed to get himself drowned.'

'Yes. I know.'

''Course you do. I suppose those two CID plods are still around?'

'I wouldn't know,' Jenny said, truthfully and gratefully.

'Hmm. Well, I've had enough of their never-ending questions, I can tell you. So I thought I'd take myself off fishing and keep out of their way for a while.'

Jenny didn't blame him. She was rather hoping to keep out of the way of the CID herself.

'Well, er…?' Justin said, rising an eyebrow at her.

'Jenny Starling,' she introduced herself with a smile.

Justin gave her another penetrating look, then began to dismantle his rod. 'I'm sure there are plenty of fish in there'—he nodded over the lake—'that could benefit from your expertise, not to mention almonds, batter and so on, but catching them is another matter. They don't appear to be biting.'

'What were you trying for?' she asked as he began to stow his gear.

'Pike.'

Pike—an excellent food fish, Jenny thought, and one that wasn't anywhere near as popular as it should be. Of course, they were vicious. A pair of teeth with a fish attached at one end as an afterthought, as one angler of her acquaintance had memorably described them. Lean and mean and absolutely delicious if boned and cooked right. Yes, she could do with a few good pike. She glanced down at his bait and her eyebrows rose. 'You're after pike with bread?' she asked, only just managing to keep the disdain from her voice. 'For pike you need worms—and a ledger.'

For the first time Justin Greer looked at her with something other than superior disdain or reluctant lust in his eyes. As he rose, he found himself staring straight into her eyes and blinked in surprise. At six feet tall, he was used to looking down on women—both literally and figuratively. But, something told him, a man looked down on this woman at his peril. And that the peril would be considerable, and real!

'I know that,' he replied testily. 'I just didn't happen to have any worms on me,' he groused, and patted his pockets facetiously. 'I might try again tonight. And if I do happen to catch a few of the beggars, oh, fancy cook, then what precisely would you do with them?'

'Bake them, of course,' Jenny said promptly. 'With rashers of fat bacon, butter and half a pint of tartar—or perhaps caper—sauce.' Well aware that she was being tested, she gazed back at him steadily, and eventually Justin began to smile. He couldn't help it.

'Perhaps my sister knows how to throw a party after all,' he acknowledged dryly.

'Of course I do, brother dear.' The voice cut across their duel of wits like the crack of a whip, and both of them jumped apart like guilty schoolchildren.

Alicia, her white dress floating around her, looked like a fairy princess as she joined them. 'Didn't I tell you this was going to be the best party ever?' She linked her arm around her brother's and gave his biceps an affectionate squeeze.

Together, the Greer siblings tended to be somewhat overwhelming, Jenny noted wryly.

'I'm beginning to believe you,' Justin said. 'Miss Starling and I have been coming to an agreement.'

'Oh?' Alicia looked at them, a little warily, Jenny thought. 'About what?'

'Pike,' Justin said.

Jenny felt like telling her not to worry. She had no intention of trying to entice her precious twin away from her.

Alicia managed to shrug nonchalantly. 'Oh, talking about the party...' she began, her voice cajoling and light as a feather.

Justin looked at her, one fair eyebrow lifting suspiciously. 'Yes?' he asked cautiously. 'I know that tone of voice, sister mine. What are you after now?'

'You really are a sod, Justin,' she said archly. 'But as it happens, I do need a new gown.'

'What, another one?' Justin's tone was scandalized but indulgent. 'You already have a wardrobe full.'

'But I've worn them all once,' Alicia said quickly. 'Come on, Juzz, this is our party, after all, and I've invited all the local press. You wouldn't want me to be seen in that Henley Regatta blue thing again, would you? Or last Ascot's taffeta horror, hmm?' she wheedled, her eyes laughing, and turned to Jenny for support.

'We ladies need to keep up appearances, don't we?'

Jenny smiled and said nothing. She had far more sense.

With an enormous sigh, Justin retrieved his wallet and extracted a credit card. 'All right, just this once. But what happened to this week's allowance?'

Jenny wondered how many women in third millennium Britain had to beg money from the men of the family and were indulged with an allowance. Reluctantly, and against all her better judgement, Jenny found herself beginning to feel sorry for Alicia Greer.

Not that she seemed to need it. For at that moment, Alicia was expertly tucking the card between her meagre breasts and beaming widely. 'I had to get Keith a new solicitor,' she admitted reluctantly. 'The old one would have let his wife get away with murder.'

Instantly, an ugly red tide of colour crept over Justin's face. 'You selfish cow,' he snapped. 'Hasn't it occurred to you that Margie Harding has two children to look after? Perhaps she needs a good solicitor too. After all, lover boy is going to be all right, isn't he, with a rich little wife to keep him in luxury?'

'Justin, shut up!' Alicia snapped. 'You know Keith isn't like that, but you're too damned stubborn to admit it. Just because Dad got lucky and rich, you think a motor mechanic is beneath me, but he's a better man than you. Oh!' she broke off abruptly.

For a second, Alicia stared at her twin, a stricken look on her lovely face. 'Oh, Juzz, I didn't mean it,' she said quickly. Impulsively, she clutched his arm tighter and smiled tremulously. 'You know you're still the number one man in my life. After Daddy, of course,' she simpered.

Jenny felt her jaw drop open in amazement. Did women still behave like this?

'And where does that leave lover boy?' Justin asked mockingly. 'Number three?'

'No,' Alicia said, her voice suddenly cold. 'He's the most important thing in the world. Oh, I don't expect you to understand,' she went on, so condescendingly that Jenny actually winced. 'But you understand, don't you, Miss Starling?' Alicia appealed, catching her completely unawares.

'Hmm? Oh, yes, of course,' she mumbled half-heartedly. Actually, she was thinking that melodrama like this should be damn well outlawed.

'You've never been in love, Justin,' Alicia stated as a

matter of fact, turning to her twin once more. 'That little doll you've pinched off poor Arbie hardly qualifies as the love of anyone's life.' She couldn't resist the dig, but then, once again, seemed to immediately feel guilty. 'Oh, Juzz, please understand. You must.' Once again she squeezed her brother's arm and leaned her lovely head on his shoulder. 'I'd do anything for Keith. You're so wrong about him, you know. Being a gold-digger, I mean. He doesn't want me for my money, he loves me. He truly does. He even made me sell my Jaguar because he doesn't want to be seen riding with me in it, like a kept man. Now would a man out to live the high life do that?'

The poor kid's really head over heels, Jenny thought uneasily. In her opinion, upcoming twenty-first birthday party or not, the Greer siblings could both do with a bit more growing up!

'So that's why you brought that little clapped-out, secondhand junk pile, is it?' Justin asked, obviously amused. 'And I thought it had something to do with your gambling debts.'

'You bastard!' Alicia yelped, but she was already laughing. 'Anyway, Keith's coming to our party, and that's that,' she returned, straight back to the attack. 'It's high time everybody got used to having him around.'

Justin said nothing for a moment, but Jenny had never seen anybody look less pleased. 'Nobody's going to get used to your bit of rough on the side,' he finally said, so callously and deliberately insulting that the colour, rather unsurprisingly, drained from Alicia's beautiful face.

'I'm not going to fight with you, big brother,' she said after a short, painful silence. 'You might be older than me by about fifteen minutes, but you're still so immature it's pathetic. But, in spite of everything, I love you, Juzzy.'

Justin seemed to be as willing to call a halt to the hostilities as his sister, it seemed, for he forced a smile onto his face. 'Come on, let's get back to the house.'

Alicia caught Jenny's embarrassed eye and laughed. 'I'm afraid you'll just have to get used to us, Miss Starling. Justin and I fight all the time. We enjoy it! Mostly.'

Jenny shrugged. 'It's all right by me. I wasn't really paying much attention anyway.' Which was perfectly true. Family infighting, as a spectator sport, held about as much appeal to Jenny as going on a diet.

THREE

THAT AFTERNOON, JENNY WENT into the village shop for some basics. As she glanced into the freezer section and eyed the rather limited range of seafood on offer, she was glad of her contacts in a little fishing village in Devon, who would be sending her order up by special courier. Expensive, of course, but it meant extremely fresh produce, very quickly delivered. But the Greers could obviously afford it, and she'd long since learned that it didn't pay to scrape on these sorts of things.

Now, as she stood dithering in the shop and checking it out for any suspicious signs such as peeling paint, or a pool of water on the floor, she became aware of two elderly ladies bearing down on her. Stepping quickly to one side before any elbows could be poked in her ribs—for Jenny had great respect for old ladies in a hurry—she watched them pass her and descend on their prey. Their target was a harassed-looking woman with frizzy blond hair and tired eyes, who watched their approach like a rabbit would watch a particularly hungry weasel. Jenny felt instantly sorry for her, and wondered if she'd be needed to come to the rescue.

'Oh, Margie, there you are. We were just hoping to catch you, weren't we, Maisie?' the first old woman began with the opening salvo. Her equally aged friend nodded wordlessly, but with such a barely repressed smile of eagerness that Jenny wondered uneasily what petty sin the luckless Margie had committed.

'I was saying just the other day, I've knitted a cardigan for Jeremy's boy, but it's too small! Can you imagine me doing something as silly as misjudging my own grandson's size? Still, they grow so fast, don't they? Anyway, so I asked Maisie, didn't I, Maisie, if she knew anyone who had a little boy who it might fit.'

The other woman nodded again.

'And she said that your Johnnie would be just the job. And I thought, of course, she's right! Margie Harding's little boy. So, you will take it off my hands, won't you, dear? No charge, of course, it was my own silly fault for not knitting the right size.' Maisie's companion gave a sudden and judicious sniff and swept on remorselessly. 'I don't know what young men are thinking of nowadays. I really don't. In my days, marriages were for life.'

Jenny winced.

Margie Harding smiled painfully. 'Thank you, Mrs Haines. For the cardigan, I mean. I'm sure Johnnie will love it. But you must let me pay you for the cost of the wool, at least.'

'Oh, no, love, wouldn't dream of it.' Jenny watched the old women beam with pride at their good deed for the day and then hurry off, no doubt to start knitting something else for little Johnnie. There was no doubt in Jenny's mind that they meant well and probably had no idea of the humiliation they had just caused.

Margie Harding watched the women out of sight with haunted and bitter eyes, then quickly turned and hurried out of the shop. Jenny, following more slowly, stepped into the deserted village street and looked around. The blond-haired young mother was just turning into a small village hall. It was not, thankfully, one of those awful 1960s boxes, but an older building, obviously donated to the village by the old squire. A large sign on the tiny front lawn proclaimed that the Rousham Green Spring Jumble Sale was 'still on'. And that more volunteers were needed to keep the village hall open until Saturday.

Jenny thought of the order of mussels, whelks and eels that she had yet to phone through to her contact in Devon, and abruptly decided that a quick visit to the jumble sale was a much more appealing idea.

Once inside the hall, she was pleasantly surprised by the quality of used goods on offer. And, from the rear of the rather dimly lit room, she could hear two women talking.

'This is the only blouse we have with a rounded collar, Mrs Harding. But it's not blue, I'm afraid.'

'Oh, that's all right. I think I can dye it to the colour I need. It has to match my suit, you see. I, er, have to go and see someone about a job.'

'Oh, yes, of course.' The volunteer who'd been roped in to 'do' Fridays was in fact the village's retired schoolteacher. She was also embarrassed by Margie Harding's obvious penury.

Did everyone in Rousham Green know everyone's business? Jenny thought indignantly on the other woman's behalf, then flushed at her own stupidity. Of course everyone did. No doubt Margie Harding's erring husband was the talk of the village.

But in that, at least, she was wrong. For now there was something far juicier than unfaithful husbands to gossip about.

'It's such a shame about Jimmy Speight, isn't it?' the volunteer said in a very theatrical whisper that would have carried clear out into the street, had the door been open. 'He was one of my ex-boys, you know. Not very academically bright, but a very nice lad, for all that.'

Margie looked up at her blankly. 'Sorry?'

'Oh, didn't you know?' the other woman gushed, hardly able to believe her luck in actually coming across someone who hadn't heard the latest news. 'They found Jimmy Speight dead in the pond. Up at the big house. They say he hit his head on a branch and fell in.' The older woman nodded her blue-rinsed head self-importantly and leaned a little closer. Paradoxically, she made no attempt to lower her voice. 'Mrs Perkins has a lad in the force, you know, and she says he told her that they found a branch in the pond floating near the body. Had blood on it, they say. And you could tell where the branch had come off one of the beech trees. That Inspector Mollineaux they've got out there was most particular about that, so Mrs Perkins says. He's had an expert crawling all over the tree, apparently. The police are so clever nowadays.'

Having successfully given out her precious gems of knowledge, she straightened up and shook her head sadly. 'Just fancy having those trees growing so close to that little bridge of theirs. And why build a bridge across a pond anyway? It was just asking for trouble, don't you think? I'm surprised somebody hasn't hit their heads on it and fallen in long before now. Still, accidents happen, I suppose,' she added doubtfully.

'Yes,' Margie Harding agreed, her voice so small it could barely be heard.

Feeling rather annoyed at herself for letting her curiosity get the better of her, and having checked that there weren't any skirts or blouses in her size, Jenny headed for the door. As she did so, two women made their way to a small table that was serving as a cash counter.

As Margie Harding cradled the precious blouse to her, she looked out of the window in the direction of the big house. Her eyes glittered oddly in the sunlight dabbled with dust motes.

'I hope your job interview goes well, Mrs Harding,' the volunteer said quietly in farewell, as she offered the blonde mother a brown paper bag containing her purchase.

Margie Harding started and then smiled.

Too wide, Jenny thought instantly. That smile's way too bright. And for some reason, she's lying about why she needs that blouse. Then, before she could get herself in any deeper, she walked firmly to the door and opened it. Jenny had a nasty habit, through no fault of her own, of getting caught up in other people's problems. This time, she vowed to steer well clear of trouble.

She glanced once more at the telephone kiosk next door to the pub, her own mobile phone having been left carelessly behind at the big house. Devon still patiently waited for the rest of her seafood order. As she walked along the pavement towards the kiosk, she nearly jumped out of her skin when a squeal of brakes shrieked in the sleepy afternoon air.

She and everyone else outside abruptly stopped and looked up the road. Two young mothers collecting their offspring from the village primary school instinctively grabbed their children's hands as an extraordinary-looking car in bottle green shot around the bend and into sight. As it screamed past and, with another squeal of brakes, turned into a tiny, single-pump garage opposite the shop, Jenny felt the heat from the machine scorch briefly across her face.

'That bloody Justin Greer is going to come to grief one of these days,' one of the young mothers said venomously. 'You see if I ain't right. He drives that Aston Martin like he's Lewis bloody Hamilton.'

'I know. He'll knock some poor sod over before long. He should realize there's old folks in this village. They ain't as quick on their feet as us. You should hear 'em go on about it at the pub.'

'Men!'

Jenny heartily agreed with the sentiments. Young men in sports cars were a menace. Except, to be scrupulously and honestly fair, she couldn't quite picture Justin crashing his car. Annoying though it undoubtedly was to admit it, he was one of those people who seemed able to do everything well. Which was a shame really. A good dose of humility would probably do him the power of good, Jenny mused sourly.

'I wonder how Jean's doing. Do you think we should go and see her?' The first young mother abruptly changed the subject.

'I heard the police were with her. Bernie too. They brought him home from work.'

'It must be awful to lose a son like that. He was only seventeen, wasn't he?'

'I reckon he was last birthday. Mind you, they don't know that that is his birthday. Not for sure, anyway.'

'What do you mean?' The second mother's voice rose in surprise, causing her companion to put a warning hand on her arm.

'He was adopted, wasn't he? Bernie Speight ain't, well, you know, quite up to it in that department.'

'Never!'

With this latest cringe-making revelation, Jenny very quickly left the two women to their gossip. She went to the telephone, punched in the Devon area code and a certain number, and then reeled off her order to the specialist fishmonger. With promises that she would receive noth-

ing but the best produce ringing in her ears, she left the
kiosk and made straight for the pub.

After the day she was having, she needed a drink.

At that time in the afternoon the pub was about to
close, since the landlord was opting not to take advantage
of all-day opening laws. But a customer was a customer.
As she took a stool at the bar, Jenny looked around and
took inventory. No noisy slot machines but a good dart-
board. Slightly uneven tiled floor, with a solid wooden
bar. And best of all—no horse brasses. Against all the
odds, the village pub had managed to stay just that—the
village pub. The landlord, a pleasant-faced man with a
broad Birmingham accent, beamed at her.

'Eh, you must be the fancy cook Alicia Greer hired for
the birthday party?'

Since she was the only other person in the place, Jenny
resigned herself to learning yet more information about
things she had no interest in. 'Yes, that's me,' she admitted morosely.

'So how's things up at The Beeches then?' the landlord asked avidly. 'You know there's been a tragedy up
there?'

Jenny sighed heavily. Was she being paranoid, or was
Fate *really* determined to get her mixed up in a suspicious
death?

SHE LEFT THE PUB ten minutes and one double vodka
later. Standing on the pavement, she began to picture
her menu. Visions of scalloped lobster with curry vied for
supremacy with fillets of sole à la Dieppe. Of course, she
couldn't decide on the complete menu until she'd finally
nailed the flighty Alicia down to actually going through
it with her. And that reminded her.

The birthday cake.

Looking across the road, Justin Greer's fancy car seemed to glow like a giant emerald in the sunshine, and she nodded firmly. That, at least, was one problem she could solve right now. Forgetting to look left or right, and as a result nearly sending a lone cyclist careening into the gutter, she marched across the road. She stood there for a moment in the garage courtyard, her sensitive nose twitching like a rabbit at the sharp astringent scents of petrol and the pore-clogging stench of grease.

It was unusual for a small garage to survive in these economic times, especially with the price of petrol at the level it was, and she wondered vaguely who was subsidizing the place. The pump was self-service, and a converted barn, that housed one or two cars in the process of being repaired, appeared to be deserted. But there had to be an office around the back somewhere.

Since a good cake needed at least a day to settle, she really had to get on with it tonight. Unless, of course, Justin was a sponge fanatic, in which case, the more last-minute the better, but she somehow didn't think so. For all his startlingly angelic good looks, he struck her as a solid-cake man.

With a sigh, she set off across the cobbled yard, carefully avoiding spanners, hoses and the odd stack of tyres. As she'd thought, a tiny office, converted from an outhouse, was located behind the repair shop, the door of which now stood open. And coming from inside, she heard the unmistakable voice of Justin Greer. It would have been hard to miss, since he was shouting fit to bring down the rafters.

'I'm warning you, Harding, stay away from her.'

'Oh, *hell*,' Jenny muttered under her breath. 'Here we go again.'

'Or what?' came back the equally belligerent reply.

Why couldn't men use the good sense that God gave them? Jenny wondered as she marched determinedly towards the open door.

'Or you'll regret it,' Justin's voice snapped out.

'I doubt it. Alicia is everything a man could want, or hadn't you noticed? She's young, beautiful and in love with me. I don't see—'

'And rich, Harding,' Justin interrupted with a sneer. 'Is that what you think? Yes, I suppose you would, that's what most people think. But the family business comes to me, Harding, *me, not Alicia*. Since Dad retired, I'm the chairman, not my dear sister. In fact, apart from her allowance, which *can be cut off at any time,* she might as well be penniless.'

'Good.'

There was a brief silence, and Jenny found herself abruptly readjusting her opinion of Keith Harding. He had actually sounded as if he meant it. A fact that Justin seemed to have picked up on also, if the startled silence coming from the office was anything to go by.

'Oh, I get it. You're relying on the house, are you?' Justin's blond/silver head abruptly came into view as he came level with a grimy window. His profile was taut with rage, and Jenny began to think that he'd have to make do with a sponge for a birthday cake after all. She was not interrupting an argument of this ferocity. She had far more sense.

Reluctantly, she began to back away. She could always make one of those towering gateaux that weren't much substance, but looked amazing. She was beginning to turn away from the office when Keith Harding said ominously, 'What the hell are you talking about? What has The Beeches got to do with anything?'

'Not the big house, you fool. I'm talking about the old

mill that Alicia persuaded Dad to buy for you as a wedding present. Don't tell me you didn't know? That I can't believe.'

Suddenly, there was a dull 'whack' and Justin was launched through the doorway, where he landed on his backside amid a clatter of tyre irons and empty petrol cans. The sight of the elegant young man, hair flapping in the breeze as he sailed past her, transfixed Jenny to the spot.

An avenging vision appeared in the doorway. The dark hair was a perfect match for the dark look on Keith Harding's face, and as he advanced with both his fists and his jaw clenched, Justin scrambled hastily to his feet, an extremely ugly gleam in his eyes. He reached down and picked up a tyre iron.

'Mr Greer!' Jenny roared, and both men jerked, as if an irritated puppet master had just pulled their strings. Jenny smiled grimly as he looked at her blankly. 'I noticed your car parked outside, and thought what a good idea it'd be to ask you about your birthday cake.'

'Birthday cake?' Justin echoed, for the first time in his life, Jenny suspected, actually looking stupid.

'Yes. Birthday cake,' she repeated firmly. 'I need to know what your favourite is. Tradition has it that it must be a fruitcake with a hard white icing, of course, but a lot of people nowadays prefer something more adventurous. After all, it is your birthday, you should have what you like.' She kept her voice even and firm, knowing that discussing something prosaic was often the best way to calm down men who were overdosing on testosterone.

She glanced across at Keith Harding and nodded politely. The mechanic took a backwards step and began, under her steady and reproving eye, to look distinctly shamefaced.

'Well?' Jenny looked archly back at Justin, and then

glanced, very pointedly, at the tyre iron, now hanging loosely and forgotten in his hand.

'Oh, bake what the hell you like,' Justin snarled, and slung down the iron. A loud clang echoed across the concrete as it hit a wall and fell to the ground.

'Lemon Madeira with kiwi fruit?' she asked mischievously.

'Good grief, no!' Justin snapped, then glanced from her to his protagonist and then back to her again. Slowly, he began to smile. 'Jenny Starling, I do believe I'm beginning to like you. And I don't think I want to.'

'I should hope not, too,' Jenny said sharply. She wanted nothing to do with rich spoilt kids. 'Now, if you would kindly tell me what kind of cake you *do* want, I can get on with it.'

'Coffee and walnut,' Justin said at last, his lips still twitching reluctantly.

Jenny nodded, surprised by his choice, but not showing it. 'Chunky walnut pieces, of course?'

'Oh, of course,' Justin said with savage sarcasm, and very nearly gave a courtly bow. The look in her eye stopped him just in time, and Jenny felt her own lips twitch. Damn him, he was such a very attractive man. And didn't he know it?

'OK. Coffee and walnut it is,' she said primly. As she turned to leave, she was relieved to hear footsteps following her, and a moment later the Aston Martin roared to life and shot past her.

At the entrance to the garage yard she turned and found Keith Harding staring after her. His darkly handsome face was a mixture of anger, embarrassment and defiance. 'What? No lecture for me?' he asked, his uneven breathing spoiling his nonchalance just a little.

Jenny saw, once again, Margie Harding being forced

into being grateful for an old busybody's knitted cardigan and turned abruptly away, her face absolutely expressionless. It was none of her business. She had to remember that. She kept getting into trouble when she made things her business.

Behind her, unseen, Keith Harding flinched at her obvious disdain. His eyes, as he watched the strangely sexy and large woman go, were bleak and hopeless.

When Jenny returned to The Beeches, she entered the cool hall through a side door, and was unceremoniously nabbed.

'Excuse me, miss,' a voice as deep as a tar pit boomed in her left ear. Had she not been so firmly anchored down by her own weight, she would have leapt about a foot into the air. As it was, she spun around, hackles bristling and prepared to repel all borders. The squat and solid policeman she had seen out of her bedroom window that morning met her glare with bland eyes.

'Oh, hello, er, Sergeant, is it?' she mumbled.

'Mollern, miss, Sergeant Mollern. Could you spare us a moment?' Although his voice put a question mark on the end, his eyes made it more of a statement.

Jenny felt her spirits take a distinctly downward turn. First she had to deal with scrapping men in garages, and now the police. What had happened to her peaceful weekend in the country? 'Yes, of course.' She sighed. 'But I don't know that I can do anything to help.'

'It's just routine,' the sergeant hastened to assure her. 'You're the only other person present in the house that we haven't questioned yet.'

'I wasn't present when the incident occurred, Sergeant,' Jenny corrected, quietly but firmly.

Sergeant Mollern, had she but known it, very nearly

smiled. However, since he so rarely smiled, and since he was so good at hiding any ability to do so, Jenny was forced to meet his bland stare with an equally bland stare of her own.

'Quite so. This way, miss.'

Jenny knew when to admit defeat, and followed him glumly to the Greers' study, where a tall, silver-haired man rose from his chair without any fuss.

'Miss Starling, sir,' Mollern said, and walked behind her as his superior politely indicated a chair.

Over the expanse of a wide, walnut desk, Inspector Mollineaux looked every inch what he was: a senior, experienced and implacable police officer, with a lean, rather pale face, and close-shaven, strong jaw. He looked, Jenny thought with a pang of compassion, as if he'd seen too much, and far too often.

Right at that moment, however, the pale blue eyes were looking at her sharply. 'We've met before, I think,' he said, his voice both modulated and quiet.

Jenny swallowed hard. 'No. I don't believe so.' For a long moment she didn't think he was going to let it go at that, but then he reached for some papers and glanced down.

'Miss Alicia Greer tells me that you arrived about quarter past nine this morning. Is that correct?'

'A little later, I think, but not much.'

'And you came from…?'

'Broadway.' For the next few minutes Jenny obliged the police by writing down the name and address of her past employers. She fervently hoped they wouldn't bother them too much—especially her last employer. She was apt to throw what Jenny's granny would have called 'a fit of the vapours'. But then, what could you expect from someone who didn't know a good Dundee cake when she saw one?

'And you were hired to cater her birthday party by Alicia Greer when exactly?' Mollineaux went on, merely glancing impassively at the addresses she'd given him, though one of the residences belonged to a lord of the realm, and the other was the home address of a rather famous American film star. And it was precisely because she'd had four months of cooking for a Hollywood darling that Jenny had fled to the relative sanity of a British guesthouse!

'Formally, today,' Jenny confirmed. 'However, she wrote to me about three weeks ago, asking if I could take the job on. She was most insistent that I try. I had originally planned to come up here, cater the party, and go straight back to Broadway.'

'But now?'

'I've left Broadway permanently,' Jenny said firmly. Nobody criticized her Dundee cake and got her to stay on. No matter how piteously they begged, or how many vapours they had.

'I see. Do you do a lot of parties, Miss Starling?' Mollineaux asked, managing not to make it sound like a leading question.

'Some.'

Inspector Mollineaux glanced once again at the illustrious names on the piece of paper she'd given him and said, 'Hmm.' It could have meant anything or nothing, and was so neutral that Jenny fought the impulse to applaud.

She wondered, idly, just how many suspects he'd prompted into incautious talk with that little prompt. She folded her hands in her lap and stubbornly said nothing. After a moment she saw, out of the corner of her eyes,

Sergeant Mollern glance across at her with some surprise. Eventually, Inspector Mollineaux looked up at her and smiled. 'I'm sure I've seen you somewhere before, Miss Starling. Any ideas where?'

Jenny had. Plenty. She'd been in practically every county courthouse in the country for a start, as a character witness. Such was the life of someone with an eco-warrior for a mother. Not that that was what he had in mind, of course, as well she knew. But she merely smiled and said artfully, 'I'm sure I couldn't say.'

'These are impressive references. I'm sure they'll check out.'

Jenny smiled, knowing he was barking up the wrong tree there. 'I'm sure they will too,' she said mildly but firmly.

'Where exactly did you do your training, Miss Starling, if I might ask? France?'

'Monsieur Gerard's School of Cuisine,' Jenny said sweetly. And didn't add that Monsieur Gerard was also known as plain Gerry Starling, one-time junior chef at The Ritz, and that the School of Cuisine had been sited in the Starling household kitchen. She didn't think to add, either, that she had been the only student, having been an only child.

A few months after her sixteenth birthday however, her father had finally taken himself off to France, minus wife and daughter, and set up in business for himself. Books, a regular television show, and numerous extremely lucrative money-making ventures had quickly followed. And while she was now a better cook than her famous father, he was the one known far and wide as 'Gerard, superchef'.

But that was life for you.

'I can't say as I know that school,' Molineaux said

thoughtfully, and Jenny smiled sweetly and mentally wished him luck in trying to find it in the telephone book.

'Could you tell me how you travelled this morning, Miss Starling?' He changed the subject so casually, and asked the question so reasonably, that once again she had to fight the urge to applaud.

Patiently she filled in the details of her van and route and was duly allowed to leave. As she did so, however, she glanced back once more and found those blue eyes fixed firmly on her.

'Thank you for your co-operation, Miss Starling,' Inspector Mollineaux said quietly. 'And don't worry. I'll remember where I've seen you before.'

I bet you will too, Jenny thought glumly, and gave him a cheerful smile.

JENNY HURRIED INTO the kitchen like a supplicant seeking sanctuary in a cathedral. Vera ducked her head over the vegetables she was scraping, and Martha began to pound the steak she was preparing with more force than a stevedore. From somewhere out of sight, the cat hissed at her, threatening reprisals.

It was bliss.

'Mr Greer wants a walnut and coffee cake for his birthday, Martha. Do you have the right ingredients?'

'Of course,' Martha shot back, immediately on the defensive, but quickly changed to attack. 'And you can't have a cake like that! Everybody'll be expecting a proper cake. With currants and raisins and hard icing.'

'Then it will be a nice surprise, won't it?' Jenny said pleasantly. 'And coffee does lend itself so nicely to soft icing.'

She reached into the pantry for flour and sugar, and hunted through the drawers for knives, spatulas and whisks. 'Perhaps you could tell me where the walnuts are, Vera?' she asked the daily gently, having come to suspect that Vera was a very timid soul indeed.

She opened an eye-level cupboard and spotted the coffee, which was, thank goodness, of a good quality, and reached for it. The next instant she very smartly withdrew her hand before the cat, hidden behind a biscuit tin, could lacerate her with a swipe of his claws. Calmly extracting a wooden spoon from the table, she held the fearsome moggy at bay and quickly snitched the coffee box from under his yowling nose. Then she neatly shut the door behind her.

As she began to cream butter and sugar together, she noticed Martha staring at her, and raised an eyebrow. The cook quickly turned away, but not before Jenny had noticed that her own hands were marred with red scratches.

Obviously the cat's owner wasn't quite as quick on the draw as Jenny Starling.

'I'll be glad when this job is over,' Jenny muttered, more to herself than to anyone else. She could no longer deny that she felt nervous, like some animals felt just before a particularly violent thunderstorm. It was almost as if the death of poor Jimmy Speight was just the opening act, and that worse was to come.

Firmly, she told herself not to be such a boob.

But, as if echoing her misgivings, the cat began to yowl once more from behind the biscuit tin, and the mournful ululating sound made the goosebumps rise on her forearms.

FOUR

JENNY TAPPED ON the door and was bid 'come in' by a hale and hearty voice that did her spirits the world of good. Doing as she was told, she entered a room full of charm and character, and immediately thought, *This is the real Beeches.*

The walls had once been bright red, she suspected, but the flock velvet wallpaper had now faded over the many years to a handsome dusky pink. Deep but nicely worn carpet cushioned the feet underneath, and large, comfortable-looking chairs welcomed you with open arms. But it was not the room so much as the people in it that gave the impression that this was indeed the heart of the house. Mr Greer Senior, he of the hearty voice, was already rising, his open and friendly face creased into a smile that sent laughter lines crinkling at the corners of his pale grey eyes. He had darkish wrinkly hair and a well-padded frame, and held out a large hand that Jenny nipped smartly across the room to take.

'You must be the fancy cook our reckless daughter has hired?' he greeted her, his eyes taking in her size with apparent approval, his eyes twinkling. 'I'm Mark, and this is my wife, Sherri.'

'I suspect, sweetheart, that Miss Starling deserves a far better title than that,' Sherri Greer admonished, smiling up at them from her seat on the settee. She was an elegant and more substantial version of her daughter, Jenny noticed at once. Her soft blond hair was greying slightly,

and swept around her skull in an artful design, no doubt
courtesy of a local hairdresser's skill with heated rollers.
Her blue eyes, however, were warmer than those of her
daughter, and life had stamped on her face far more in
the way of character.

'Please call me Jenny, but fancy cook will suffice,'
Jenny acknowledged cheerfully, 'although I'm not sure
Martha would agree.'

'Oh, dear. Yes, I rather thought Martha might be a
little put out.' Sherri sighed. 'I do hope this rotten business about poor Jimmy hasn't upset you too much? It's
such a shock, you know.'

Jenny murmured that indeed it was shocking.

'Apart from that, I hope you've settled in all right?'
Mark Greer asked solicitously.

'Oh, perfectly. I've been around the garden and noted
all that I could use from the vegetable patch, and I've
also put in orders with the various grocers, butchers and
fishmongers that I use. I insist on the best quality food,
and such things aren't cheap.' She thought she should
warn them now. 'But I really do need to get the menu
confirmed now and, well, to be blunt, I've been having
trouble pinning your daughter down. Perhaps the party
co-ordinator would help?'

'Goodness, you have been quick,' Sherri said, impressed. 'And you're not the only one having trouble holding on to our daughter these days.' She laughed, but the
look she gave her husband was distinctly troubled.

Jenny looked politely blank, even as she marvelled at
the trouble a handsome face could cause.

'You'll have no trouble tonight,' Mark said comfort-
ingly. 'I've ordered the little minx to join us for dinner.
She should be down any minute, Miss Starling—sorry,

Jenny—so perhaps we could all collaborate on the menu together then?'

Just then the door opened and a well-preserved middle-aged woman came in. 'Excuse me, Mrs Greer, are you still going to entertain the Women's Institute tomorrow?'

'Oh, Daphne, I totally forgot all about that—how clever of you to remember. But I don't think, really, I can cope with them just now, with poor Jimmy and everything that's happened.' Sherri Greer glanced at her husband for help.

'I think you'd better cancel the meeting, Mrs Williams,' he said crisply, a man evidently used to taking charge. 'The good ladies of the village won't mind going without their sherry and scones for one week. Oh, have you met the lady who'll be catering the twins' birthday party?'

Jenny smiled and walked towards the other woman, trying to place her in the hierarchy. Secretary? Housekeeper? Combination of both, perhaps. She put out her hand and smiled. 'I'm Jenny Starling,' she introduced herself quietly, and showed not a flicker of emotion as a pair of very cold hands briefly touched hers.

'How do you do,' Daphne Williams said.

'Daphne will help us all to see that the party runs smoothly, Miss Starling,' Sherri said confidently. 'She keeps the old house and daily routine ticking along through all kinds of crises.'

Jenny secretly wondered. The lovely blue eyes of Daphne Williams looked dead. Not clouded, or worried, or even just tired, but dead.

'I don't know how we managed without her before she came to us,' Mark agreed cheerfully. 'How long have you been with us now, Daphne?'

'Four years, Mr Greer,' Daphne replied, her voice as

dead as her eyes. Her usual manner must always have been so markedly reserved, Jenny surmised, for neither of the Greers seemed to sense that something was terribly amiss with their paragon.

Jenny watched, feeling utterly helpless, as the elegantly silent and suffering Daphne Williams murmured an almost whispered goodbye and left the room. Then, just a few seconds later, the door suddenly flew open again and a vision in sea green appeared in the doorway. In marked contrast to the woman who'd just left, she seemed to vibrate almost obscenely with health, youth and life.

'Oh, here you all are. I was wondering why the house looked as deserted as a morgue.'

Despite Alicia's renewed good mood, Jenny found herself going cold at her choice of words. Nevertheless, she hastily whipped out her trusty notebook and gave Mark Greer, whom she'd already picked out as her greatest ally, a telling look. Catching on at once, he didn't let her down.

'Right, before dinner, let's get Saturday's banquet sorted out,' he said, and in spite of Alicia's moue of displeasure and protestations of being ravenous, they all sat down while Jenny determinedly held court.

She'd already planned the menu, of course, but she did so like to give her employers the fantasy of having had a hand in it. 'I take it your twenty guests are of a mixed age?' she began.

'Indeed they are,' Alicia said regretfully. She would obviously have preferred a younger group altogether, but Jenny suspected her mother of having put her foot down.

'In that case, may I suggest a mixture of the traditional and novel?' she began. 'That way everybody must, if only by the laws of mathematics, come across at least one course that they thoroughly enjoy.'

Alicia sighed somewhat rudely, as the two older Greers looked at Jenny with relieved approval.

'Perhaps we could start with soup.'

'Soup!' Alicia groaned. 'Oh, that's so boring.'

'Cream of asparagus, perhaps, with Parmesan fingers as a garnish?' Jenny ploughed on, reminding Mark of a battleship he'd once known. 'Then, of course, a sea-food savoury. I'd like to suggest crab, mixed with melted butter, some finely chopped gherkins, breadcrumbs and some cream. Served (very hot, of course) on either hot biscuits or toast.' If she didn't push forward with her campaign for real food, who would?

Jenny trusted modern chefs about as far as she could throw them. And her father was top of the list. Ever since he'd published an extremely popular book of low-fat menus that took roughly three minutes to prepare and were full of macrobiotic politically correct ingredients, the relationship between father and daughter had been very rocky indeed.

Hence the hideously expensive gift of the jewelled Swiss watch currently residing on her wrist, which he'd given her for her last birthday. Jenny had contemplated sending the bribe back, but she wasn't that stupid. Besides, it was battery-free and kept perfect time.

'Sounds delicious,' Mark said heartily, who was very fond of gherkins.

For the next half an hour they batted forth a range of possible courses, finally agreeing on Jenny's selection, naturally. This consisted of steak with lemon and cucumber, followed by small but tasty helpings of mutton chops à la jardiniere. And for puddings, a raspberry fruit cream to clear the palate and make way for a chestnut and pineapple trifle, the whole to be rounded off with cheese and biscuits and fine coffee.

'Well, I think I shall have to stop eating right now if I'm to get through all of that.' Sherri Greer laughed. 'I must say, though, it all sounds wonderful.'

'What does?'

They all turned as Justin strode into the room, hands thrust nonchalantly—but so *effectively*—into his trouser pockets, and Jenny wondered with a reluctantly fond amusement how many actors could have staged an entrance so perfectly.

'Our birthday banquet, as if you didn't know.' Alicia laughed. 'I'll bet you had your ear plastered to the door all the time we were talking.'

'Rubbish. I'd trust Miss Jenny Starling with my life,' Justin said, then glanced at the granite-faced cook. 'Well, with my stomach, anyway.' Jenny, having been paid the ultimate compliment, very nearly beamed. 'That is, if all these flat-footed policemen swarming all over the place don't put her off her baking,' Justin added, with a wry grimace. 'They've had me in yet again, wanting to know this and that. Honestly, it's getting beyond a joke.'

'Somebody probably blabbed about that ticking-off you gave poor Jimmy,' Alicia said sweetly and just a shade spitefully. 'They've been talking to anyone and everyone they can nab all morning.'

Justin flushed angrily. 'Well, he deserved to be ticked off, the little sneak. It was about time somebody put him right.'

'What on earth do you mean?' Sherri asked in some alarm, looking from one of her twins to the other, her pretty face genuinely bewildered.

'Oh, Mother!' It was Alicia who replied first, her voice both amused and exasperated. 'You seem to go about in a world of your own! Everybody knows Jimmy Speight was nothing more than a little snooper. He was always poking and prying around. That mother of his said he wanted to go into the newspaper business, and he was only practising! I ask you! A reporter? He didn't have a brain in his head. Just a big fat nose.'

'Which he regularly poked into places it didn't belong,' Justin added moodily. Seeing the quiet censure on his mother's face, he added defiantly, 'I caught him rifling through your handbag once.'

'No!' Sherri gasped, utterly shocked. 'And he did such a good job on the begonias!'

'He did such a good job on ladders too,' Alicia added, her eyes sparkling in remembered outrage. 'I caught him looking into my bedroom window on more than one occasion. And when I confronted him he had the cheek to say he was pruning the wisteria.'

'Perhaps he was,' Mark said heavily, who was obviously old-fashioned enough to disapprove of talking ill of the dead. The young lad had died in his garden, after all. The family owed some loyalty to the Speight memory.

'Oh, yes? And how could he prune and read my diary upside-down at the same time, I might ask?' Alicia snapped.

There was a cold silence for a moment. Then Alicia sighed deeply, and cast a mischievous glance at her brother. 'Anyway, I can't be the only one he snooped on. If he hoped to get some juicy bits of gossip from my diary and write them up and sell them to some gossip-mongering society rag or other, he must have really done something to get into your bad books, brother dear.'

Justin gave his sister an I-could-strangle-you look, but managed a nonchalant shrug. 'Not really. It was just the usual snooping. I got sick and tired of it and told him either to cut it out or he would find himself without a job at all. Then he could devote all his time to trying to persuade the local *Clarion* to take him on.'

Alicia laughed. The local *Clarion,* Jenny assumed, was not exactly a racy or particularly adventurous type of newspaper. A big report on the church bazaar would probably have been the topic of its front pages for days.

'I'm glad you think it's funny,' Justin said, miffed. 'The police seem to think it all most significant. Although why, I can't say. Perhaps they think I topped the little sod.'

'Justin!' Sherri Greer said, shocked.

'Justin!' her husband roared in echo, knowing that his son had gone too far this time. Mark probably didn't roar all that often, since there was another long, and this time definitely sheepish, silence.

'Well. The police get on your nerves,' Justin said defiantly. 'Implying this, insinuating that, and all with that sickeningly polite look on their faces. That Inspector Mollineaux, for instance, is a particularly officious sod. Still, at least he didn't try and hint that we should postpone the party. But I was beginning to wonder if he might.'

'Well, I should think not,' Alicia said hotly, and with such injured outrage it made everyone smile, including Jenny.

'That reminds me,' Mark said, his voice suddenly serious enough to make everyone's smile fade, 'I meant to tell you, Jenny, that there will be twenty-two for the feast, not twenty. I've invited Tom Banks and his wife to join us.'

Alicia shot her brother a half-curious, half-appalled look. 'Daddy!'

'Why the hell did you do that?' Justin asked, just managing to keep his voice on an even keel. One look at him, however, showed his extreme anger. The smiling nonchalance was gone, and in its place was a white, pinched, furious expression that was all the more unnerving for being held so severely in check.

'I thought it was the least we could do.' Mark stared at his son levelly. 'Tom's worked for Greer Textiles for twenty years, eight of those as assistant manager. Since he's now *retired*'—he gave the word a strange emphasis that his son couldn't fail to miss—'this is the perfect opportunity to see him go in style.'

Justin's lips twisted in a parody of a smile at his father's words, and Jenny found her memory being jolted.

When she'd been in the shop, thinking about whelks, hadn't some of the other customers been talking about a somebody-or-other Mr Banks who'd been fired by Justin Greer? She hadn't been paying much attention at the time, and had promptly forgotten all about it.

'I still don't think that our birthday party is either the right time or place.' Justin's voice interrupted her thoughts. 'Tom has already left the company, remember?'

'Left? That's not the way I heard it.' Mark, confirming all of Jenny's misgivings, was openly challenging now.

'Regretting your own retirement, Dad?' Justin asked, almost on a sneer. 'You have seen this year's figures, I take it?'

'I'm well aware that profits are up.'

'I've made our competition look feeble,' Justin openly boasted. 'And our blanket-making division is more than holding its own.'

'I'm well aware of that.'

'And I did it all without Tom Banks.'

'I'm also aware of that.'

'Well, then, I think…'

'Tom Banks was a loyal employee and a friend. He still is, I hope. And he's coming to your party.' There was a finality in the elder Greer's voice that nobody could mistake, and Justin flushed. He would not, Jenny was sure, be magnanimous in defeat. And she was quickly proved right.

'Oh, have it your way,' he said savagely. 'You always do.'

Jenny watched him stomp out, and sighed deeply. Did the Greers actually intend to invite any friends to this party of theirs?

THE ATMOSPHERE IN the kitchen as Martha, Jenny, Chase and the almost monosyllabic Mrs Williams dined on Martha's delicious steak and kidney pie was hardly conducive to good digestion.

'Wonderful pie, Martha,' Chase said and helped himself to some more mashed potato.

'Thank you,' Martha said smugly, and gave Jenny a telling look. A discreet electronic buzzer sounded, puzzling Jenny for a moment, before Martha jumped up and retrieved a piping-hot jam roly-poly from the oven, and she realized that it indicated a summons from the dining room.

'I do so like your flower arrangements, Mrs Williams,' Jenny said, deciding that if you couldn't beat 'em, you might just as well join 'em. 'It's becoming rare nowadays to find somebody who knows how to handle flowers.'

Daphne Williams gave her a dead-eyed look, and forced a smile. It managed to make Jenny feel both sad and scared at the same time.

'I daresay you'll be busy soon, Chase, with all the weekend visitors arriving?' Jenny ploughed on, and rose a questioning eyebrow in the butler's direction.

'Indeed,' Chase said flatly, and reached for an extra pat of butter. Martha returned, and when everyone was finished, retrieved a second roly-poly pudding from the oven and cut out pieces—Jenny, to nobody's surprise, receiving the last and smallest piece.

'I daresay you were discussing the menu earlier then?' Martha said at last, her own cook's curiosity demanding satisfaction.

'Yes,' Jenny said, and spread out her pudding to allow the jam to cool off. Both Chase and Martha glowered at her silence. Two, after all, could play at that game. Jenny smiled sweetly, and began to eat her pudding.

'Well, I don't think we should be having a party at all,' Martha sniffed, now in a right old hump. 'This thing about poor Jimmy has right upset me, it really has. The police are all over the place. It's like being in an episode of *Crimewatch.* And they've been on to poor Justin, just because he told Jimmy off that time. And it wasn't as if he didn't deserve it.' Martha was in full spate now. 'I heard Justin found him poking about in his room one time. I know that mother of his always said he was going to be a newspaper man, but if you asked me, he just liked knowing other people's business!'

Chase coughed discreetly and directed a telling look in Jenny's direction. Martha flushed guiltily.

'I understand Miss Greer has hired an army of waiters and waitresses for Saturday night,' Mrs Williams said, obligingly changing the subject and at the same time uttering the longest sentence Jenny had ever heard her say. She glanced at the older woman, surprised that she had even been taking notice. She'd seemed so distracted before.

Now, however, two spots of colour had miraculously appeared in her cheeks and her eyes were glittering. But Jenny could have sworn that it was anger that animated her.

'Hmm. They'll be needed, I expect,' Martha said crisply. 'All this fuss.' She gathered the empty plates together and then stacked them in the sink before running the hot-water tap and squeezing in a dash of soapy detergent. She plunged her arms in without a second thought. Evidently, she didn't believe in dishwashers, or else the Greers would have coughed up for one long ago, Jenny surmised. And the absent Vera was obviously a morning-only helper.

When Jenny appeared at her side, washing-up cloth in hand, Martha almost gaped at her. Jenny took a plate from her unresisting fingers and began to rub, vigorously. Unclean crockery was an anathema to her, as it was to all good cooks.

Martha sniffed but began to frown uneasily, and Jenny sympathized. It was disconcerting, when you'd got a good hate going, to have your foundations for dislike given a hearty wallop.

The clearing away done, Jenny left, intending to go to her room and get a good night's sleep. Tomorrow was going to be a busy day. The meat should arrive early, but it had to marinate for at least eight hours. And that would only be the beginning of her preparations.

As she crossed the hall, the family emerged from the dining room, and at the same instant the front doorbell rang. Chase, moving with much more speed than anyone probably suspected him capable of, opened the door just as Jenny was halfway up the stairs and therefore in the best position of all to witness the scene that was about to unfold.

Had she known what was coming, of course, she'd have galloped up the stairs like a Grand National winner, but alas, she was not blessed with foresight, a disadvantage that very often caused her grave inconvenience indeed.

'Darling!' From the first happy and ear-piercing cry, Jenny felt her heart sink.

Chase, mortally offended at not being given a name, and therefore unable to announce the visitor, watched her sweep past him with a comically dismayed look on his face. Not that the human hurricane in designer gear seemed to notice.

The impression of force, Jenny saw at once, was largely projected, for the woman herself was tiny—standing in high-heeled shoes at not more than five feet tall. Her hair was the colour of rich corn, yellow and probably natural. Under the coat, a very curvaceous figure was hugged tightly by a blue silk dress, and tall stiletto heels made a staccato tapping on the tiles as she all but flung herself into Justin's arms.

Justin, perforce, had to catch her, or who knows where she might have landed. 'Babs?' he said, and obviously couldn't have been more surprised if Father Christmas had just rushed in, ho-ho-ho-ing, six months early.

'Pet, I've missed you so much. I simply couldn't stay away another day.'

Alicia, Jenny noticed, was having a great deal of trouble keeping her face straight. The elder Greers, however, were looking, in contrast, distinctly nervous at this latest development. From her aerial view, Jenny watched as the young woman bussed Justin's cheek, leaving a fine smear of powder on his face. Her lips, painted a deep, luscious red, brushed his ear and she saw her teeth give him a nifty nip.

Jenny's eyebrow rose.

'Babs, what on earth are you doing here? I thought you were coming tomorrow night.' He sounded anything but pleased and welcoming.

'Oh, petal, don't be so banal,' she accused. 'Oh, yes,

before I forget, I have some cases outside,' she said, noticing the butler for the first time. 'Could you be a dear and bring them in for me?'

Chase went white, then red. Jenny wondered if anyone had ever before dared to even *think* of Chase as 'a dear' and doubted it. Doubted it considerably. 'Certainly, er, madam,' he said, the hesitation between the two words making it as near to an insult as Chase would ever come, but both the elder Greers noted it at once, of course, and their anxiety visibly deepened.

It was obviously a bad sign, Jenny realized, when Chase became antsy.

'A suitcase?' Justin said sharply. 'I thought I told you I'd booked a room for you at The Bell?'

The woman laughed. 'Oh, you and your jokes!' Her eyes were a rather surprisingly deep pansy brown that looked almost black, and they met his with an expression in them that would have made a rock think twice about claiming to be hard. 'Justin, are you going to introduce me to the parents or what? After all, they do need to get to know their future daughter-in-law.'

Alicia, at this, guffawed out loud, then, at her brother's furious look, clapped a hand firmly across her mouth. Sherri Greer swayed in shock, and Chase, who had just returned, dropped the cases on the floor. He stared at them for a second incomprehensibly then quickly retrieved them, hoping nobody had noticed such an unforgivable error.

'Timbuktu,' Jenny whispered under her breath. 'I could just do with a nice trip to Timbuktu about now.' She'd welcome a journey anywhere, in fact, that got her away from this madhouse.

'You must be Mark,' the blonde hurricane said, instantly zeroing in on the elder Greer. A wise choice, of course, for Mark Greer would always be polite to any lady. Of course, older men could also be very silly about pretty little blondes, as the blonde hurricane and, unfortunately, Mrs Sherri Greer, also knew. As a consequence, the irresistible force of Babs found herself facing the unmovable object of Justin's mother, who stepped very neatly into her path.

'I'm Sherri Greer. How do you do, Miss...er...?'

'Walker, Barbara Walker. I'm sure Justin's told you all about me?'

'That name sounds familiar,' Mark said thoughtfully.

Again Alicia laughed, but since she still had her hand clasped to her mouth, it came out in a series of choked snickers. Once more her brother shot her a killing look, and Alicia nearly bent double. Evidently, there was a good joke going on, but nobody else besides the twins seemed to know the punchline.

'Chase, take Miss Walker's case up to the green room,' Justin said, evidently in an attempt to regain the upper hand. 'Then perhaps you could serve brandy in the lounge.'

Chase, relieved to have orders to follow, gave a dignified nod. Jenny smartly made way for him on the stairs and, as the butler passed her, glanced down. For an instant the tableau froze.

Sherri and Mark Greer were staring at the petite blonde, with varying expressions of dismay on their faces. Alicia was propped against the doorjamb to the dining room, evidently awash with mirth. The blonde in designer-everything was looking around the house with avid, hungry eyes, and Justin, in turn, stared at the interloper, a look of raw desire on his face mixed with a combination of exasperation, anger and amusement.

Jenny shook her head and sighed deeply. Here was yet

more tension and strife coming into a house that was already awash with it. She really didn't like the way things were shaping up.

She didn't like it one little bit.

FIVE

'WHERE DO YOU want these crates of bubbly stacked then, missus?'

Jenny, up to her armpits in potatoes, turned her head and sighed wearily at a somewhat scruffy-looking delivery man. 'Don't ask me, I'm only the cook. It's the party co-ordinator you need.'

The party co-ordinator had descended on The Beeches that morning and had made it very clear, very quickly, that she was going to vigorously defend what she regarded as her turf.

'Where can I find him then?' the delivery man wondered aloud.

'You'll find her somewhere in the house, organizing something or other. She'll tell you where to put it, believe me!' Jenny said, with feeling.

It was 10.30 in the morning, the meats were marinating, and she, Vera and even Martha were beginning to make a sizeable dent in the huge mountains of vegetables that needed preparing. Nevertheless, Jenny's timetable was tight, and she didn't need any distractions.

'A blonde lady told me the crates were to go in the kitchen,' the delivery man insisted stubbornly.

'There's no room in here,' Jenny pointed out reasonably, feeling her patience beginning to wear thin. 'We'll be tripping over them all day. Martha, is there a wine cellar in the house?'

'Of course there is,' Martha said flatly and returned to

her carrots, her glee evident. She was enjoying the spectacle of the unflappable fancy cook beginning to show signs of strain, just like the rest of the mere mortals.

The party co-ordinator couldn't have chosen a better moment to put in an appearance. She was whippet-lean, dark and business-suited, a forty-something only recently divorced.

'The catering staff will be arriving shortly, and they'll help with the decorations and so forth,' she announced, to no one in particular. 'Ah, the champagne has arrived, I see.'

'It needs to be stored in the wine cellar. I have to keep the kitchen as uncluttered as possible,' Jenny said firmly.

'Alicia wants the wine stored in here, I'm afraid.' The co-ordinator shrugged one padded shoulder. 'She's worried that the catering staff might start dispatching Mr Greer's best wines and ports by mistake if the party wines are also allowed into the cellar.'

'Oh, for…' Jenny began ominously, but was interrupted before she could get in full flow.

'That's all right.' Daphne Williams, entering the kitchen at that moment, quickly proved her worth. 'I cleared a space in the back pantry for it last night. It's cold enough in there, and the catering staff will be bringing wine coolers for the bulk of it anyway. Follow me, please.' She turned to the delivery man, who obeyed instantly.

The co-ordinator went off to co-ordinate something and Jenny promptly forgot their existence. She had to ice the cakes. Alicia had opted for a traditional fruitcake with white icing for her own cake, and it was always best to do that five hours before eating.

Justin and Alicia, apparently, had an arrangement. On their birthdays they shared a party, but each got their own toast, each got an individual cake and so on, and took it in turns to open their presents. Originally designed, no doubt, to save childish arguments and tantrums.

Jenny began to think about which sauces needed to be made first, especially those that needed to chill.

'Hello, Mr Chase,' Vera piped up timidly and tearfully from behind a mound of onions.

'Vera,' Chase responded with a brief smile as he headed straight for Martha. 'You heard about that woman's unexpected arrival last night?' he asked, his voice lowered to a whisper but carrying clearly across the quiet room.

'From Daphne, yes. She had to take in fresh towels this morning. Apparently she was in bed in the nude!' Martha's voice lowered to a scandalized hiss. 'I think that's so *common,* don't you!'

Chase sniffed. 'I'm not surprised. I do hope Justin doesn't… Well, that he isn't at all *serious* about the, er, lady.'

'I don't think he is,' Martha said judiciously, moving closer as Chase leaned eagerly forward. 'I was up early this morning—well, I had to be, didn't I? Couldn't expect that one'—Jenny didn't look up, but knew in which direction they were now looking—'to do any of the real work herself, could I? And I had the family breakfasts to think of. Anyway, I was passing Mr Greer's study, as you do, like, when I heard him and Justin arguing something rotten.'

'No!'

'Yes! Mark was asking him what on earth did he think he was doing, bringing a girl like that into the house, and Justin said he had a right to invite her to his party if he wanted to.'

They broke off as Mrs Williams walked the delivery

man back through the cavernous kitchen and out into the hall.

'So, Mark says, yes, that's all right, but why invite her for the whole weekend? Well, that's when Justin gets really angry, see? He says of course he didn't invite her to the house, did his father think he was stupid? He was going to put her up in the pub. Then Mark says, well, that's all very well, but couldn't he see that she was the kind of girl who wasn't going to take no for an answer? And what was all this daughter-in-law business about? Were they engaged or what? Well, Mark put it better— you know how nice he talks.' Martha broke off, more to take a much-needed breath, Jenny suspected, than through any real desire to praise her employer.

Chase nodded encouragingly.

'Anyway, Justin, he's getting really hot under the collar now, and says that no, of course they aren't engaged. His father says that she obviously thinks differently, and then Justin laughs, and says that's her problem, since he never promised her nothing.'

'Ah,' Chase said, beginning to relax. 'I must say, I always credited Justin with greater taste than seemed evident last night.'

'I know. But young men and women like her can get themselves into all sorts of trouble.'

'Well, at least it looks as if we're over the worst of it,' Chase said with some relief.

From her growing pile of mixed veggies, Jenny sighed deeply. Over the worst, my eye, she thought inelegantly. From what she had seen of Babs Walker last night, she was only just beginning to fight, and Justin was obviously in the grip of a powerful lust for her. And when a strong-minded woman was desired to that extent, she could do an awful lot of damage. Babs Walker was obviously angling to live the good life, that much had been obvious, and she wasn't likely to settle for anything less. Not if Jenny was any judge of character.

No, she rather thought that marriage to Justin would suit Babs very well indeed, as Justin was no doubt going to find out when he tried to dump her.

Just then Daphne, who had returned to the room unseen, coughed discreetly and Chase flushed guiltily.

'Anyway, mustn't gossip,' Martha said lamely, and worsened her gaffe by clumsily changing the subject. 'I'm glad those police have finally gone, anyway. All those blue uniforms about—it was enough to give you the shivers all over.'

'They've not all gone,' Daphne corrected her quietly. 'The plain clothes detectives are still here.'

'Oh. Those two,' Martha said glumly. 'I don't know what they keep hanging around for. It was obviously an accident, wasn't it? They should talk more with Jimmy's mother, if you ask me. That Jean Speight.'

Chase gave a very loud cough, overdoing it somewhat and sounding as if he was coming down with a severe case of laryngitis. It made even Martha stop in mid-flow.

'I'd better go and see to the flowers,' Daphne said, her face once more white and tight. Jenny watched her go and frowned. She was riding an emotional seesaw, that one, Jenny mused uneasily, and wondered what it was that was making her so miserable.

'You'll have to be careful what you say around Daphne, Martha,' Chase prompted once the door had closed behind the housekeeper. 'You know what good friends she is with Jean Speight.'

Martha sniffed. 'Yes, I know. I can't understand it myself. I'd never have thought that a woman like Daphne would have much to do with the likes of Jean Speight. Her husband's only a dustbin man, after all.'

And with that parting shot, she turned back to her sink.

'WOULD YOU LIKE TO inspect the dining room, Miss Starling?' Daphne Williams asked about an hour later, once more firmly hidden behind her 'perfect housekeeper cum private secretary' persona. 'It seems the party co-ordinator knows what she's doing, after all.' She smiled gently. She also watched with interest as the Junoesque cook mixed some stuffing that would later be encased by rashers of bacon and cooked with the chops.

'I'd love to,' Jenny agreed, pushing aside her qualms about the organizer's taste in dining rooms. She had to keep reminding herself that she was there to do a job and nothing more. And if the Greers had warring Vikings for offspring, a suffering ghost for their housekeeper and dead gardening boys in their pond, it was nothing to do with her.

'I've just got to finish this stuffing first or it'll harden too much,' she carried on. 'Vera, can you bring me some more sage and tarragon from the herb garden, please?'

With the stuffing finally mixed to her satisfaction, she checked on all the stocks, tasting and adding a little more freshly ground black pepper where needed, and then watched Vera for a moment, just to be sure she was coring the horseradishes properly.

As she stepped out of the kitchen, Jenny took several deep breaths then checked her hugely expensive watch. She noticed Daphne start then stare at it, her blue eyes widening appreciatively. It was nearly noon. A long way to go yet, but so far, everything was coming along nicely.

'Hello, Miss Starling, have you seen'—Alicia came

upon them, then hesitated for a moment as she too caught sight of the gold and diamond watch—'er, Mummy?' she finished.

At her lilting voice, Jenny jumped around guiltily. Whenever she was caught out of the kitchen on zero day, she always felt absurdly traitorous. 'I'm afraid not, Alicia.' She used the woman's first name deliberately.

Daphne Williams discreetly excused herself.

'But now that I've run across you, could you come to the kitchen and check the birthday cakes for me?' Jenny pounced. 'I need to know the exact wording of what you want on yours, and what style you'd like. Italics are always nice, but I can best show you by demonstrating on a cold marble board.'

Alicia laughed. 'Oh, Miss Starling—I mean Jenny— that won't be necessary.' She took a backwards step, as if afraid the cook would force her inside. 'I trust you completely. Just put the usual kind of thing. I'm sure it will look just perfect.'

Jenny watched her go, feeling vaguely annoyed, then shrugged and made her way to the dining room. There she paused, looking around with pleasure. Long, dark green velvet curtains hung at French windows, and a deep peach carpet lent the huge dark mahogany table a complementary splendour. Paler peach walls, with apple-green alcoves, gave the impression of walking into a blossom-laden arbour. When Daphne had placed the flower arrangements at strategic points in the gaps evident on the table, it would look magnificent.

She walked to the table itself and checked the settings. It was, as she'd half-suspected, immaculate. A dainty, circular lace tablemat was set at every place, along with a crisply folded snowy-white napkin. The lines of knives, forks and spoons were laid out correctly, and crystal wine goblets, dusted and buffed, stood in perfect formation. The tablecloth was of a deep bottle green, which was not only a perfect foil for the room's colouring but would also make a perfect backdrop for good food, red wine and flowers.

She toured the table from one end to the other, checking the line with her eye, and was coming up to the far end when she noticed something white on the floor. As she bent down to retrieve it, she saw that it was a napkin. A good job she'd checked after all, though whether any guest would have noticed it was debatable.

She had just taken it between her fingers when she heard the door open, and voices, in mid-conversation, echoed across the empty room. '…and I really do think you should see our point of view,' Sherri Greer said, her voice chiding. 'Oh, doesn't it look lovely.'

Jenny was just starting to straighten up when a spasm of cramp crossed her back, making her wince.

'What? Why?' Alicia said airily. 'I really don't see why I should see your point of view at all, Mummy dearest. I told you, Keith and I are going to get married. And since we've been sleeping together for ages anyway, I don't see why finally making it legal should worry you all so much.'

Jenny dropped back to her haunches and almost groaned aloud. The cramp was killing her! Unfortunately, she was prone to attacks of it now and then.

Obviously exasperated by the look on her mother's face, Alicia laughed grimly. 'Don't tell me that you and Dad didn't do it before you got married,' she challenged scornfully.

'We were far more careful then,' Sherri admonished. 'Besides, Keith's a married man, Alicia! With children too. And if, well, anything should happen, he wouldn't be free to marry you.'

Jenny's left leg started to twinge warningly and, wincing and gritting her teeth, she very carefully, and very slowly, began to stretch out flat on the floor. It was agony.

'You mean if I get pregnant?' Alicia said bluntly, then laughed. 'Oh, Mum, don't be daft! There's the morning-after pill nowadays, as well as every contraceptive under the sun. They've even invented flavoured condoms!'

Under the table, Jenny felt her muscles slowly beginning to relax. It was utter bliss.

'Alicia!' Sherri said again, as if repeating her daughter's name in a pained whisper was all that she could manage.

'Well, it's true,' Alicia said defiantly. 'And what's more, where Keith and I go, to this nice little hotel in West London, there's this huge new chemists that has huge stocks of everything you could imagine. So you see, you needn't worry about being made an accidental grandmother.'

Sherri groaned out loud and Jenny felt like doing the same. The only good thing about pain that Jenny had ever discovered was when it stopped. Finally, with the pain receding, Jenny began to relax, and then concentrate on the important things once more. She needed to clarify some butter, and if she didn't get out of here soon, she might forget.

'Oh, don't worry, Mum, I know how to take care of myself. I always go into the shop myself and get what I need. I'm not so naive as to leave it up to Keith. Men are so lax about that kind of thing, aren't they?'

'I'm not listening to this anymore,' Sherri said grimly, and from her somewhat unconventional position lying flat under the table, Jenny saw one set of high heels turn smartly and leave the room. Alicia quickly ran after her, and after waiting a cautious moment or two, Jenny was able to climb stiffly from off the floor, the offending napkin still clutched tightly in her hand.

Once mobile again, Jenny made her way briskly to the kitchen. There, as she'd suspected, the butter hadn't yet been taken from the fridge and would need to soften a little first. 'Vera, can you open the windows, love?' she called, her round face flushed from the heat of the stove. 'It's already so damned hot in here.'

Vera quickly agreed and Martha smiled happily. 'Want some help with that?' she asked sweetly.

'No thanks,' Jenny said stiffly. 'You can chop me some mint, though, if you're not doing anything.'

Martha gaped at her, then marched out of the kitchen in high dudgeon. Vera giggled.

A dark shape jumped up onto the windowsill outside, and the cat stared in, his tail flickering angrily.

Vera moved hastily away.

Out on the front lawn a huge marquee was being erected, with the party co-ordinator in close attendance, and Jenny glanced up, distracted, as a couple of busy young men flitted past the window.

'Doesn't the tent look pretty?' Vera said. 'I love those stripey ones, don't you? It always reminds me of a fair.'

Jenny glanced towards the marquee. The party staff were certainly hard at it all right, and she only hoped they'd still look fresh come the evening. It was a hot day and all that running about couldn't be doing them any good. The uniforms were smart though. Dark blue trousers for the men, and pencil-line skirts for the women, with white shirts or blouses, with rounded blue collars. They looked cool and elegant, and Jenny only hoped they'd stay that way.

If there was anything guaranteed to put a guest off his food, it was having it served by a waiter with a sweaty armpit.

'Yes, very nice, Vera,' Jenny muttered absently, and was about to carry on stuffing some tomatoes when she just caught a glimpse of a frizzy blond head, and turned back sharply to look once more.

That particular waitress had her back towards the cook, though, and quickly disappeared behind the half-erected marquee, her tight blond curls bouncing in the sunlight. And yet Jenny knew that she had seen that frizzy blond head somewhere before, and quite recently. But where had it been? Then she shrugged, and promptly put it out of her mind.

She needed all her concentration for the prawns she was using to make Prawns Magenta. She took them out of the fridge and gave them a careful, suspicious sniff.

OUT IN THE GARDEN, Inspector Mollineaux, with Sergeant Mollern at his side, stood on a pretty little rustic bridge and stared down into the pond.

The body of Jimmy Speight had been autopsied and was due to be released to the local undertakers soon. A light rain during the night and now the bright sunshine had all but obliterated the traces left by the heavy boots of the policemen who had crowded around the pond yesterday. All was peace again. A boy might never have died there.

'Looks like an accident, sir,' Mollern said, with no inflection at all in his voice.

'Yes,' Mollineaux agreed. 'The blood we found on the branch floating beside him matches his and is perfectly consistent with him hitting his head on it.'

'And he could very easily have grabbed at the branch,

half-dazed, like, in an attempt to stop himself falling in and broke it off,' Mollern continued, still in that emotionless way so many people found disconcerting.

'Oh, yes. It's all very feasible. Very neat and tidy,' Mollineaux agreed. 'Except the boy was a nosy little sod. Everyone agrees on that. And when nosy people end up dead in ponds…' He shrugged graphically but didn't voice out loud the conclusion of his train of thought.

Mollern sighed. After a while he said thoughtfully, 'Justin Greer had that big barney with him.'

Mollineaux stirred. 'You know, I've been hearing some interesting things about Justin since he's taken over the running of the company,' he replied thoughtfully. 'He's getting awfully rich, awfully quickly. He's into computers and selling on the internet and all that. Well up too on foreign trade, the European market and taking advantage of the subsidies system and so on. I just wonder if it's all strictly on the up-and-up.'

Mollern nodded. 'A clever man on a computer can hide all sorts of things nowadays, if he knows what he's at,' he agreed. 'Justin might only be just twenty-one, but the money market is traditionally a young man's game, isn't it? Look at all those young rogue traders who lost banks millions. And I understand Jimmy Speight was a bit of a computer whizz himself. If he managed to get access to Greer's computer, who knows what a clever hacker might have found out?'

For a long while, the two policemen stood on the pretty bridge, looking into the pretty pond, and saying nothing.

SIX

AT THREE O'CLOCK the band arrived, and Jenny watched a scarecrow look-alike carry a red and black electric guitar across the lawn and enter the ballroom through the open French windows. A skinhead followed, carrying and dropping a drum kit, then a very beautiful young man indeed who carried nothing at all. Must be the lead singer, Jenny surmised. On his heels came a small troop of roadies, electricians and other technicians.

Sherri Greer, who was attempting to stay out of the party co-ordinator's way, while at the same time seeing that nothing went amiss, was looking more and more frazzled by the minute. Eventually, she flopped down on the garden bench next to the roses in front of the kitchen window, and blew out her cheeks in a gesture of defeat.

As Jenny began to slice potatoes wafer thin, which were to be placed on top of a vegetable-layer stack, she watched Alicia emerge from the herb garden at the far end of the greenhouse and smooth down her badly wrinkled dress. No prizes for guessing what she'd just been up to, or with whom.

Jenny hastily bent her head and began to brush melted butter on top of the vegetable layer. Now all it needed was a few hours in the fridge before cooking, to harden it slightly.

'Oh, Mum, there you are. I was hoping I'd get you at a good moment. Have you seen my outfit for tonight?

Justin lent me the money for it, since I'm short. I really don't know why you and Dad don't just let me have a credit card.'

'No, I haven't seen it,' Sherri hastily cut across her daughter's whining recital. 'Perhaps Mrs Williams is pressing it for you.'

'No, Mum, I don't mean that it's gone missing. I meant have you *seen* it? It's a gorgeous electric-blue silk, with a silver-thread motif. It's absolutely fabulous. I got it from this wonderful boutique I know in Chelsea.'

'I don't wish to know about your haunts in London, dear,' Sherri said sharply. But Alicia pretended not to understand the chilly reference to her favourite trysting spot, and when Jenny happened to glance up, it was to see her nestle beside her mother, twirling a carnation absently between her fingers.

'I was just thinking how well your sapphire and diamond set would go with it. Being dark blue, I mean,' she said casually.

'*I* was going to wear those,' Sherri said sharply, and Alicia shrugged an elegant shoulder.

'Oh? What dress were you going to wear?'

'My orange taffeta.'

'And you were going to wear sapphires with it? Oh, Mum, come on! I always said you had no dress sense, and this proves it.'

'Really?' Sherri said mildly. 'And what would you suggest I wear?' Her silky words gave Jenny the satisfying sensation that Alicia could not quite fool her mother as well as she thought.

'With an orange dress? Well, that amber and silver set you have, for instance. Or even emeralds, but you'd need other green accessories. Have you got a green bag and shoes?'

'Somewhere.'

'Well, there you are then. Then I can have the sapphires.'

'You can *borrow* them, yes,' Sherri corrected tellingly.

'Thank you, Mumsie! Although, you know, I really ought to have *some* jewellery of my own.'

'All my gems will come to you in the will,' Sherri said with a finality that was unmistakable, and then rose with a sigh. Jenny smiled over her carrot julienne. 'Now I'd better go and see how that band you hired is getting on. I'm sure our small ballroom is not at all what they're used to.'

As the two women wandered to the French windows and disappeared, Jenny checked her watch for about the thousandth time and sighed in relief. Back on schedule.

'What do you want done with this stock, Miss Starling?' Vera piped up from the stove. 'It's been barely simmering for hours now.'

'Good,' Jenny said with a satisfied smile. At last, things were coming together. 'Did you put in the fresh basil, like I said?' In the ominous silence that followed, Jenny glanced over her shoulder, took one look at Vera gnawing industriously on her lower lip and shook her head. 'I'll go and get it,' she said, wondering at the same time where Martha had disappeared to. No doubt the resident cook was endeavouring to teach her a lesson by making herself scarce just when things were beginning to get hectic. Jenny could have told her it would be a wasted effort. She was used to working alone under pressure, and much preferred it to having people under her feet.

She was just returning from the herb garden, crossing the pleasantly cool hall with a sizeable bunch of basil grasped firmly in her hand, when Babs Walker appeared on the landing, swathed in black silk and emanating a cloud of expensive French perfume.

She peered over the balcony in such a way that Jenny wondered if she secretly needed glasses. No doubt the young lady would rather go blind than cover up those huge pansy eyes of hers. Someone should sit her down and persuade her to buy contact lenses.

'Oh, at last. You must be the cook.' Babs let her eyes flicker briefly and disdainfully over her. 'I'm absolutely ravenous. Bring up a sandwich, will you? Smoked salmon, I think.'

Jenny, her mind reeling as it tried unsuccessfully to grapple with the concept of placing delicately smoked salmon between bread, let the girl slip away before she could properly vent her spleen. Slamming into the kitchen, she barked at Vera to slap a single layer of the smoked salmon from the fridge between some bread, and stormed to her soup pot. She was so incensed, she didn't even stop Vera from putting margarine on the bread. Instead she smiled and took the plate from the baffled daily's hand and marched back into the hall.

There she stopped dead at the sight of the stranger in the hall, and blinked. The man was dressed in full evening dress, but of the white-suited variety, and was so enormously fat that the outfit served only to make him look like a giant meringue. His hair was of an unfortunate crinkled black, but his skin was quite pleasantly tanned. His appearance, however, might have been more quickly assimilated had it not been for the huge and odd bouquet of flowers he was carrying. In his hand was the biggest bunch of bird-of-paradise flowers and assorted greenery that Jenny had ever seen. They looked about as out of place in the genteel and ever-so-British hall of The

Beeches as a pair of exotic parrots would have looked in
a Liverpool dockyard.

'Arbie!'

Alicia Greer sailed into the tableau, and Jenny watched,
fascinated by the combination they made. Alicia went
straight to the stranger and kissed him on both cheeks.
'Are these for me? Oh, Arbie, you shouldn't have,' Alicia
said, then laughed at the disconcerted look that passed
over his moon-like face. 'Oh, Arbie, I'm only teasing.
Don't worry, I know just who they're really for, and I must
say I wish you loads of luck. You're gonna need it.'

Although Jenny had no idea what was going on, she
had the sudden and unshakeable feeling that Alicia Greer
was being very spiteful indeed. 'Have you brought the
rest of the flowers with you?' she carried on, glancing
over his shoulder to the driveway, where a dark green van
was parked. 'I see you have. I hope they're all as lovely
as these.'

'They're just what you ordered, Alicia. Would I ever
dare bring anything else?' His voice was very nearly
amused.

Jenny began to sidle around them, a little difficult for
a woman of her stature to accomplish, but luckily the pair
seemed too intent on their business to pay her much heed.

'Orchids, lilies, loads of roses of course, carnations.'
The man was ticking them off on the fingers of his left
hand—not easy when his other hand encased what looked
like a whole Borneo jungle.

'And freesias. Lots of freesias,' Alicia prompted. 'I
adore their scent.'

'I've emptied the greenhouses of them,' the unusual
and mysterious Arbie assured her.

Jenny, having gained the stairs, nipped smartly up
them and then began to knock on doors. At last, from

behind one, a small voice piped up. Jenny entered and stared at an empty room. Just then, Babs emerged from the bathroom, her hair swathed turban-like in a towel, a Japanese silk bathrobe wrapped around her curvaceous body. 'Ooh, lovely. Put it in the sitting room, will you? Wasn't it thoughtful of Justin to give me a suite?'

Jenny didn't think a comment was called for, and did as she was told, mainly because she felt such a sudden and strong sense of pity for the woman. She was so desperate to make the move from working to upper class; so needy for all the good things in life. And so determined to appear to be something she so obviously was not, and could never be. Jenny could only hope that when the time came, Justin would let her down lightly, but she rather doubted it. She doubted it a lot.

She'd just put the plate of foul sandwiches on a rather nice table when she heard a knock on the door and Babs grunt in exasperation. An instant later, she heard the door click open.

'Hello, Babs. Guess who?'

Jenny instantly recognized the voice as belonging to the man with all the flowers.

'Arbie! What the hell are you doing here?' Babs's voice suddenly lost all the imitation dulcet qualities, and the raw edge of real anger grated through.

'Why wouldn't I be here? I've known the Greers for years. It was me who introduced you to Justin, remember?' The pause between the last two words was a distinctly bitter one.

'Arbie,' Babs sighed, and a cajoling note crept quickly into her next words. 'I wasn't expecting you to be invited. Surely you don't want to come? Wouldn't it be easier on everyone if you stayed only for a little while, just to be polite, and then went home?'

'Better for whom?' Arbie asked, his voice so soft and yet so full of repressed rage that Jenny actually shivered. A caterpillar of real fear and unease began to creep up her spine.

'For all of us, of course,' Babs said, her tone of voice full of coo and confidence. It made Jenny shake her head in amazement. Was the girl blind or just without any common sense at all? Couldn't she tell she had a tiger by the tail in there? Obviously not, for Babs carried on as blithely as a butterfly. 'You know it's no good, don't you? Be a little angel, Arbie, and, oh, are these for me? They're lovely, really.'

Evidently Arbie had handed over the blooms in an attempt to forestall her, for she saw Babs briefly cross the open doorway in order to lay the bouquet on a table by the window before turning back to her visitor.

'I'm glad you like them. They always remind me of you.' Arbie's voice was softer now and genuinely smitten.

'Oh, Arbie, don't,' Babs said. 'It's all over. Please, just accept it.'

'No.'

It was that simple. Jenny knew it, even though she couldn't even see the expression on his face. He was not the kind of man who said one thing and meant another. Moreover, he was obviously the kind of man who could become obsessive. Babs would have to tread warily. Very warily indeed, she thought.

'Well, you'll just have to,' Babs snapped, her voice rising as her temper did likewise. 'Justin and I are to be married. So you'll just have to accept it.'

'Do you want me to do the wedding flowers?' Arbie asked, his voice so mockingly amused and vicious now that even Babs, at last, seemed to get the message.

'Don't be so cruel!' she gasped. 'I wouldn't dream of asking you. Do you think I'm so heartless?'

'As a matter of fact, yes,' Arbie said, and in that moment Jenny realized that she should never have pictured him as a meringue. A meringue crumbled at the onset of a spoon, but there was nothing soft about Arbie the florist. Rock cake, perhaps.

'Not that it matters, of course,' he carried on, and from the sitting room Jenny could picture him prowling around the room. 'Because he'll never marry you, not in a million years. I know Justin. Better than you do, it seems.'

'Liar!' Babs shot back. 'You're just saying that, hoping I'll take you back.'

'Hoping you'll settle for a rather less rich, less handsome catch, you mean,' Arbie corrected her. 'You might as well say it. You see, Babs, I know you too. Inside and out. And it still doesn't matter.'

Jenny glanced at her watch. Damn! She was behind schedule *again*. She'd never had a job go so unevenly before. Why couldn't Babs Walker have the good sense to marry Arbie and have done with it? He must have money to have attracted her in the first place, and he evidently loved her something stupid. He'd put up with her infidelities, shower her with gifts and never cheat on her. An ideal husband, in fact. But no, she had to try for Justin Greer, of all men. Just because of his pretty face and lean, sexy body.

'Get out,' Babs said, her voice wavering. Perhaps, at last, she was beginning to see the real Arbie, not the fool she thought she'd hooked and then discarded for a better catch. For now there was something approaching real fear in her voice.

'Oh, I'll go for now. I have to oversee the flowers, but as you can see, I'm already dressed for the banquet, so

I won't even need to go home to change. Oh, yes, Alicia invited me to it. Didn't you know?'

And with that excellent parting shot, the door opened and then slammed shut. Taking a big breath, Jenny stepped out into the bedroom. Babs Walker stared at her, her pansy eyes widening in dismay as she watched the Junoesque cook bolt for the door and realized she must have heard every word.

'Oh, Alicia.' Jenny, having just escaped Babs Walker's room, noticed Alicia and Justin coming out of the library. 'I need you to check the cake. I've iced it in a way I hope you'll like.'

'Oh, lovely. Where is it? In the ballroom?'

'No, the kitchen.'

'Oh. Well, I think Justin should be the one to check it, don't you? Then it can be a surprise for me,' she said with an offhanded laugh, and promptly disappeared back into the library. Jenny sighed deeply. Honestly, anyone would think Alicia was allergic to the kitchen.

'Lead on, Macduff,' Justin said, giving her a knowing grin. 'And don't try to domesticate my sister. It's a wasted effort.'

Jenny shot him an arch look. 'My dear Mr Greer. I wouldn't dream of trying to teach your sister, or yourself for that matter, anything at all.'

Justin was still laughing when he stepped into the kitchen and looked around with impressed eyes. 'Everything seems to be going well. Hello, gorgeous,' he said to Vera, who blushed to the roots of her hair. If they'd been able to see them, her toes would probably have been beetroot too. 'So where's this cake of my sister's?'

'In the back pantry, keeping cool,' Jenny said, and led the way. Justin looked first at all the crates of champagne, and then his eyes saw the cake, and widened. He stepped closer. It was six layers, artfully held up by white columns, almost like a wedding cake. Except that the icing was a lovely deep cream colour, and was decorated with lemon and orange icing sugar roses. On the bottom and largest tier, in flowing orange lettering, were the simple but exquisitely rendered words: *Happy 21st Birthday Alicia.*

He held out a finger, intending to snitch an orange rose, and found his wrist smartly encased in a grip of steel. He turned and found himself not two inches from Jenny's nose. For the first time he really noticed her eyes, and was amazed at their deep blue beauty.

'Don't even think about it,' Jenny advised him, and smiled sweetly.

Justin straightened up and grinned. 'You know, Jenny Starling, if you were six stone lighter, I think I'd marry you.'

Jenny, mortally offended, stared at him for a shell-shocked instant, then spun on her heel and stormed into the kitchen. The grey cat, prowling around the waste bucket for scraps, took one look at her and hissed massively. Jenny hissed back.

Marry her indeed, Jenny fumed. Hah! Did she look as if she had so little taste that she would actually marry a man like Justin Greer?

'I do hope you can get that monstrosity into the ball-room without an accident.' Justin's laughing voice followed her across the room, and a little while later he emerged from the pantry, closing the door behind him. 'I'd hate to see that marvellous edifice, like Humpty Dumpty, having a great fall.'

'Don't worry,' Jenny said grimly. 'I'll see to it. It only needs myself and one other to handle it. Perhaps the florist. He looks as if he could handle anything,' she said, more to herself than to anyone else. She was still subconsciously worrying about Arbie and the grasping Babs.

'Florist?' Justin said, his voice sharpening.

'Hmm. Arbie-somebody-or-other.'

'I doubt he'll be around for long. You'd better be quick. I saw them unloading the last of the flowers just now. Daphne's in seventh heaven.'

'But he's staying to the banquet,' Jenny said, looking around in surprise. 'Your sister invited him.'

Justin stared back at her, his handsome face darkening. 'Did she now?' he said, his voice suddenly low and ominous, all good humour vanishing. 'Did she really?'

Jenny turned and began rattling pots and pans in a tellingly loud manner. 'I imagine Alicia felt that she could invite who she liked,' she said diplomatically, her voice deliberately vague. From behind her, Justin laughed harshly.

'No doubt she did, the little mischief-maker. But then, two can play at that game. And I can invite who I like as well.'

Jenny spun around sharply, not at all sure she liked the sound of that, but he was already halfway out the door. Jenny threw her head back and gave a yell. Vera dropped the pan she was stirring and the cat shot two feet in the air, turned, landed and streaked to the door.

After her shriek of pure frustration had finished rattling around the rafters, Jenny felt much better, and calmly began seeing to the various sauces, while Vera watched her anxiously.

She'd be glad when this damned party was over. But she didn't realize, then, just how permanently 'over' the party was going to be—for someone.

SEVEN

'HELLO IN HERE. Anything I can do to help?'

Jenny looked around and smiled vaguely at Mark Greer as he came down the few steps that led into the kitchen and took a deep, appreciative sniff.

'Thanks, no. Everything's just about ready, final touches notwithstanding.'

'Ah, it's those final touches that sent me down. Alicia wants to make sure that the flat wines are uncorked and breathing. She doesn't trust the wine waiters to do it, apparently.'

Jenny, taking a delicate taste of her cherry sauce, nodded and then quickly showed the elder Greer to the back pantry. 'Look at all that champagne!' Mark gasped, turning a shade green. Then he forced a laugh. 'I'd better get someone to take a few crates into the ballroom. My daughter must think people are going to bathe in it.'

Jenny smiled distractedly, her mind on her Prawns Magenta. She mustn't forget the final squeeze of lemon.

'These are the reds then. And the whites are, oh, yes, over there. Why are these two dozen champagne bottles set aside?' Mark asked.

Jenny glanced in, and shrugged. 'I don't do wine,' she said firmly.

'I believe, Mr Greer, that Al wants those for the toast.'

Both Jenny and Mark jumped at the unexpected interruption, with Mark going slightly stiff-backed at the sight of the young man in front of him. Not that Keith

Harding didn't polish up well in an evening suit. He did. The black and white ensemble only served to make his hair more richly thick, his athletic body more manfully elegant and his handsome face even more pronounced and undeniable.

'Oh. Ah, right. I'd better leave it here then.'

'I saw you come in,' Keith said, by way of explanation, 'and wondered if there was something I could do. Al asked me to come early. I daresay she thought an extra pair of hands around the place wouldn't hurt.'

'Er, no. Well, perhaps you could lug a crate of this champagne into the ballroom for me then?' Alicia's father obliged. 'We can't have the waiters traipsing in and out of the kitchen too often tonight.'

'No,' Jenny said quickly and loudly. 'We can't.' She went to the fridge to check on her mousses.

As the two men left, Keith Harding carrying the crate with a telling ease, Jenny watched them go, her eyes troubled. Things were all topsy-turvy in this house. Nobody wanted Alicia and Keith to marry, except Alicia and Keith. Arbie-the-florist was a powder keg getting ready to explode, and Justin, unless she missed her guess, was about to pull a fast one on his sister. It all made her deeply uneasy. She sighed, trying to talk herself out of her doom-laden mood, and checked her watch. One hour until the banquet was due to begin.

'Hello. Alicia sent me down for some champagne.'

Jenny swung around, annoyance leaping across her face. The kitchen was like Piccadilly Circus tonight.

'Sorry,' Arbie said, obviously and accurately reading her expression. 'I wouldn't bother you otherwise—I know how annoying it can be when you're trying to work—but Alicia insisted. Champagne?'

'In there.' Jenny nodded to the pantry and watched him

go, then gave a start and rushed to the oven to check the various meats. They were, as she'd really expected, cooking perfectly. Arbie appeared a little while later, puffing slightly, just as Mark and Keith came back.

'Hello, Arbie,' Mark said cheerfully. 'Alicia has you working as well, I see. She seems to think guests are invited for her private whims, rather than to be entertained.'

Arbie smiled such a knowing smile that Jenny felt disconcerted. Here was a man who missed very little, and understood a great deal about human foibles, she thought. She wondered how such an obviously sensitive and intelligent man coped with life's blunt instruments. She wondered, too, how he felt about Alicia Greer and her cruel little games. As she watched his white-suited, comical figure stagger under the weight of the wine, she wondered even more how he felt about Justin Greer's golden beauty, inherited wealth and easy elegance.

'I don't mind,' Arbie, the easygoing friend of the family said lightly. 'I daresay I shall be drinking my fair share of the stuff tonight, anyway.' And he laughed, joining in Mark's happy acknowledgement.

Jenny nodded, finding it all very interesting. Arbie was obviously a 'good sort' to Mark Greer. To Alicia he was a joke. To Babs Walker he was a meal ticket. Jenny got the weird feeling that he could be all things to all men. But when he looked in a mirror, who did *Arbie* see?

As he struggled up the steps and nudged open the door to the hall, Jenny sighed in relief at the sight of a gaggle of catering staff coming their way.

'Well, I suppose we'd better let you get on with it,' Mark said jovially to the impressive cook. 'We'll leave the champagne for the toast until the final minute, if you don't mind. Ah, here they come. Don't they look smart,'

Mark said as the waiters and waitresses, indeed looking very smart and crisply clean and tidy, filed past.

Keith Harding, looking and no doubt feeling uncomfortable, pressed back into the wall to let them pass, then suddenly froze.

Jenny clearly saw his eyes widen and his face muscles collapse in total surprise. And a moment later, she saw why.

Margie Harding, carefully standing at the back of the group and trying to look as inconspicuous as possible, stared grimly at the floor in front of her. And then Jenny remembered seeing her frizzy blond head earlier on that afternoon, in the garden. Hard on the heels of that memory came another. Jenny's glance fell to the rounded collar of her blouse. The one she'd been buying in the jumble sale. The one that she had indeed dyed, for her uniform looked exactly the same as the others. But surely legitimate members of the catering firm had their uniforms supplied? Jenny felt a cold chill run down her spine. What the hell did she think she was doing?

Margie glanced up at her husband, who was staring at her blankly, a peculiar expression in his eyes.

'You wanted to speak to us, Miss Starling?' The head waiter, a very competent individual named Georges, grabbed her attention, more with his fake French accent than with his actual words. Jenny smiled automatically, dredging up her pep talk from memory, and out of the corner of her eye saw Mark Greer leave the room. Keith Harding, she noticed, stayed exactly where he was.

'Er, yes. I'm sure you all know the routine. And the party co-ordinator has gone over things with you.' There was a general, well-repressed groan of agreement. 'However, I just want to go over the menu, just to get the timing right. The soup needs to be served quickly, so I suggest…' Jenny rattled through the procedure, her mind and her eyes on the husband and wife standing only yards, but light years, apart.

Georges, knowing and always impressed by professionalism when he heard it, listened intently, but Jenny, who would normally have been pleasantly flattered, hardly noticed. When she was finished, Georges reassured her that he would follow her instructions to the letter then clapped his hands imperiously and collected his brood. As they trailed past him, Keith reached out and grabbed Margie's arm. She didn't, Jenny noticed, make any move to pull away.

It became deathly quiet in the kitchen as the last of the staff left. Vera had been asked to stay on, just to help with any little emergencies—spilt drinks, dropped plates, and such—but she and Martha had disappeared about an hour ago, no doubt to sulk somewhere out of the hurly-burly and sip some of the Greers' finest port. Now, only the sound of simmering saucepans and spitting meat disturbed the silence. From the shadows at the top of the stairs, Margie finally spoke. 'Hello, Keith.'

'Margie.' His answering voice was quiet and unbelievably tired. 'What are you doing here? Have you gone completely round the bend?'

'I had to come. You wouldn't talk to me. You wouldn't come to the phone at work. Every time I saw you on the street you ran away from me. You moved from your mum's house, and she wouldn't tell me where you'd gone. The only place I knew where to find you is here. Tonight.'

Jenny saw him run a hand wearily through his hair. 'I moved out. I left you. Don't you understand?'

'Other men leave their wives, but they don't avoid them. It's just childish, that's what it is.' Margie's voice was getting tearful now, and Jenny shifted uneasily. She wished they'd go. She'd had enough of fraught human relationships to last her at least a month. What was it about The Beeches that seemed to ferment unrest?

'I tried that. Remember? Coming to see you and the kids. And what happened?'

'Well, what did you expect to happen?' Margie asked, anger and tears now in equal proportion. 'I wanted you back. I still want you back. Did you expect me to just give up? To not even try to get you to come back home where you belong?'

'I tried to warn you it was no good. I tried to tell you if you didn't stop that I wouldn't come again. But you wouldn't listen.' His voice rose to a kind of hopeless wail.

'And what about the kids?' Margie asked, all trace of tears now gone. 'You stop coming to see me, you stop coming to see them. Or are you so wrapped up in your new life that you didn't notice?'

'Of course I noticed,' Keith snapped, his own voice bitter now. 'I hate not seeing them. But you didn't think of that when you drove me away, did you?'

In the silence, Jenny clearly heard the other woman gasp. 'You think it's all my fault?' Her voice was incredulous. And the tears were back. 'I love you. Oh, Keith, I've always loved you. Ever since we were kids at school, there was never anyone else. There won't ever be anyone else. You know that. Why are you being so bloody stupid?'

'Oh, Margie, don't.' Keith sighed deeply. 'Why can't you just accept it? I have to have her, Margie. It's like it is for your old dad and his whisky. I can't stop. I can't give her up. Don't you understand? I just can't.'

Margie began to cry. Soft, heartbroken sobs that had her husband reaching for her and holding on, but not giving in. 'It's no good, Margie,' Keith said softly. 'It's no good. We're through.'

'Don't say that!' Margie howled, pulling away. 'You'll never become one of them, no matter how much she tries to make you one. You'll always be poor, and they'll always have money. Just because of that, they'll never accept you. Everyone else knows it except you! You're the laughingstock of the village.'

The harsh words rang around the quiet room.

'I know,' Keith said, his voice flat and bitter. 'You think I don't know all that? But it doesn't matter. That's what you don't get, Margie. What nobody gets. Alicia and I can't live apart. We can't *be* anything if we're not together.' His voice was passionate now. Desperate, almost possessed.

Jenny winced. She stared at the oven, then at the fridge, then out of the window. The marquee was up, she noticed vaguely. The tables would be set up, and she really should set about transferring the buffet. She wished these two young people would go. Just take their pain and their tragedy, and get out of her kitchen.

'She's a witch, that's what she is,' Margie said bitterly. 'If we'd lived 300 years ago I could have had her burned alive for putting a spell on you. And I would do it too. Just give me the chance!' There was such hate in her voice that her husband stared at her, as if at a stranger. Finally, he shook his head.

'Go home, Margie. Go home to the kids and just forget about us. OK? I'll see you and the kids don't suffer. You've been getting the money all right?'

Margie began to cry in earnest now. It was obviously more than her husband could take, for he suddenly roared, 'Go home!' making both women jump. Jenny, having thoroughly had enough, picked up a tray of Bengal eggs and very loudly slammed it down on the table.

The voices above her promptly lowered to become a

whisper, but such were the acoustics that Jenny could still clearly hear them. 'I won't let you go,' Margie warned. 'You may think I will, but I won't.' And there was something maniacally stubborn in her tone.

Jenny heard a door open somewhere in the hall, and looked over her shoulder. Then they all heard a blithe voice calling Keith's name. Then 'Oh, Daphne, have you seen Mr Harding?'

'I believe he's in the kitchen, Alicia.'

'The kitchen?' Alicia's voice came sharply. 'What on earth's he doing in there?'

'Helping your father with the champagne crates, I understand.'

'Oh, hell!'

As Jenny began to move rapidly across the room, to do what, she wasn't quite sure, Margie backed away, her face white and pinched. At the same time Keith opened the door and left quickly. Nobody, it seemed, wanted a confrontation. When she was sure the coast was clear, Margie left as well, looking stiff and drained. She never gave the cook so much as a backwards glance.

For a long time Jenny stared at the closed door, her heart thudding painfully. When the door suddenly flew open again she nearly screamed, but only Martha, Georges and two of the waiters appeared in the doorway. 'Time to load up the marquee, yes?' Georges said, eyes twinkling and moustache twitching. 'The dining guests are already arriving. The party crowd will not be far behind, and they must have their nibbles, yes?'

'Yes,' Jenny agreed automatically, and watched them unload the food from fridges, ovens, cupboards and table tops, never once remonstrating at the proper way to transfer stuffed tomatoes from baking tray to platter.

'Getting worried, eh?' Martha Vaughan said smugly.

'Don't worry. They won't dare complain. Not about such an accomplished cook as yourself.'

Jenny glanced at Martha and smiled. 'Thank you,' she said sweetly. 'Perhaps you'd care to give me a hand with the giblet gravy?'

Martha paled but gave in gracelessly. 'I wouldn't have thought the likes of you would have known what good old-fashioned giblet gravy was,' she sniffed. 'I thought you fancy cooks always dined on them foreign sauces?'

'You can't beat giblet gravy,' Jenny said sincerely.

'No,' Martha said, stunned into agreeing with her. 'Oh. Well. That's all right then.' Then, realizing that an olive branch had been offered, and feeling strangely obliged to take it, the resident cook said as pleasantly as she could manage, 'That cake of Alicia's looks a treat.'

THE NOISE LEVEL WAS beginning to filter through to the kitchen now—a low, rumbling sound of conversation. Jenny glanced at her watch. It was 6.15 and everything was ready. The first course was simmering, ready to be served, and the meats were going to be ready at the optimum moment. Chase had reported that all the dining guests had arrived. Georges was primed, the wine had breathed, and the Greers had descended, resplendent in tuxedos, gowns and jewels. The band had been told to stop their noisy and tuneless 'warming up' in the ballroom, and were despatched to the marquee. The marquee itself was installed with food and wine and the party lights were twinkling away in the garden.

Everything was ready.

And Jenny, like a horse at the starting gate, was waiting for the flag to be raised. She should be happy. The food was perfect. The tables were beautiful. There had been no major mishaps. She should have been feeling a serene sense of satisfaction. Instead she was afraid. She simply couldn't help feeling that there was something very wrong. She'd tried to shrug it off, reminding herself to simply take care of the food. That was what she was being paid for, after all—to cook.

'I'm going to check on the guests,' she said abruptly, and Georges, who had become convinced of her culinary sainthood, nearly fainted. Martha gaped at her, then hissed, 'Are you mad? You're not supposed to go out there until Mr Mark makes his speech and thanks the staff.'

Jenny knew that. She was flying in the face of etiquette, and nobody would like it. She didn't like it herself. 'I'm going to check the guests,' she said again, and marched briskly out of the kitchen. She knew she was going to regret it, even as she did it.

She just didn't know, then, how much.

EIGHT

DESPITE HER DETERMINATION, Jenny stood in the hall for several moments, glancing nervously at the ballroom doors. The sounds of gaiety clearly emanating from within made her fears seem suddenly ridiculous. And yet there was the dead gardener's boy. But what, really, did an accidental death have to do with a birthday party? Jenny shook her head.

Then a dull thud from across the hall made her turn and frown. A door stood slightly ajar. Giving the ballroom a final anxious glance, she sighed and crossed the hall, pushing the door open and glancing in. For a moment she thought the room was empty. Perhaps it was only the cat, exploring and knocking something over. Then a shadow moved, and Jenny felt the back of her neck prickle.

The room was Mark's study. A large desk was covered in papers, and a comfortable-looking swivel leather arm-chair was positioned behind it. The room was gloomy, for the heavy velvet curtains had been drawn across the windows. Now who would do that? Not Chase, she was sure. It was his last job of the evening to close windows and draw curtains, and generally lock up, and she could see no reason why a member of the household would want the curtains closed on such a lovely and still-light May evening.

Then she realized that the window overlooked the large lawn with the marquee. And so anyone looking in from there would be able to see clearly what was going on inside the study.

The shadow moved again, and this time the sound of rustling papers carried clearly across the room. Jenny realized that whoever was inside must have drawn the curtains in an effort to conceal what he was doing. But what exactly was that? From the sound of it, he was rifling through the papers on the desk. Not a burglar then. Even if the timing had not been so wrong, the visitor was ignoring the other valuable objects in the room; even from the doorway, Jenny could see the gleam of silver candlesticks on the fireplace mantel, for instance.

Then the stranger did something that almost made Jenny change her mind. He picked up something that glinted even in the dimmed light of the room. Something jewel-like. She was just about to demand to be told what was going on, when the stranger lifted his hand and she saw the object clearly. It was a decorative paper knife, one of the dagger-like, jewelled objects people brought back from their holidays in places like Spain and India. The shadowy figure slipped the object, handle first, into his inside pocket.

Jenny opened her mouth to speak just as a blast of noise hit her from behind. The ballroom doors had been pushed open, and a stream of chatting guests began to file into the dining room opposite. Jenny automatically shot a glance at her watch.

Six-thirty. For the first time in her career, she was not present when the first course left the kitchen. She turned back to the stranger, who had stopped halfway across the room, and was staring at her in slack-jawed dismay. She could see now that he was an older man, much older than she had previously thought. He was sturdily built, with a bluff and, she was sure, normally friendly face. Now he looked only surprised and disconcerted. He walked to meet her with reluctance in every step.

'Tom! There you are!' From behind her, Mark Greer's voice sounded wonderfully normal and unconcerned.

'Hello, Mark. I was just taking a breather.'

'I know what you mean!' Mark said, with a surprising gentleness. 'Don't much care for parties myself. Hello, Jenny, is something wrong? Don't tell me the soup has burned and we're all going to have to start off with corned beef sandwiches!'

Jenny managed a tight smile. 'Oh, I always check everything is ready just before the off,' she lied with all the assured panache of a politician. 'Make sure all the guests are seated, that the pathways are clear, that sort of thing,' she elaborated, and glanced tellingly at the stranger. 'Like this gentleman here,' she said softly. 'He didn't seem to know his way to the dining room.'

'What! Tom not know the way to food?' Mark took his friend by the shoulders. 'We can't have you missing the best meal of your life, eh, Jenny? Especially since it's partly a celebration of your own retirement as well.'

Jenny glanced sharply at the man she now knew must be Tom Banks, the recently sacked executive, and wondered exactly what he wanted with a sharply bladed paper knife. She began to open her mouth to warn Mark, and then closed it again as the two men entered the dining room. After all, what could she say? 'Oh, excuse me, Mr Greer, but did you know your friend is a thief?' Or, even better, 'Excuse me, Mark, but I think your old friend is about to stick someone with your paper knife?'

'And what are you doing here, pray tell?' a voice asked from just an inch behind her left ear, and Jenny spun around. The kitchen cat would have recognized the hiss she gave. But Justin merely grinned at her mockingly. His blond hair and blue eyes set off the black and white of his evening dress in a manner that wouldn't have looked out of place in a Hollywood movie.

'I thought you were supposed to be panicking in the kitchen, making sure every morsel is perfect. What happens if a waiter leaves the kitchen with a splash of soup on the soup-bowl rim? Won't the world come crashing to an end?'

'I never panic,' Jenny corrected him sharply, 'and if Georges lets a waiter out of that kitchen with the soup anything more than the regulation two inches below the tureen rim, I'll boil and eat Martha's cat.'

'Now that I'd like to see.' Justin guffawed with laughter. 'I can't see *that* animal standing for being plucked and seasoned.'

'Why aren't you in the dining room?' Jenny counterattacked sharply, exasperated and angry with him. He was making her like him again, and that was just too much.

'Family has to take care of guests, you know. Mother went in with the early birds. Father took care of his cronies. Alicia and I have to round up the stragglers and get them seated before the soup.'

'As if you'd care,' Jenny growled.

Justin grinned. 'How well you know me, darling Starling.'

Jenny stared back stonily, and Justin laughed. 'All right, if you must know, I'm waiting for my date. I want to make sure she behaves herself.'

'And why wouldn't she?' Jenny asked archly. 'I'm sure Miss Walker wants only to impress.'

Justin laughed. 'How well you know us all, darling Starling. Actually, Babs *would* have wanted to impress the daylights out of everyone, reassuring them all that she knew which fork to use, and demonstrating that she would never, *ever* put her peas on her knife. But that was when she actually thought she might become one of the family,' he added, his voice now both grim and vicious.

Jenny stiffened. 'You've broken off your engagement?' she asked quietly. *'Now?'* And again that sense of impending doom washed over her.

'Engagement? Hah, we were never engaged, except in Babs's own mind. And I told her so, in no uncertain terms, not an hour ago. Now I'm not so sure that she hasn't planned a little revenge of her own. She can be a trifle wild, can Babs,' Justin acknowledged, with such cheerful disregard that Jenny felt like throttling him.

'You should be more damned careful!' she said instead, and with such a note of genuine fear that Justin gaped at her, all amusement draining from his face. 'I mean, women don't like to be used.' Jenny felt compelled to justify herself. 'And Alicia's gone to so much trouble to make this party a success for you both. It would be a shame to have it ruined because of your awful timing. Not to mention lack of basic human compassion,' she added drolly.

'Darling Starling, are you telling me off?' He half-laughed. But his eyes were narrowed, and he was clearly unhappy with her lecture.

'Yes. I am.' Jenny looked at him levelly.

Justin laughed then. Whether or not it was genuine, Jenny couldn't tell. 'Darling Starling! Oh-oh, here she comes. Doesn't she remind you of a tigress?'

Babs Walker, a vision in flaming-red silk, slunk across the hall, very much reminding Jenny of a tigress. Her dark eyes were blazing with black fire.

'Does Arbie know about this?' Jenny suddenly asked, surprising herself almost as much as Justin.

He stared at her, the amusement definitely genuine now. 'I doubt it. Although I daresay Babs will get around to telling him eventually. Oh, not the truthful version, of course. She'll tell him *she* dropped *me,* and he, like a fool, will believe her. Or pretend to. Not that she'll stay with him long, of course. Arbie makes a good safety net, but she'll be on the lookout for another meal ticket soon. Won't you, darling?' he added in a slightly raised voice as Babs finally reached them.

She glanced sharply at the cook, although Jenny knew she hadn't overheard their conversation. Then she smiled at Justin, showing her lovely white fangs, and looped her hand under his elbow. Her nails, long and red, curled around the black satin of his sleeve. Her smile was indeed animalistic, and Jenny wondered just how well Babs had taken her dismissal by Justin Greer—how she had re-acted to having the dream of the good life taken away, and of being made to look a fool in front of her ex-lover.

As they headed to the dining room, Justin turned back and winked at Jenny over his shoulder. The cook shook her head at him angrily, her lips grimly tight. Torn be-tween her intense desire to return to the safety of the kitchen, and her unremitting conscience, which de-manded that she do something, she stood there wavering.

The dining room was now almost full, but she simply couldn't go in there. A cook in the dining room was just asking for trouble. Instead she walked to the ballroom, where only a few guests remained, and she hastily stood to one side as they passed, glancing at her curiously. She was not dressed as a party guest, nor was she in a cater-er's uniform. All the guests were strangers to her, and Jenny ignored them, sure that the threat, whatever it was, did not come from their quarter.

Finally, only Alicia and an older couple remained, Alicia clearly trying to chivvy them towards the door. She glanced up and saw Jenny, and a peculiar expression crossed her face.

'Everything's all right in the kitchens, Miss Greer,' the cook reassured her quickly, and Alicia laughed.

'See, Moira? Even the cook has come up to try and hurry you along. Frank, you're going to love this banquet. Miss Starling here is one of the best cooks in the country.'

'As right?' Frank leered at her, obviously already well away on the wine. No wonder Alicia was having trouble with them. 'Wouldn't miss it for the world'—he burped—'in that case.'

Jenny stepped aside to let them pass, and Alicia paused beside her, watching the couple sway their way into the dining room. 'Is there something wrong, Miss Starling?' Alicia asked, turning to her. She looked spectacular in her blue dress and borrowed sapphires—young, vibrant, alive and beautiful.

Jenny sighed and shook her head. 'No.'

'Good. Well, then, I'll go and join the others and announce dinner is served. Everything set?'

'Everything's set,' Jenny echoed, and hoped she was right. It might be chaos down in the kitchen by now for all she knew. As she watched Alicia sail into the dining room, queen of the evening, Jenny had never felt more oddly depressed. Perhaps she should see a doctor. Perhaps her hormones were out of whack or something.

She was about to return to the kitchen where she belonged when a figure stepped through the French windows and into the ballroom. He was a tall man, lean and dark, and aimlessly began to wander around, looking at the paintings and ornaments, then pausing beside a buffet table to take a nibble. Then the man turned her way, spotted her, and his face became as still as rock. He looked almost unreal for a moment. She felt a purely instinctive desire to run, and quickly quashed it. She raised her chin and one eyebrow, stiffened her back and her resolve and waited.

'Hello. Looks like I'm not the only late arrival around here. Oh, you can't be a guest, can you?' he added, as he ran his eyes over her in a thorough inspection, noting more her luscious curves and beautiful eyes then her plain summer dress. 'I can't see Alicia allowing the competition somehow.'

'I'm the cook,' Jenny said stiffly. 'If you're dining, you're a little late. Miss Greer has just gone in.'

'I'm not.' His lips twisted in what, Jenny supposed, was meant to be a smile. 'And I doubt, very much, if Alicia even knows I'm here.' He dug his hands deep into his pockets and pulled out a pack of cigarettes and a fancily engraved silver lighter. 'Smoke?'

Jenny reared back. 'Hell, no! They ruin the taste buds.' He might have been offering her opium, for all the shocked disdain her tone carried. The man looked at her in surprise, and twisted his lips again. Then his eyes seemed to narrow, although she could have sworn none of his facial muscles actually moved. 'I've seen you somewhere before,' the stranger said matter-of-factly, and Jenny felt her heart jump.

'I don't think so. I would have remembered you had we met.'

'I didn't say we'd met,' the stranger corrected softly. 'Only that I'd seen you before. I never forget a face.' The man paused, considering, and Jenny began to have difficulty breathing. 'Ever had your picture in the papers?'

'Do you have an invitation?' she asked coldly, neither denying nor confirming his question.

'You mean a written one? One of those elegant square bits of paper with gold italics on it? My name, and everything?'

'Yes.'

'No.'

Jenny watched him light the cigarette. He was, she suddenly realized, very attractive, in a strange and dangerous sort of way.

'I think you should leave,' she said.

'Do you?'

'Yes.'

'You could always chuck me out,' the man agreed. 'You're a veritable Titan. Who knows, you might even manage it.'

'Yes—I just might,' she agreed pleasantly.

Behind her, a door opened and Georges appeared from the kitchen, carrying aloft a lovely Spode soup tureen. Behind him a line of waiters and waitresses marched past, several of the men carrying matching tureens. Georges spotted her but never even paused in his stride, and Jenny almost wilted in relief. She could trust the fake Frenchman to keep things on track.

When she looked back, the ballroom was empty. Jenny blinked and dragged in a breath. That was quick! The man must have moved like greased lightning. No doubt the gatecrasher, once caught, had thought better of it.

Jenny looked once more around the deserted ballroom, then stepped back and closed the doors. Then she glanced through the open dining-room door, watching the waiters and waitresses expertly ladling out the soup, Georges pouring from a great height with deft ease. She stayed only long enough to watch the first few diners take their first sip and make happy noises over its texture, taste and general excellence, and then turned back for the kitchen and sanctuary.

MARTHA LOOKED UP as she walked down the few steps and stopped in the middle of the now-deserted kitchen. The resident cook opened her mouth, no doubt to say something snide, but the look on Jenny's face stopped her. Instead, she nodded to the oven. 'Better check them lobster thingummies,' she reminded, almost kindly, and Jenny nodded absently.

The cat, from the top shelf of the condiment cupboard, watched her take the lobster dishes from the oven and leave them to cool on the worktops. The cat licked his whiskers and waited.

'Did anyone say anything?' Martha asked, and Jenny absently shook her head. 'Ah, well. Perhaps it's just as well.'

Jenny, even more absently, nodded. She saw again Justin's cheeky wink over his shoulder. The strange look on Alicia's face. She saw, in her mind's eye, Tom Banks putting the paper knife in his pocket. And she recalled the stranger, asking if she'd ever been in the papers.

'I just feel so damned unsettled,' Jenny muttered out loud, more to explain her own behaviour to herself than anything else.

'Don't we all, love,' Martha said with feeling. 'This business with Jimmy Speight has left me feeling as if everything's changed somehow. I dunno, it feels as if the whole house is different. I'm beginning to think it was a bad day when the Speights moved into Rousham Green. That I am.'

The cook frowned. 'You mean they aren't locals?'

Martha sniffed. 'That they're not. Moved down here

from somewhere in the west about four years ago. Wouldn't be surprised if they weren't Welsh,' she added gloomily.

Jenny frowned again. Four years ago. Now where had she heard that before? Somebody else had done something four years ago too. But she just couldn't quite seem to remember—oh, yes. Daphne had come to The Beeches four years ago too. Now that…

Her thoughts broke off as, out of the corner of one eye, she saw the cat bunch his muscles, ready to make his move on the lobster morsels. Just as he leapt, she deftly lifted the tray away and the stunned feline found himself landing on an empty worktop. There he stared at her with dumbfounded eyes.

'You've got to be quicker than that, my good moggy,' Jenny informed him gently, and actually gave him a chuck under the chin. But even as she stroked the astonished feline, Jenny had the uncanny feeling that someone out there in the house, somewhere, somehow, had been very much quicker off the mark than even Jenny Starling, supercook. And that before long, everyone was going to know about it.

NINE

JENNY WAS FEELING pretty stupid. It was not a feeling she was accustomed to, and it was the only thing that had the tendency to make her gush. Mercifully aware of this foible, however, she now firmly clamped her lips together as Georges and his army departed with the final course.

It was nearly eight o'clock, and all was well. Nobody had complained about the meat being undercooked. Nobody had choked to death on her soup. Everyone had roundly admired her seafood dishes. Disaster had never seemed so far away.

So, she'd made a fool of herself for nothing. She'd just have to think of it as one of life's painful little lessons and chalk it up to experience. Unless, of course, somebody keeled over during the dessert, while gasping out curses on the cook's head.

But nobody did. Fifteen minutes later, Georges came back with empty plates and a beaming face. 'Ees a triumph, Mademoiselle Starling. Never 'ave I heard the guests rave so about the food.'

Martha harrumphed loudly, and her cat yowled. Georges quickly stacked the dishes, noting with stunned surprise that the previous dirty plates were washed and dried and ready to be packed away. He glanced at Martha, who glowered at him, and slightly shook his head. No, definitely not that one. Then he turned to Jenny, and nodded. He'd been right the first time. A real professional. That momentary madness earlier must have been just nerves. And Georges could allow that. All great creative artistes were allowed nerves.

'The coffee ees ready?'

'Of course,' Jenny said, and whipped out a plate of crackers, biscuits and wafers, freshly cooked and as crumbly as good soil after an experienced gardener had been around it. Georges let himself have a crafty sniff as he held a tray aloft. Bliss.

'Well, that's that then,' Martha said gloomily. She'd been hoping the fancy cook would fall flat on her face all day.

''Fraid so,' Jenny acknowledged, almost sympathizing with her.

'Mr Greer would like the staff to put in a brief appearance at the table,' Chase announced from the top of the three steps that led down into the kitchen, stiff-backed and so dignified he almost crackled. Martha got to her feet quickly. 'I'm all for that, Mr Chase,' she said, determined that no one must forget that the resident cook had played her part (even if she hadn't) and that she hadn't taken offence at being so rudely usurped by a stranger in her kitchen (even if she had).

Jenny followed them out.

The dining room was replete with satisfied diners. At the head of the table, Mark Greer rose formally and tapped his spoon against his glass. 'Ladies and gentlemen, I'd like to thank you all for coming'—there were muted sounds and rumbles of acknowledgement—'and trust that you've all had a good time. I'd like to thank our caterer, Miss Jenny Starling, for producing such a truly wonderful and memorable meal.' He paused and raised his glass to her, and Jenny beamed as everyone looked her way and applauded. 'I'd also like to thank our own resident cook, Martha, and all the catering staff, who served us so well. The staff.'

Mark and the guests raised their glasses in a toast, then Chase led them all out again, probably miffed at not having been given a mention. Jenny caught Tom Banks staring at her, and she met his eyes briefly. He looked away first. Out in the hall once more, she could hear the band revving up in the garden, and the sound of a hundred voices raised in conversation. Large Chinese lanterns were now being lit out in the gardens, and would look lovely once true darkness had fallen.

Again, she felt stupid. Everything was going swimmingly. There was not a hitch in sight.

VERA WAS SITTING in the corner chair, dozing. The last of the dishes were stacked away, and a waiter came in to collect more champagne and the special vintage for the toast to the birthday boy and girl. It was nearly midnight.

Jenny watched Martha tuck into a piece of lemon tart that Chase had brought down from the buffet tables, and smiled.

She glanced once more at the clock ticking away on the wall, and thought of tomorrow, when she would be off. There was a hotel in Taunton that she knew would always welcome her with open arms. There was, if it came to it, a hotel in practically every county in England that would take her on, on the spot, should she show up on their doorstep. Or she could go north—Edinburgh was nice, this time of the year.

The kitchen door burst open so quickly that it slammed against the wall and ricocheted back. Vera leapt out of her chair, and Martha's last few bites of tart shot out of her spoon. The door, being pushed open for the second time, revealed only Chase.

But a vastly different Chase from the one Jenny knew. His eyes were huge, like those of an owl, and all colour had fled from his face. His lips moved, but no sound came out, and he staggered down the steps as if he were drunk.

'Whatever is it?' Martha cried. If Chase were in such a state then the world must be coming to an end, at the very least, she was clearly thinking. Jenny's heart also pounded. Once again that feeling of disaster pounced on her, chilling her blood and mocking her previous relaxation.

'They're dead,' Chase finally managed to croak.

'What?' Martha gasped. Her trembling lips made her next words almost inaudible. She looked ashen. 'Who's dead?'

'The twins! Justin and Alicia,' Chase said wretchedly. 'They're dead.'

Jenny groped her way to the kitchen chair and sat down heavily. In front of her was a half-empty bottle of champagne that Martha had opened and guzzled, glaring at the upstart cook as she'd done so, and daring her to object. Jenny, of course, hadn't. Now she reached for an empty glass and poured herself a good dollop. If ever she'd needed a drink, now was the time.

Jenny took a hefty gulp.

'They're saying it was the champagne,' Chase carried on, totally stripped of all his authority and suddenly appearing heartrenderingly human. 'They say it was poisoned. At least, that's what young Dr Bannister thinks.'

Jenny promptly sprayed the contents of her mouth towards the sink. Some of it actually reached it. The cat, getting some of the fallout, flattened himself against the tiles and growled.

All three heads turned her way, their eyes straying to

the champagne she was holding. Jenny hastily put the glass down and pushed the chair away from the table, wiping her mouth with the back of her hand and staring at the bottle of finest Moët and Chandon as if it was a spitting cobra, getting ready to strike. For a second or two nobody spoke. Then Martha began to sob. The sight of the usually stalwart cook, so overwrought, was too much for Vera, who began to shake and tremble like a leaf in a hurricane.

Chase merely stood there, looking blankly at the wall.

Jenny slowly rose, and found somebody had transplanted her kneecaps with jelly. She nevertheless managed to walk to the steps, and emerged into a hall that was eerily silent. The doors to the ballroom stood open, and from the study she could hear somebody calling for an ambulance. As she crossed the floor, the phone was put down and picked up again, and the same voice, young, harried but admirably firm, called for the police.

Jenny pushed open the doors, which were already ajar, and looked around her. It was an eerie, almost unbelievable scene. A hundred people stood about in total silence. Some were clinging to the walls, some of the women were weeping. Men looked at each other, and around, then down at their feet. The atmosphere was leaden. In bizarre contrast, gaily coloured balloons swayed from the ceiling, and party streamers, all the bright colours of the rainbow, festooned the walls, draped over the tables and lay on the floor.

The only signs of movement came from one corner where a small semicircle of stout-hearted or ghoulish souls had gathered.

Jenny found herself walking towards them, compelled by some force she couldn't have named if offered a million pounds. People parted easily to let her pass. Being so tall, Jenny could clearly see between the shoulders of two male guests the sight that had changed the ballroom from one of gaiety to tragedy.

Mark and Sherri Greer stood to one side, their hands clinging tightly together as they stared, white-faced and too shocked to weep, at the sight of their children, lying stricken on the floor.

Justin lay on his back, his eyes wide open and staring at nothing. His hands were clenched into fists, but whether it was pain, rage or fear that had clenched them in those final moments of life, Jenny would never know. His legs were bent, his head thrown right back. His mouth was open, and just a trace of saliva gleamed on his chin. He'd obviously had some kind of convulsion before dying.

It seemed to Jenny, still reeling under the influence of shock, that it was a very inappropriate way for someone of Justin's elegance and beauty to die, and she felt a sudden and overwhelmingly fierce rush of rage wash over her.

She remembered him alive, winking cheekily at her over his shoulder as he led his just-jilted ladyfriend away, and she too wanted to weep. Instead she took a deep breath and straightened her back, then lifted her eyes from the dead man and searched out Babs Walker in the crowd.

She was standing not far away, clinging to a broad shoulder and staring at her dead lover with apparently genuine horror. Not grief. But then, Jenny wouldn't have expected that. Her eyes moved to the man she was leaning against. It was, of course, Arbie, who had wasted no time in becoming a pillar of support.

But just how quickly, Jenny wondered, had he seized the advantage? Had he given even a single thought to anyone but himself, or Babs Walker? He was not even looking at Justin, Jenny noticed with bitter eyes, but was instead staring down at the blond head leaning against his upper arm.

He looked very, very happy.

A small sound had Jenny's head swivelling around. Alicia Greer was lying on the floor not a foot away from her twin, but she was being cradled in Keith Harding's arms. He held on to her fiercely, only moving at all when another young man, kneeling in front of them, checked Alicia's small white neck.

It seemed a bizarre thing to do, until Jenny's dazed mind finally began to work at something like its proper level. The stranger was obviously the doctor that Chase had mentioned, and he was checking her pulse. Which meant that Alicia Greer, at least, was not dead. Not yet.

But as Jenny looked at her deathly pale face, she thought she had never seen anyone more close to it. She could only barely make out the very slightest rise and fall of Alicia's slender breasts as she breathed, as shallowly as a robin. Her long, white, lovely limbs also had a bent, thrashed look, but her convulsions were now obviously over. Her delicate eyelids looked blue, and her painted lips hung obscenely open. She was a pathetic sight.

Jenny raised her eyes to Keith Harding, and took an involuntary step back. He looked ferocious. Stricken. And vastly terrified. In fact, she'd never seen a stronger, wider range of overpowering emotions on any one human face before. Tears streamed from his eyes unnoticed, for he did not heave with sobs, or gulp, or in any other way express his grief. Instead he stared down at Alicia's head, his hands shaking as they held on to her.

Keith looked across at the doctor, his eyes pleading. 'Don't let her die.' His voice was choked, but urgent, and

several of the people around them looked away, unable
to bear such raw emotion.

'An ambulance is on the way,' the doctor said reassuringly. 'It will have a stomach pump. We have to hope…'
His voice trailed off, and Jenny understood. Alicia looked
so beyond hope it was pitiful.

Keith bent over his love, and let his tears fall on her
unknowing head. 'Don't leave me,' he whispered, so quietly that only the doctor, Jenny and probably Sherri and
Mark Greer were close enough to hear him.

Keith hadn't, as far as Jenny knew, even looked in Justin's direction either. Nobody, it seemed, was looking at
Justin. With the exception of herself and his parents, did
anybody even care that he was gone? Aware that such
thoughts could only lead her to hysteria, she shook her
head, clearing it and getting a strong grip on herself. She
turned away, quite deliberately, and met only blank, disbelieving faces.

Except for the man who stood by the mantelpiece.

Jenny recognized him immediately. The gatecrasher.
So he hadn't left after all. He was smoking, and his face
was merely thoughtful. It came as such a shock to see that
level of indifference amongst so much shock and bewil-
derment, that Jenny actually shivered. The gatecrasher
met her gaze, hesitated, as if unwilling to acknowledge
her, then smiled, as if recognizing the inevitable. His eyes
narrowed on her, sensing trouble.

Jenny looked away. Later, she thought grimly. Later.

Unable to stop, and feeling like a magnet drawn by
some macabre force, she found herself once more looking down at Justin Greer. The rage was still there, deep
in her soul, but she was channelling it now. Nobody deserved to die like this. In convulsions, in pain and fear,

at their own birthday party, and seeping out their life in front of hundreds of gaping people.

Whoever had done it would not get away with it.

A nagging feeling of something being missing had been teasing her subconscious ever since she'd entered the room, and suddenly she knew what it was. Jenny looked around but, as expected, she could not see the face she was seeking.

Where was Tom Banks?

Jenny's lips thinned. She would be glad when the police arrived. This was all getting too much—way too much. Turning back for the final time, needing to get back to her kitchen, wanting with a longing that was almost physical to return to her normal, safe world, she glanced once more at Justin and Alicia Greer, and shook her head.

It was just as she started to turn away that she noticed that Keith Harding was staring now into the crowd, and the look on his face was so strange, so enigmatic, that it stopped her dead. Tracing the path of his eyes, feeling almost afraid to see, but knowing that she must, she realized that Keith Harding was staring at his wife.

Margie.

Jenny had almost forgotten about Margie. Now, as she too looked at the frizzy-haired blonde woman, she saw that Margie Harding stood statue-still, her eyes wide and dark with a strangely triumphant expression. She looked neat and efficient in her forged waitress's uniform. To complete the picture, she was still holding her tray, professionally steady and at the recommended waist level.

The tray, Jenny noticed with deep and grim dismay, was full of champagne glasses.

TEN

THE KITCHEN WAS so quiet that Jenny could hear the cat snoring. She wasn't sure where he was—perhaps in the big mixing bowl under the sink, a favourite ambush spot—but the wheezy sleeping sound was offset only by the mechanical precision of the ticking clock. Chase put the kettle on for the fifth time. It was nearly two in the morning. The ambulance had arrived and taken Alicia away. Nobody yet knew whether she was alive or dead.

The police had followed on shortly after, and everyone had been ushered from the ballroom into side rooms. Constables were now taking the names and addresses of the last of the guests, who'd been leaving in small numbers during the early hours.

Jenny had pointed out to a very young-looking constable the gatecrasher, and recommended that he take good care in checking his identity before allowing him to leave. She wouldn't have put it past that cold-thinking, slippery individual to leave a false name and non-existent address. She could only hope that the constable was not as inexperienced as he had appeared.

Chase handed out yet more cups of tea. Vera was asleep in the chair and he left her cup on the sideboard beside her. It was an oddly touching gesture. In normal circumstances, Jenny suspected that not even torture would have made Chase do something as menial as make the daily a cup of tea. Jenny smiled her thanks as she was given her own cup, but left it cooling on the kitchen table.

Everybody started nervously when the door opened, and a constable asked them to come to the library. Martha shook Vera awake, and they all trooped out like weary and chastised schoolchildren.

The library was crowded with catering staff. Faces were white with exhaustion and lips were pinched tight in tension. Even Georges seemed to have lost some of his verve and vim. Wearily, one or two on the sofa moved over, allowing Martha to sit, and a young waiter hastily took his feet off a chair as Chase gave him a killing glance. Vera disappeared to a window seat, shrinking back behind the curtains as if they could hide her from the hideous events of the night. Jenny took one of the wooden-backed chairs, no doubt scrounged from various rooms, and sat with her back to the wall.

It was, as it was to turn out, a very apt choice.

For a while, nobody spoke. The constable standing at the door and looking as if he expected one of them to try and make a bolt for it at any moment stifled the inclination to talk very effectively. Finally, it was Martha who could bear no more.

'Have the police talked to you yet?' she asked the limp waitress next to her, who shook her head wordlessly.

'Any word on Miss Alicia?' Chase asked, of no one in particular. Nobody spoke. It came almost as a relief when the door opened and Inspector Mollineaux walked in, with Sergeant Mollern at his side. The resident staff knew them at once, of course, but the catering staff eyed them both with a mixture of relief and apprehension. Jenny could well imagine what they were thinking. Sergeant Mollern looked as if he caught (and ate) perpetrators for breakfast, whilst Mollineaux looked formidably intelligent.

'Sorry to keep you all waiting. I'm Inspector Mollineaux,' the grey-haired policeman introduced himself, his accent totally lacking any inflexion whatsoever. 'This is Sergeant Mollern.'

There were half-hearted murmurs of greeting, but nobody was surprised when Inspector Mollineaux remained standing. The polite greeting was as socially relaxed as the policeman intended to become. 'There's no need to tell you all that there's been a tragedy here tonight,' he began, looking around. His eyes, Jenny noticed, were of a peculiarly colourless variety tonight. If pressed, she could only call them grey.

No doubt being called to The Beeches for a second time, to deal with a second death, had left him feeling in a rather grey mood as well. 'Mr Justin Greer is dead. I have no news, yet, of the condition of Miss Alicia Greer, but at the moment we are working on the assumption that Mr Greer was murdered.'

There was a ripple of sound, but nobody was really surprised.

'I have been talking to the guests, and now have a good general idea of the events of the night. However, since this was a birthday party, and you, as staff, had much more to do with the actual running of the show, so to speak, my sergeant and I now want to hear from you in much more exact and precise details, concerning the events of this evening.'

The group looked around uneasily but Mollineaux seemed impervious to the fear in the room. No doubt he was used to it. Sergeant Mollern, Jenny noticed vaguely, was jotting down notes so quickly it could only have been in shorthand, and she felt herself relax a little. They might have been forced to tread warily around the Jimmy Speight case, but now they had the bit well and truly between their teeth, and it boded well for the investigation. No policeman was at his best when he had superiors constantly breathing down his neck to take it easy and not upset the VIPs.

'Since we are not yet totally sure of the cause of death in Mr Justin Greer's case, we'll begin, tonight, with the arrival of the first guests. I shall ask questions, and whichever of you feels most able to help should answer. Is that clear?'

Jenny found it very clear indeed, but wondered how many of the others did. His reference to what they would discuss 'tonight' could only mean hours and hours of more questioning in the days to come.

'Very well. We'll begin with the first guests. Who is the butler here?' As if he didn't know!

Chase coughed once, then stiffened as the eyes of the inspector fell on him. 'You are?'

'Chase, sir.'

'Oh, yes, of course, Chase. You admitted the first guests?'

'Yes, sir.'

'Who were?'

'Mr and Mrs Drake, sir.'

Jenny noticed Mollern glance at a list of guests and mark their names. He gave the inspector nothing more than a look, but it spoke volumes. Jenny relaxed even more. These men had obviously worked together a great deal, probably for years, and she was glad. She had the feeling that discovering Justin's (and possibly Alicia's) killer was not going to be easy. And Jimmy Speight's killer? The thought slipped into her mind so craftily it almost made her jump. But just because there'd been a murder tonight, did it really necessarily follow that Jimmy had been murdered too? She rather thought that it did. If not, then it was one hell of a coincidence, Jenny mused sourly. Perhaps Jimmy had seen the soon-to-be killer of Justin doing something incriminating, and so had had to be silenced beforehand? Or had Jimmy Speight been in on the plan all along, and his accomplice had decided that he couldn't be trusted to keep his mouth shut, and so had silenced him before the murder investigation of Justin could get underway?

Things were beginning to get very complicated.

'Can you tell me, as near as you can remember, the sequence of arriving guests that followed?'

Chase did admirably well, all things considered, and Jenny could see that the inspector thought so too. He was already mentally noting down Chase as an excellent witness.

'Now, the dinner, not the party, began when?'

'Six-thirty.' Again, it was Chase who appeared to have been elected spokesman and nobody seemed keen to disagree with the unspoken decision.

'Right. And it was served by whom?'

Chase pointed out the waiters and waitresses. As head waiter, Georges was obliged to take over the description and progression of the meal. This he did in great culinary detail, with neither policeman attempting to stop him. Each course was described, the method of transportation and order of serving, plus the approximate time of arrival in the dining room.

'And this was all prepared by?'

Jenny sighed deeply and rose a hand. 'Myself, Inspector.'

Mollineaux turned and looked at her. Getting no reaction from his superior, Mollern looked again at his boss, then glanced sharply at the cook. 'Refresh my memory, Miss Starling,' Mollineaux said slowly, although they were both aware that it needed no such jogging. 'You were hired by?'

'Alicia Greer.'

'When?'

Jenny obligingly told him. She then went on to describe in detail where she'd purchased every single item of food, and Mollern made a separate list of the foodstuffs that came directly from the garden. Mollineaux then had the temerity to inquire about what lengths she went to to ensure hygiene, and was given a very precise lecture that had Georges beaming with approval, and left neither policeman in any doubt whatsoever that food poisoning could not possibly have originated from neglect.

Jenny had no doubt, however, that an army of police specialists were even now ransacking the kitchen and taking samples of anything and everything they could find. She wondered what they'd make of the cat when they found it. Not that she'd ever allowed its presence to compromise her food.

'I see,' Mollineaux said neutrally as Jenny's stint finally came to an end. 'So, after the dinner was over, the guests joined the others in the ballroom and marquee. What time did the party guests—as opposed to the diners—begin to arrive?'

Once more, Chase stepped into the breech. Apparently, the rooms had begun to fill as early as seven o'clock. Various waiters and waitresses reported circulating with the food, wine and champagne. Everyone agreed that the party was a roaring success. The band had already been questioned, and Jenny could only guess at the mental collations going on in Sergeant Mollern's head. Who had done what. When. Where. Who had become drunk. Who had left early. Slowly, over the next few hours, the map of the party was being painstakingly spread out before the police.

The diners had left the dining room at about eight, and then the party really began to swing. Everyone agreed that Alicia danced mostly with 'her young man', as Chase so elegantly put it. Babs Walker, it seemed, had danced with almost every male in the room, with the exception of Arbie Goulder. Every guest, as far as the waiters and waitresses could remember, had eaten of the savouries, a satisfying number of them complimenting the unknown cook. Everyone had drunk the champagne and wine, with the exception of two guests—one due to medical reasons, the other on the grounds of religion. Most had had the forethought to come in taxis, and thus weren't driving.

'Very well.' Although dawn was by now beginning to break beyond the library windows, Mollineaux still looked as fresh as a daisy. 'Now, it's getting on towards midnight at the party. We've got the names of the guests who left early—Judge Wainwright and his wife, due to their age, and Miss Lucy Jones and her escort due to, er, probably amorous intentions.' Nobody snickered. It was not a snickering occasion. 'What happened next?'

'The cakes came in, sir,' Chase said, and Jenny remembered the two waiters who had come to the kitchen to carry Alicia's fancy cake out. It was, to all intents and purposes, the 'main' cake. Justin's, a more modest affair, had been carried out just after.

'It had candles?'

'Yes. I put them on,' Jenny admitted. 'And lit them.'

'It looked a lovely sight,' Georges piped up, his remembered admiration for the cake overriding momentarily his desire to be as inconspicuous as possible. There was a low murmur of agreement.

'Indeed it did, sir,' Chase agreed, taking up the story once more. Jenny began to suspect that he was beginning to enjoy his moment in the limelight. 'With the lights off, and only the candles burning, everybody applauded.'

'The lights went off?' Mollineaux prompted.

'Yes, sir. It was one of the highlights of the evening.'

'Of course. And who gave the signal? For the lights to be switched off, I mean?'

'Miss Greer.'

'Alicia Greer?'

'Yes, sir.'

'I see. And she was stood where?'

'By the table with the presents, I think,' Chase said.

'No, you're wrong,' one of the waiters spoke up. 'She was by the champagne table.'

'Was anyone else with her?' Mollineaux turned to the young man, who scratched his head in thought.

'Her boyfriend. And that funny fat bloke in the white suit.'

'Mr Goulder?'

'Dunno his name. He was the only one wearing a white dinner suit.'

Mollern nodded.

'Anyone else? This was the table that housed the champagne that was shortly to be used in the toast?' Mollineaux clarified.

'Yes, it was.' Yet another waiter spoke up. 'I'd just popped the corks on them. Miss Greer told me the toasts were to come straight after the cutting of the cake.'

Mollineaux nodded. 'So, standing around this table were Miss Greer, Mr Keith Harding and Mr Goulder. Anyone else?'

'That tiny blonde lady was there,' a waitress's timid voice piped up from the back. 'The one in that lovely scarlet dress.' After a quick debate, they all agreed she was referring to Babs Walker.

Jenny could feel her heart begin to pound sickeningly. This was terrible. Were all the prime suspects gathered at that damned table? And why was the inspector so interested? It seemed to confirm that it was the champagne that had been poisoned after all, that it wasn't just a melodramatic rumour doing the rounds.

'Anyone else?'

'Mr Banks, sir.' Chase spoke up. 'I remember now. I was looking at Miss Greer so's not to miss her cue to turn off the lights, and I remember her turning and saying something to Mr Banks.'

'You were the one to turn off the lights?'

'Yes, sir.'

'And Mr Banks is?' Mollineaux asked, although he already knew the answer.

For the first time, Chase began to look uncomfortable. 'He is, or was rather, an employee of Mr Greer's company, sir.'

'Was?'

'He retired, sir. Some weeks ago.'

'I see. Anyone else?'

It was generally agreed that several guests had been or were near to the table, the ballroom being so very crowded. 'That man that was arguing with Miss Greer, earlier. He was there,' Georges said thoughtfully, then flushed as all eyes turned to him.

'Arguing?' Mollineaux said sharply. 'Why didn't you say this before? What man?'

Georges shrugged, suddenly very Gallic and very afraid. 'I didn't think, sir, Inspector, sir. I thought nothing of it. I was returning from the table with a tray of glasses when I saw Miss Alicia and the gentleman by the big alcove of flowers. They had no drinks, so I approached, but then I saw they were arguing, so I went away again.'

'Arguing about what?' Mollineaux asked, with no trace of tension in his voice, which Jenny found herself admiring.

She hadn't been present for most of the time when Mollineaux had been questioning the others about Jimmy Speight. Now she could understand why they'd been so rattled. She couldn't imagine him leaving a stone unturned concerning their movements on that tragic morning.

'I could not tell,' Georges said, indignant now that he was suspected of eavesdropping on the guests. 'Miss Alicia had her teeth clenched, like this'—he gave them all a graphic demonstration—'and she was sort of hissing her words. Her face was flushed and angry, that's how I knew they were arguing. So, naturally, I do not intend to embarrass the hostess by offering drinks, so I go elsewhere.'

'Naturally,' Mollineaux said dryly, and a brief glance of annoyed disappointment flickered over the face of the sergeant. 'How did the man seem to be taking all this?' he asked remorselessly, and again Georges gave a Gallic shrug.

'He didn't seem to mind,' he said, very nearly smiling in remembered admiration of the other man's machismo. 'He looked, you know, amused. The ladies can be so combustible, yes?'

Jenny wished with all her heart that Georges would drop the fake accent. He was really going over the top now.

'Yes,' Mollineaux said, so tonelessly that Georges' man-of-the-world smile collapsed like a bad soufflé.

'Did anyone else witness or overhear this argument?'

Nobody had.

'Does anybody know the name of this man?'

Nobody did.

'Can you describe him, please?' Mollineaux turned once more to the now downcast Georges, who did his best. And as details of the man's description slowly emerged, Jenny found herself stiffening. She coughed discreetly, but needn't have bothered. Neither Mollern nor Mollineaux had missed her reaction.

'Yes, Miss Starling?' Mollineaux prompted.

'I think that sounds like the gatecrasher,' she said, and Mollern quickly flicked back through his notes. For the first time, he spoke.

'A lady told one of our constables about a gatecrasher earlier on. That you, Miss Starling?'

'Yes.'

Mollern glanced at his superior. 'Trevor Watkins, sir.' He said the name as if it were in capital letters and inverted commas. Several of the waiters gave one another uneasy glances. The name was not totally unfamiliar, it seemed. Even Martha recognized it.

'What, that crook?' she gasped, before she had time to choose her words more carefully.

Mollineaux smiled at the resident cook, but there was no humour in his eyes. 'I should point out, madam, that no formal criminal charges have ever been levied against Mr Watkins.'

No. That was probably true, Jenny surmised. She felt instinctively that he was too slippery by half. But the police knew about him all right. A lot of people did, apparently.

'You were right to warn us, Miss Starling,' Mollern continued. 'Mr Watkins has quite a reputation.'

'Yes. So I gathered. But for what, exactly?' she couldn't help but ask.

'Oh. This and that,' the sergeant replied, unhelpfully. Mollineaux shifted from one foot to the other, and Mollern abruptly fell silent. 'Are you sure that Mr Watkins was at the table with Miss Greer?' he asked Georges, who nodded. 'Very well. Now, to continue. The lights went out and the cake came in. What happened next?'

'Mr Justin gave a short speech and cut the big cake. Several guests took photographs,' Chase said. Apparently, Alicia had left the speechmaking to her brother. It figured.

'And then?'

'The lights went back on, and Miss Greer joined her brother. She called for champagne for the toast.'

'Who served the glasses that the Greer twins drank from?'

There was a long, pregnant pause. Eventually a voice spoke from somewhere near the back. 'I did.'

It was a waitress with frizzy blond hair. None of the other catering staff knew her by name, but Jenny recognized her at once. She was, of course, Margie Harding.

'And after the toast was given?' Mollineaux carried on, seeming to give no undue importance to this piece of information.

'Everyone drank,' Chase said, beginning to lose colour.

'And then what happened?'

'Mr Justin fell to the ground. A moment later, Miss Alicia did the same,' Chase continued. He said the words stiffly, and with little emotion, but they dropped like leaden weights into the sudden, silence.

'Yes, I see,' Mollineaux said heavily.

ELEVEN

JENNY DIDN'T BOTHER going to bed after the catering staff were let go and the rest of the household regulars were dismissed. It was already 5.30 a.m., and bed didn't seem worthwhile. Besides, who could sleep?

She learned from the inspector that Sherri Greer was upstairs, and sedated. Mark Greer was still at the hospital, but there had, as yet, been no word of Alicia. The police were everywhere, not surprisingly, and the library had been commandeered as an 'incident room'. She'd noticed Chase practically tiptoe past it the last time he had brought tea to the troops.

Finding herself at a loose end, she took herself off for a walk around the village that was, as yet, still asleep and largely in ignorance of the events at The Beeches. She knew that wouldn't last long. Once word got around about the sensational happenings, the quiet country village would resemble an ants' nest. And the arrival of the press wouldn't help. Jenny shuddered. She didn't like the press. Not one little bit.

Leaving the village behind, she began to traipse across the meadows, finding herself facing the large lake an hour or so later. There she stopped and sighed. It was nearly seven now, and the sun was beginning to generate a little more warmth. Birds, with hungry mouths to feed, dashed everywhere, and out on the well-stocked lake, a carp jumped. It looked idyllic. But a sense of darkness still hung over her. She sat down on the dry grass and arranged her voluminous skirt around her knees. Then she sat, stiff-backed, staring out across the lake.

There was no point in trying to pretend it hadn't happened, she mused grimly. Facts had to be faced. And, as far as she could see, there were three strong possibilities. One: someone had intended to murder Justin Greer, and had succeeded. Two: someone had intended to kill Alicia Greer, and may (or may not) have succeeded. Only time would tell. Or three: someone had intended to kill someone else entirely (identity yet unknown) and had failed.

Three seemed very unlikely, and although she put it to the back of her mind, she knew she would still have to consider it. Even as improbable as it seemed, stranger things happened at sea—as her grandmother had always insisted on pointing out.

So, was it one or was it two? Of course, it could be a combination—maybe someone had wanted both the twins dead? Either way, it was an undoubted fact that Justin was dead. And who wanted him that way? Arbie for sure, Jenny thought sadly. Babs Walker possibly. Cliché or not, it was often true that a woman scorned was a very dangerous animal indeed. And add to the fact that Babs had just lost out on her dream of a rich and easy life, then Jenny could well see the self-absorbed and single-minded Babs exacting a horrible revenge.

And then there was Tom Banks. The disillusioned, fired, but once-loyal company man. What thoughts ran through the mind of an otherwise decent, ordinary man when his working life came to an abrupt end? His loyalty rewarded with unfairness. His livelihood cut off. Just what lengths might he go to? And, Jenny reminded herself grimly, shifting on the hard earth and trying without success to find a comfortable spot, just what on earth had he wanted with a paper knife? Justin had not been stabbed. And if it had been poison (and Jenny really had no doubts about that), what use was a knife?

Unless it had been dipped in poison and then put in a glass or a bottle? Jenny sighed angrily. Now that really was far-fetched, and a very depressing indication of how lost and floundering she was.

So, supposing Alicia had been the intended target? Well, only Margie Harding would want her dead. Her husband was besotted with the beautiful blonde, that much was obvious. Unless love had turned to hate somewhere along the line, in which case, had Keith secretly begun to resent the break-up of his once happy marriage? Did he miss the love and companionship of his children more than he let on? Had he come to resent Alicia and her money and her possessive ways? Perhaps he was riddled with regrets. In which case, Keith Harding was a very fine actor.

And then there was the gatecrasher, the very unwelcome, very shady Trevor Watkins. Had his argument with Alicia been serious? Deadly serious?

Jenny sighed. It was no good—she had, as yet, nowhere near enough information to go on. And pointless speculation would only drive her up the wall.

She wished she had lunch to prepare; that would at least give her something to do. But Martha had reclaimed the kitchen the moment the last of the police had left. And, of course, she mustn't forget Jimmy Speight. Had he been murdered also, and if so, why? Gossip had it that he was a prize snoop. Had his long nose sniffed out some trouble somewhere? Had Justin's argument with the boy been more than that? Had Justin in fact killed him? And if so, had someone known it, and killed Justin in revenge?

If the death of the gardening boy had been no accident, Jenny mused, then the perpetration of it pointed firmly towards the residents of The Beeches. But she couldn't see how either of the boy's parents, intent on revenge, could have turned up at the party without being spotted. A dustbin man and his equally lowly wife would have stuck out like a sore thumb at the party of the local lord of the manor. And who could there have been at that party who even knew Jimmy Speight, let alone wanted to avenge his death?

There were just so many unanswered questions. Still, she couldn't sit here brooding all day long, she acknowledged, and got slowly to her feet.

WHEN SHE RETURNED TO the house, the first person she saw, in a group of people milling aimlessly about in the hall, was Mark Greer, who'd obviously only just returned from the hospital. He was holding a glass of brandy and looked almost happy. It made Jenny stop dead in her tracks.

'Another glass, sir?' Chase asked, and it was then, noticing that the bounce was back in the butler's step, that she realized there must have been good news from the hospital.

'Thank you, Chase. I really shouldn't—it's such an ungodly hour for it. But I will. To Alicia, my darling daughter, and may she have a speedy recovery. I just can't tell you what it meant when the doctors finally told me she was going to live.' His voice, drained and exhausted though it was, was full of the joy and relief he must have felt, and Jenny felt herself swallow. Hard.

Inspector Mollineaux, she noticed, drank to the toast with a mug of tea. Martha was dabbing her eyes on her apron, and even Sergeant Mollern allowed himself a smile. It was at the high point of this heartwarming scene that cold reality intruded with an abruptness that was shocking.

'Ah, Miss Starling. Where exactly have you been?'

Jenny jumped guiltily, and immediately felt angry at doing so. She gave Inspector Mollineaux, who had spoken with such sharp suspicion, a cold glance. 'I took a walk around the village and lake.'

'I see.' The inspector was obviously not best pleased. 'I was wondering if you had any objection to staying on for a few days. I know you're due to leave today, but I've asked Mr Greer and he assures me they have the room.'

'To be sure,' Mark agreed wearily. 'I'm sure Martha would appreciate the extra help.'

Jenny was sure that Martha would do no such thing, but she smiled absently at him. For a moment she said nothing. Finally, she turned to Mollineaux, her chin angled at a slightly higher degree than normal. 'I imagine you've asked others to stay on as well?'

Her voice held a distinct challenge. If she was a suspect, she wanted to make damned sure she was not the only one.

For a second, Inspector Mollineaux looked startled at her quick wits, then his eyes narrowed. For a long moment the two of them stared at one another, he looking at her like a fox might contemplate a buzzard. He knew it was no ordinary bird he had here, and the talons and beak made him pause.

'Yes. That is, I will, once they rise,' Mollineaux conceded reluctantly. 'The overnight guests have very wisely tried to get some rest.'

'And…' Jenny hesitated and glanced at Mark. But there was no help for it. 'And Mr Banks?' she asked quietly.

Mollineaux nodded. 'I have told Mr Banks not to leave his hometown.'

'Eh? What's Tom got to do with it?' Mark roused himself, the enormous strain of the last few hours beginning to tell in the shortness of his temper. 'Tom's a good man, and Justin should never have fired him. He wouldn't have, if I'd known in time what was going on. I won't have Tom upset like this.'

'Just standard procedure, Mr Greer,' Sergeant Mollern interrupted, soothing ruffled feathers with an expertise that was surprising in such a blunt-looking individual. 'We must keep tabs on all the guests at the party.'

'And what about that Watkins man then?' Mark demanded belligerently. 'I hear from one of your constables that he's an out-and-out crook. You don't want me to put him up in the house as well, do you?' he asked, but heavily, as if he already knew the answer.

'If you wouldn't mind, sir. I've already had a word with our Mr Watkins and told him that I would appreciate it if he stayed available for questioning for a few days. A constable's escorted him back to London, but he'll be returning with a bag.'

Sometimes, living deep in the countryside had a price, like no nearby hotel being available to put up unwanted guests, for instance. Mollineaux was sympathetic but firm, and Jenny suspected that it wasn't often he didn't get his own way.

'Very well.' Mark gave in without a fight. He seemed drained of all energy suddenly. 'Now, I really must go and see if my wife's awake yet. If she is, she'll want to know about Alicia.'

'Of course, sir.'

The small group watched him in silence as he made his way upstairs, a stoop-shouldered, broken man. Then, as if on cue, Chase headed off and Martha scurried for the kitchen, and Jenny was just turning to head for the sanctuary of her own room when Mollineaux called her back.

'Just a moment, Miss Starling.'

Reluctantly, she followed him into the small lounge off the library, which he appeared to have made his own private office. He waved her into a chair, which she took, and noticed that Sergeant Mollern had entered and stood by the closed door. She glanced warily at Mollineaux, who smiled at her. He was a handsome man, and he had a handsome smile, but Jenny wished heartily that he was smiling at someone else.

'I must just make a phone call. I won't be a moment.' He lifted the receiver, and dialled once. 'Hello, get me Vanchester 305621, please. Inspector Hopcroft.'

Jenny almost groaned out loud. She'd known this was coming, ever since she'd seen the look of recognition in his eyes earlier on. Oh, well. Best to get it over with, she supposed.

'Hello? Clive? This is Randolf. Yes. Mollineaux.'

Jenny had never thought of Mollineaux as a Randolf. A Lawrence, perhaps. Or maybe even a Geoffrey.

'Yes. Oh, I'm fine. What's it like up north?' Mollineaux dispensed with the pleasantries without taking his eyes off the woman seated, so composed, in front of him. 'The thing is, we've had a particularly nasty murder down here. A young man at his birthday party was poisoned. His sister very nearly died along with him. Yes. I know. The thing is, we've got problems, as you can expect, with a house full of guests, staff and whatnot, and as of yet we're not even sure who the intended victim was. We've also got another, rather peculiar, fly in the ointment, and that's why I'm calling you. You've come across this particular fly before. She goes by the name of Jenny Starling.'

Mollineaux paused, then nodded. 'That's right, a cook. A rather, er, striking lady. Now if I remember right, wasn't she a suspect in that murder you had up there a year or so ago?'

There followed an even longer silence, during which time Mollineaux's eyes widened, narrowed, and widened again. Finally, he sighed heavily. 'I see. So Chief Inspector Gunn was... Yes. And it was really like that? Yes. I see. Right. And she had nothing to do with it at all? Not even a doubt or two? No. Right.' Mollineaux sighed again. 'In this case the family is rather prominent, and I'm already coming under pressure from the top brass for a quick solution. But yes, I'll bear it in mind. 'Bye, and thanks.'

Mollineaux hung up and leaned back in his chair. 'That was a very interesting call, Miss Starling,' Mollineaux began, and she had no trouble at all in picking up the undertones of sarcasm. 'According to our mutual friend, Chief Inspector Gunn and his team didn't solve the Enderby murder at all. You did.'

Although she couldn't see him, Jenny had the distinct impression that Sergeant Mollern had just shifted uneasily behind her.

'Well, I wouldn't say that,' she demurred faintly.

'No? According to our friend Inspector Hopcroft, Enderby's killer would have got away scot-free, if it hadn't been for you. Only you, it seems, managed to sift through the clues and come up with the name of the killer.' Mollineaux's voice had been getting progressively tighter, chillier and more sardonic as he'd talked, and now Jenny sighed deeply.

'Oh, damn,' she said forlornly.

'Yes, Miss Starling. I think "oh, damn" sums it up very

well. And now, here we are, with yet another murder. Tell me, Miss Starling, do you collect them? Like stamps?'

'Oh, damn.'

'I don't have to tell you, do I, Miss Starling, that I don't want you running around like some kind of female Sherlock Holmes wannabe, out-thinking and out-sleuthing us poor old coppers?' Mollineaux was getting downright irate now.

'No, Inspector, you don't,' she said meekly.

'Good. So there will be no questioning of the suspects?'

'No, Inspector.'

'No sifting through the rooms for clues?'

'No, Inspector.'

'No accusations, no following of suspects. No interference, in fact, of any kind whatsoever?'

'No, Inspector. And if you would kindly let me get in a word or two, I'd like to point out that I never intended to do any of those things. Contrary to the impression you may have received, Inspector Mollineaux, I am a cook. That's all. That's all I've ever wanted to be, and that is all I ever intended to do when I worked for Mr Enderby. It was just unfortunate that Chief Inspector Gunn was...' She tailed off, unsure of how to put things delicately.

'Incompetent?' Mollineaux offered helpfully. 'According to Inspector Hopcroft, that is.'

'Well, let's just say that he was, er...' Jenny stopped, aware that she had talked herself into a corner, and tried again. 'I'm sure that what happened at Enderby Hall will be nothing like what happens here,' she finished, somewhat lamely.

'I should hope not, Miss Starling,' Inspector Mollineaux said coldly. 'Otherwise I might start to think that the murder of Enderby gave you ideas. That it might have inspired you, so to speak. Do I make myself clear?'

'Oh, quite,' Jenny said quickly. She was tempted to ask how the murder of an old man, stabbed to death in a locked pantry in a deserted house, could possibly give her ideas on how to murder a young man by poison in a house crammed full with people. But, very wisely, she managed to resist the impulse.

Instead, she smiled. 'Is that all?'

'Hmm? Oh, yes,' he agreed vaguely, dismissing her with a brief wave of his hand.

Jenny rose and was halfway to the door when Mollineaux stopped her. 'Oh, Miss Starling. About putting us on to Trevor Watkins. I want to thank you for that. If he'd been allowed to leave we might never have known about him. And it may not come as much of a surprise to know that we would dearly love to get something on our Mr Watkins.'

'No. I'd already guessed that he was not the most popular of men with the police. I was glad to be of help.'

'Yes. But no more help of that kind, all right, Miss Starling?' he added firmly.

Jenny looked at him, blinking the blink of the innocent. 'Of course not, Inspector. As if I would.'

Randolf Mollineaux looked at her and shook his head wearily. 'Good day, Miss Starling.'

Jenny needed no second prompting, and was out the door like a greyhound. Given her full and rounded figure, it was an impressive accomplishment, and Sergeant Mollern watched her cross the hall and hare up the stairs with wide and wondering eyes.

He shut the door, still smiling. 'She's an impressive woman, sir,' he said, deadpan. 'And quite beautiful and sexy too. Have you noticed?'

'Yes,' Mollineaux said, shooting him a warning look. 'Unfortunately, she's also a very clever woman, Sergeant.

I thought as much the first time she opened her mouth. And our friend Clive Hopcroft has just confirmed it. In spades.'

'You think she really did solve the Enderby case then?' Mollern asked, interested. He always liked to know the latest gossip.

'Well, did you really believe that Chief Inspector Gunn, of all people, had actually pulled it off all by himself?'

'Well, no,' Mollern said. 'I just assumed it was Hopcroft who'd solved it.'

'As did everybody else. But according to Hopcroft, it was our friend there.' Mollineaux pointed at the door, through which Jenny had so recently departed.

'So, do we take her off our suspect list?'

Mollineaux smiled. 'She was never really on it. And I, for one, don't think for one minute that she poisoned the Greer boy. But let's not tell her that.' And he grinned evilly.

Mollern grinned back. 'Right. And in the meantime, I take it that I keep a close eye on her?'

'Oh, yes,' Mollineaux said quickly. 'If Hopcroft is even only half right in singing her praises, she's got a brain like a steel trap. Which might prove very useful to us, but very dangerous for her.'

'If the killer realizes just how sharp our cook really is, you mean? But it's not all that likely to happen, is it?' As Mollineaux glanced at him inquiringly, Mollern cleared his throat. 'Well, I mean, nobody really takes her seriously, do they? A voluptuous woman cook, I mean, well, nobody would ever dream she could be a danger to them.'

'I hope you're right,' Mollineaux said feelingly. 'Because whoever killed Justin Greer is still in this house, or at least in this village. I can feel it in my bones. And if Jimmy Speight wasn't murdered by someone either living in this house, or strongly connected to it, I'll be very much surprised as well.'

Mollern sighed. 'The trouble with the Speight case is, we've got nothing solid to go on. Both Mr and Mrs Greer say they were in bed between five and seven, and so they probably were. I can't see why either of those two good people would want to bump off their gardener.'

'And of course Justin and Alicia claimed the same thing.' Mollineaux took up the train of thought. 'Although in Justin's case we at least have the inkling of a motive.'

'And then there's the other staff,' Mollern carried on. 'I can't see that the cook, butler or that nice housekeeper had any kind of motive either, although they were all annoyed at his snooping. Yet somebody bashed that lad on the head with a branch and pushed him into the pond.'

'And if I'm not mistaken,' Mollineaux said grimly, 'our clever friend, Miss Starling, has already come to the same conclusions. And if she starts to get some good ideas, and the killer realizes that she has, then…'

Mollern nodded. 'She'll be well and truly up a well-known creek with paddles in short supply,' he agreed glumly.

TWELVE

'I'M GLAD YOU'RE feeling better,' Inspector Mollineaux said heartily.

Babs Walker, descending the stairs and holding on to Arbie as if he were a lifeline, tried her best to look pitiful and pale. She didn't quite succeed. 'I can't say as I really do, Inspector.' She smiled wanly at the policeman, ignoring Chase and Jenny, who were also in the hall, one passing on to the lounge with a tray of brandy, the other just on her way out.

'I'm sorry to hear that,' Mollineaux said blandly. 'I shall have to take this opportunity, however, to ask you to stay on at The Beeches for the time being. Perhaps Chase will take your bags back upstairs?'

The butler nodded gravely, settled his tray, and headed purposefully up the stairs. No one failed to see how Babs's hand clutched her case more tightly, nor did they miss the pleading look she cast Arbie's way.

Arbie, in immediate response, tightened his hold on her other cases. 'Exactly why do you want Miss Walker to stay, Inspector?' he demanded. 'Surely you can see she's upset? She's just lost her fiancé. The last thing she wants to do is stay around and be reminded of the tragedy. I have offered to drive her back home and—'

'I'm afraid that's not possible, sir, at the moment. I have also asked all the outside staff and overnight guests to remain in the vicinity as well, if possible.'

There was such steel in Inspector Mollineaux's voice

that Arbie was forced to concede. 'Oh, very well,' he agreed reluctantly. 'But I insist on staying also. Miss Walker needs a friend. Especially in this environment.'

Mollineaux smiled. 'I'm so glad you feel that way, sir. I was about to ask you to remain also. You may, of course, leave to collect a few belongings.'

Arbie didn't miss the significance of the statement. But whereas Babs Walker looked down at them with fear and consternation on her pretty face, Arbie Goulder very nearly smiled. His eyes held those of the inspector for a long moment then he nodded. 'I shall, of course, be pleased to stay,' he said affably.

Mollineaux turned away. As he did so, he caught sight of Jenny, watching it all with a lively interest, and his lips twisted wryly. They were, no doubt, both thinking much the same thing. Arbie might look ridiculous in his white suit, and may appear as a figure of fun with his round girth and strange hair, but inside he was as hard as iron. There would be no cracking Arbie Goulder, of that Jenny and Mollineaux were in silent accord.

'Oh, Arbie, I'm afraid. I don't want to stay. What if I'm next?' The pitiful wail came from Babs Walker, who in stark contrast to her escort, looked as if she were about to come apart at the seems.

'It's all right,' Arbie said soothingly. 'I'll be with you. I promise. I won't let you out of my sight.'

Jenny winced at what seemed to her to be more of a threat than a comfort, but Babs didn't seem to mind. As she watched the couple return back up the stairs, the travelling cook felt almost sorry for Justin's erstwhile fiancée. Babs might have been able to handle Arbie with ease in the past, but now, Jenny sensed, the shoe was on a very different foot indeed. And if Babs thought she could use him a second time and then cast him aside for someone else, she had better think again. Arbie was far too wily a bird to be fooled twice.

JENNY DIDN'T GO FAR. She didn't, in fact, leave the garden. It was nearly noon, and the village was now boiling with the news, and the last thing she wanted to do was be pumped for information by the locals. Instead she toured the garden, watching as the gardener, an old man with a remarkably subtle back, set about planting the autumn dahlias.

She was worried about Margie Harding. No doubt the police had insisted on taking everyone's name and address. Had she lied? Given a false name, or compromised and reverted to her maiden name? If she had, the police were sure to find out in the end. And if she'd told the truth, surely one of the eagle-eyed young police constables would have noted that her last name was the same as that of Alicia Greer's unpopular lover. What would the police make of it all?

Jenny was sure it wasn't looking any too good for the abandoned wife and mother. No matter whether she had lied or told the truth, her illicit presence at that party was going to prove a major stumbling block. Jenny could only hope that she hadn't done the actual murder.

Sighing deeply and unable to find peace of mind even amongst the flowers, she lingered for a while longer in the herb garden and then returned to the house—and promptly wished she hadn't, for something was most definitely up.

'Ah, Miss Starling.' Mollern pounced on her the moment she set foot in the hall, and on his face was such an expression of polite neutrality that she knew instantly that she was in trouble. 'The inspector has gathered all the staff together in the library. Perhaps you could join us?'

Jenny smiled. 'Of course,' she agreed, her voice even more polite and gracious. So that's why the gardener had suddenly disappeared. She'd wondered why he'd left a row of chrysanthemums undone.

The library was quiet when she entered, as if the very walls had absorbed the tension emanating from its residents, and Jenny had a sense of deja vu as she looked around. Chase was sitting, stiff backed, in one of the chairs, and looked uncomfortable. By the unlit fire, Martha and Vera sat on a small sofa, Martha actually holding Vera's hand. So they'd gone into the village and got Vera, had they? That seemed a little cruel, as Vera's timid soul must have been terrified. The daily had gone home at the first opportunity and no one had really expected to see her set foot in the house again.

The gardener stood by a large bay window, as if he could not bear to be out of the daylight for long. Daphne Williams was staring at one of her own flower arrangements, looking, as ever, the epitome of genteel British womanhood. The party co-ordinator glowered beside her, looking most put out, and Jenny wondered what important function she'd been hijacked from.

The Junoesque cook took the only other available chair, by the desk. It was instantly apparent why it was the only one free. Inspector Mollineaux was sat on the other side of the desk.

'Now that we're all here, I'd like to ask you all some questions on the actual running of the house,' Mollineaux began, and Jenny shot him a quick, surprised glance.

He's lying, she thought instantly. He couldn't care less how The Beeches was run. Something had broken. She suspected that the police had had to send the samples of food and wine to London, which had the sophisticated laboratories needed to analyse poisons. And no doubt the murder of the prominent businessman's son at Rousham Green had been given top priority. Even so, they must have been very quick off the mark to come up with the goods so soon. And yet, here they all were.

Jenny's heart sank. This did not look good. It did not look good at all.

'Mrs Williams. Perhaps you could start. You have help in cleaning the house?'

'Yes. Two girls come in from the village on Mondays, Wednesdays and Fridays.'

'And you use what? Furniture polish? Wax? Disinfectant?'

The tension in the room escalated as the others finally caught on. Mrs Williams frowned, but looked not at all uneasy. She proceeded to give the inspector a thorough and calm outline of the materials used to keep the house clean, where they were kept, where they were bought, and who had access.

'And Chase. Your duties would include the upkeep of the silverware? Shoes? That sort of thing?'

Taking his cue from the housekeeper, Chase also gave a thoroughly calm account of where the cleaning materials he used were kept. He tended to guard his territory a little more fiercely than did Mrs Williams, but all the materials were kept in unlocked cupboards where anybody, with a mind to it, might find and use them.

'And, Thorne, isn't it?' Mollineaux turned to the gardener, one eyebrow raised.

So that's his name, Jenny thought. And how apt it was. His face was creased and darkened with the long years spent working out of doors, and his fierce scowl made him look like a prickly character.

'Yes.'

'You're the head gardener here?'

'That's right.'

'You work in the greenhouse? Amongst other places?'

Jenny knew a leading question when she heard it, and stiffened. The greenhouse? What, exactly, was kept in the greenhouse? Unbidden, her mind flipped back to the first day she had arrived, when she'd toured the greenhouse in search of edibles. What had been in there exactly?

When she remembered, she almost groaned out loud. The gardener, however, seemed oblivious. 'I do, yes.'

'You buy the fertilizer. And other substances?'

'Ahh.'

'Weedkiller, for instance,' Mollineaux prompted silkily, and glanced at Jenny out of the corner of his eye. His lips almost twitched. She was staring morosely out of the window, already miles ahead of everyone else in the room—with the exception of the two policemen, of course.

'Yes.'

'You made the stuff in the bottle Sergeant Mollern found this morning. A derivative of rhubarb leaves, he tells me.'

'That's right. Powerful good stuff it is an' all,' the old gardener conceded comfortably.

Mollineaux smiled. He couldn't help it. Across the table, Jenny stiffened even more. Here it comes, she thought glumly.

'And the paraquat. Did you buy the paraquat, Mr Thorne?'

Even as the rest of the staff, alerted by the gentle tone Mollineaux had suddenly adopted, began to look anxious, the gardener only leaned complacently against the windowsill. 'Ahh, but that was more'n twenty years ago

now. They don't make it nowadays, see? T'weren't much
of it left, I reckon. I stopped using it ages ago.'

Chase and Martha exchanged quick, assessing glances.
Two natural allies, they were already thinking alike. How
best to wangle out from under, while dropping somebody else well and truly in it. And Jenny didn't need two
guesses in order to name their first choice.

'I see. Tell me, Thorne, apart from yourself, who else
had access to the paraquat?'

At the need for a more than one syllable word in answer,
Thorne sighed. 'Any 'un who went in t'greenhouse, I
reckon.'

'Hmm.' Mollineaux wrote the observation ostenta-
tiously in his notebook and Jenny felt like slapping him.
'Chase. Do you go into the greenhouse?' he suddenly
asked sharply.

'No, sir. It's not my province,' the butler replied instantly.

'No. Mrs Williams? You must go in. For flowers and
such?'

Daphne Williams cocked her head very elegantly to
one side and thought for a moment. 'Not really, sir. The
greenhouse is mostly used for vegetables and fruits. Mr
Greer insists on it. He's a very practical man. I mainly
gather flowers and such from the garden itself.'

'I see.' Mollineaux scratched his nose. 'And your
young girls? Would they have reason to go into the greenhouse?'

The housekeeper, for the first time, looked angry. 'Of
course not. I supervise my girls very well. They get paid
wages to clean the house, Inspector. I don't let them go
mooning off to the greenhouse.'

'No. Quite. So that leaves you, Mrs Vaughan. As

the cook, I imagine you're in and out of the greenhouse a lot?'

Everyone looked at Martha, who paled visibly. 'Not recently I didn't,' Martha said shortly, expelling her breath so explosively she almost shouted. 'I didn't need to, did I? Not with *her* coming to do the party and all.' Martha sniffed. 'I didn't have nothing to do with the food, did I?' she reiterated, just in case she hadn't hammered home her point quite enough. 'In fact, there's only one person here that I knows of that went into the greenhouse, because she came back with a list in her fancy notebook.'

And with that, Martha went suddenly quiet. Not that she needed to say anything else, Jenny thought glumly. No siree. As if they were one, everybody suddenly looked at her.

'Miss Starling?' Mollineaux prompted.

It had to be paraquat, didn't it? Jenny allowed herself the luxury of a quick, quiet fume. It couldn't have been good old-fashioned arsenic, could it, that once popular poison that regularly saw off unwanted Victorian wives and husbands? Or even one of those untraceable South American blow-dart poisons that were so popular in classic whodunnits. Oh, no. It had to be paraquat.

'Miss Starling?'

She looked up, one eyebrow raised. 'Hmm? Oh, the greenhouse. Yes, I went in there. I wanted to see what was available. Not much, as it turned out. Some tomatoes and courgettes, but not much else.'

'Hmm. And did you happen to notice the paraquat?' Mollineaux asked blandly.

Jenny looked resolutely across at him. 'Yes,' she gritted through her teeth. 'I did.'

'Was the bottle full or empty?'

'More than half gone, I would say,' she answered sweetly.

'Did you notice if the top was on or off?'

'On.'

Mollineaux glanced at her, silently impressed by her no doubt accurate observations. 'I don't suppose you noticed if the dust on it had been smudged?'

'No. I didn't notice that,' Jenny said slowly, and thoughtfully.

'Hmm.'

'I take it, sir…' Chase, unable to stand it any longer, cleared his throat. 'I mean, was Mr Justin killed by paraquat?'

The room held its collective breath.

'Yes, Chase. He was,' Mollineaux confirmed quietly.

Now why, Jenny wondered, suddenly confused, did he confirm it? The police didn't usually go around volunteering information. In fact, the less the general public knew, the better they liked it. Except, of course, that the people in this room were not exactly the general public. And no doubt Mollineaux was playing a very clever game. He wanted the killer to know that they knew. He wanted, in fact, everybody in the house to know. The more nervous everyone was, the more likely things were to come out. It was a clever ploy, but dangerous, and Jenny gave him a disapproving look.

'Well, that's all for now. Thank you for your co-operation. I do, of course, expect you to keep this knowledge to yourself.' Mollineaux glanced at Vera and Martha. 'No gossiping in the village, yes?'

The two ladies quickly ducked their heads and eagerly followed old Thorne out the door. 'Not you, Miss Starling,' Mollineaux said as she made to rise, and Mollern saw the look of satisfaction that passed between butler and resident cook.

Noticing it, Mollern realized grimly that their Miss Starling didn't have many friends in the house. And that was too bad. She might well need a friend before this affair was cleared up.

'So,' Mollineaux said, when the room had emptied and quietened down, 'it's a very nasty business, Miss Starling.'

'I noticed,' she said dryly.

'The staff seem to think you're the number one suspect,' he mused, leaning back in his chair and looking suddenly tired.

'I noticed that too,' she agreed, even more dryly.

For a while the three very disparate people were silent. The police didn't seriously suspect her, and she knew it. But they had to keep an open mind. She knew that too. Finally Jenny said, 'There's no doubt then? About the paraquat?'

'None at all. The coroner's report was most clear. Death by paraquat poisoning. It's ancient stuff, of course, and they hardly ever come across it now. The hospital was informed at once, but Alicia Greer seems to be over the worst already. They're thinking of releasing her as early as tomorrow. It's a good job she didn't drink all her champagne, as her brother did.'

'Yes,' Jenny agreed absently. Her mind was on something else. 'Can they tell if the paraquat that killed Justin was the same as the stuff in the greenhouse?'

Mollineaux looked at her curiously. 'Justin? I didn't know you were on first-name terms with the deceased.'

Jenny could have kicked herself for making such a slip. 'He was an informal sort of man.' She shrugged casually.

'Did you like him?' Mollineaux asked sharply.

'I did my best not to. To have liked Justin Greer, Inspector, would have shown very poor taste on my part.'

Mollineaux's eyes narrowed for an instant. He'd had several conversations with Justin before his demise and knew exactly what she meant. 'Yes,' he said judiciously. 'And to answer your question, the lab is still working on it. Once they break the poison down further, I'm confident that they'll eventually be able to make an identical match, if it's the same stuff that's in the greenhouse. But we are working on the premise that that's what the killer used. Why?' he asked suddenly, sitting up straighter in his chair, Clive Hopcroft's warning about her clever intellect suddenly leaping up and hitting him in the face. 'What are you thinking?' he demanded sharply.

Jenny shrugged. 'It's nothing specific. It's just that paraquat is very much a gardener's province, isn't it?'

'Yes, but you heard for yourself. Anyone could have gone to the greenhouse and siphoned some off.' He was not about to tell even Miss Starling about the startling discovery they had found in one of the waste bins in the ballroom. 'And you can't really see old Thorne bearing a grudge against the young master of the house, can you?'

'No,' Jenny said quietly. 'But Arbie Goulder runs a very large nursery business. He must have acres of greenhouses in order to accommodate all those orchids and bird-of-paradise flowers of is.'

Jenny glanced down at her nails innocently.

By now, Mollineaux would be well clued in on all the gossip. He must know about Babs Walker being snatched from him by the more handsome, not to mention much wealthier, Justin.

'And Mr Goulder, of course, had all the reason in the

world to bear a grudge,' she pointed out gently. 'You're assuming the killer went to the greenhouse for the poison. But have you considered the fact that he may well have come already fully equipped?'

THIRTEEN

TREVOR WATKINS ARRIVED back in time for lunch. Martha promptly refused to cook for him, and Jenny was torn between the itch to get her fingers on some minced beef, and distaste at the thought of who was going to benefit from her excellent, own-recipe shepherd's pie. Eventually the minced beef won, which didn't really come as a surprise to anyone.

'I don't know what the police are coming to,' Martha sniffed to Vera, who, to everyone's surprise, had not gone straight home after the questioning but had decided to stay on. The poor thing probably needed the wages, Jenny reflected. She'd heard somewhere that Vera had two aged parents to support. 'Fancy asking a man like that to stay here. I mean, here, of all places. This is a respectable house, this is.'

Vera nodded. 'It's terrible,' she agreed.

'I've heard all sorts of nasty things about that cockney,' Martha went on wrathfully. 'My Dave says he stabbed a bloke in a nightclub once. Not that they ever had him up for it, of course. Too many witnesses said he was somewhere else.'

Martha broke off to watch Jenny carefully as she added tomatoes and carrots to the minced beef mix. Jenny didn't mind. A good shepherd's pie recipe should be passed on. 'That's the trouble with men like him,' Martha continued to bend Vera's willing ear. 'Nobody dares stand up to him. I even heard'—her voice lowered in a passing nod to delicacy—'that he arranges for girls who need abortions to get it done without going to proper doctors and stuff.'

'Ooh, Mrs Vaughan!' Vera said, shuddering. 'I thought it was easy enough to get terminations nowadays.'

Martha patted her shoulders gently. 'Not always it isn't, Vera, not always. Not if you're desperate to keep it a secret, for instance, or if you're a Catholic or whatnot. And there's still some doctors as won't give permission easily. But, there, I'm just saying, I won't cook for the likes of him, and that's that. My Dave said that Trevor Watkins cut some chap's ear off once, just because he owed him money.'

'Well,' Vera said, recovering somewhat. 'What can you expect when you run one of those casino places? Of course people will owe you money.'

'Casino?' Martha echoed, her voice raised so many octaves that Jenny thought the glass lampshade might splinter. 'Nothing so fancy, my dear. Gambling dens, that's all his establishments are.' She sniffed judiciously. 'What I can't figure out is why he was at the party at all.'

Jenny, who was busy adding oxtail soup to her bowl, had a good idea about that. She hadn't forgotten Justin teasing his sister about her gambling debts that day at the lake. Nor had she forgotten Justin's wrathful tone of voice when he'd pointed out to her that if Alicia could invite Arbie, he too could invite whomever he liked.

Although she had no proof, Jenny would have bet a considerable amount of her payment for this job that Justin had telephoned the reviled Trevor Watkins and invited him to the party in revenge for his sister's mischief-making.

Not that Alicia's sins were any of her business, Jenny reminded herself hastily. She'd promised the police she was going to stay out of it. But that didn't mean she couldn't *think,* did it? Next to cooking, thinking was one of the things she did best.

She sighed and headed for the potatoes. Mashed with milk and lots of butter and some parsley and garlic, that was the secret for a really good shepherd's pie.

CHASE RETURNED FROM the dining room, looking his years. The events of the last forty-eight hours were beginning to take their toll, Jenny noticed with a pang. 'Compliments to the cook on the shepherd's pie, Martha,' Chase said, unknowingly heaping praise on the enemy.

Martha gave him an exasperated look, but when he sank heavily onto a chair, her expression softened. Without daring to give Jenny a glance, Martha rose and dished out a good plateful of the pie for Chase, who sat staring at it morosely, making no effort to eat. Jenny didn't take it personally. The poor man had obviously lost his appetite.

'I don't know what to do, I really don't,' Chase said. 'The dining room was always a place of gentility before. But Mrs Greer's still in her bed, and Mr Greer sits there hardly saying a word. Then there's that awful woman, who came down to lunch dressed in a cocktail dress. Can you imagine?'

Jenny could. No doubt Babs, in her naivety, thought the rich always dressed for dinner. Even if it was lunch.

'Praise be for Mr Goulder, that's all I can say,' Chase said. Obviously a businessman who ran something as British as a nursery was not in the same class as other businessmen, Jenny assumed. Besides, Arbie had the mark of a man who had gone to all the right public schools, even if he had never managed to totally fit in. And in the gloomy atmosphere of the dining room that

Chase had just described, she could well see how the butler would latch onto Arbie as a lifeline. The world at The Beeches was coming apart, and it must be painful to watch.

'I suppose that Watkins man was there,' Martha said, unable to let go of her favourite pet hate.

Chase sniffed. He didn't need to say anything more on that subject. 'Inspector Mollineaux was there.' He changed the subject, leaving Martha wrong-footed. Obviously the cook wasn't on such sure ground with Mollineaux as she was with Trevor Watkins.

'It's so difficult,' Chase said. 'Knowing how to deal with the police. Especially with Mr Greer actually present.'

Martha frowned. 'In what way?' she asked curiously.

'Well, I mean, what does one say, or not say?' Chase asked plaintively. 'I certainly want to do my duty,' he began, his pomposity easily forgiven, since it came mixed with such obvious sincerity. 'I do so want the police to catch Justin's killer. But how does one know what helps, and what doesn't?' he appealed helplessly. 'Take Mr Banks, for instance…' The butler suddenly hesitated, and Jenny realized she was sitting tensely on the edge of her seat now.

She forced herself to relax, knowing that she could rely on Martha to ferret out the juicy bits.

'What about him?' Martha asked anxiously. 'I like Mr Banks. He's one of the last of the real old-fashioned gentlemen.'

'Exactly,' Chase said, relieved to find someone who understood his dilemma. 'And Mr Greer is very fond of him too. After all, they worked together for so many years. So should I tell the police that I saw Mr Banks coming from Justin's bedroom on the night of the party, or shouldn't I?'

Jenny licked her painfully dry lips and forced herself to wait patiently for Martha to ask the question.

'Did you?' Martha asked, right on cue but obviously surprised. 'When?'

'About 11.30. That's just it, you see.' Chase's impassioned cry made Vera start nervously. 'I can't see how that could possibly have anything to do with the murder. Justin died in the ballroom, not his bedroom. So it might just embarrass Mr Greer if I told the police. On the other hand, how do I know that it might not be important? I don't want to do anything to make the job harder for the police, do I?'

Martha gnawed her lip, finally understanding his dilemma. Jenny cleared her throat and Chase looked at her instantly, his face hopeful rather than resentful, for once. As an interloper, Jennifer Starling was not to be tolerated. But in times of crisis, Chase was learning— as quite a few others had learned before him—that there was something comforting about the impressively large cook. Something honest and decent and, well, *dependable,* that you could rely on.

'If I were you, Chase,' Jenny said gently, 'I should take Inspector Mollineaux discreetly to one side and tell him all you know. If you ask him to, I'm sure he won't tell Mr Banks or Mr Greer where his information came from. It'll probably turn out that Mr Banks has a perfectly rational explanation anyway,' she continued bracingly, even though she secretly rather doubted it. 'In which case, the matter can be cleared up quickly. It's far better to be honest about these things. Don't you agree?'

Chase sighed. 'I expect you're right,' he agreed reluctantly, and glanced at Martha for further guidance. But not even Martha could find fault with the advice. Chase sighed and rose, his food untouched. Jenny watched him go, and wondered what Mollineaux would make of the news.

As for herself, she couldn't see how it was particularly relevant. Unless it transpired that Justin had left the party and gone to his room for some reason. And even if that was the case, she couldn't see how Tom Banks could have done something in Justin's room that would have resulted in him dying half an hour later in the ballroom.

The man was not a magician, after all.

Was he?

THAT AFTERNOON, the weather changed. The sun, as if ashamed of itself for shining so brightly on a house of tragedy, took itself off behind a bank of lowering, thunderous-looking clouds, and the temperature dropped dramatically. In the ballroom, the police presence had dwindled considerably now that all the rifling, tidying, cataloguing and general sniffing around had been completed. There were still two constables left, however, to make sure that no one interfered with what evidence remained.

When Jenny entered the room, a tray in hand, she was the immediate focus of their attention. 'Hello, lads,' she said cheerfully, firmly establishing herself as the adult in charge. 'I thought you boys would appreciate some tea and scones. I made them fresh this afternoon and they're still warm. I have apricot and strawberry jam. I know you boys don't appreciate gooseberries, though why I can't imagine. Although, as a matter of fact, wild damson jam is my all-time favourite.'

Before she'd even finished she could almost hear their saliva glands beginning to stir. The slightly older constable glanced at his companion and nodded permission. 'Can I put the tray on that table there?' She pointed at the table which had hosted the champagne, but which was now totally bare. Again the older constable took charge. He still looked ridiculously young and uncomfortable in the stiff blue uniform, and his rather ruddy complexion had paled a little at the cook's choice of table, but the inspector had said all the evidence had been collected. He could see no harm. Besides, the smell of the scones had wafted over the air and his stomach was in danger of rumbling.

'Certainly, Miss Starling,' he said, deliberately using her name. He'd been taking careful note of all that had been going on, and had memorized everyone's name, and was rather proud of the fact.

Jenny found the gesture oddly touching. 'Sugar? Milk?' She poured the mugs of good strong tea as specified, glad when the two lads sidled closer to take them. She cut into the scones and reached for the jam pots. 'Apricot?'

'Strawberry, please,' the youngest constable spoke at last. To Jenny's eyes he looked as if he should still have been at school, but then, she supposed, even Mollineaux must have started out like this, although that was almost impossible to picture.

'There you go.' Jenny handed out the plates and watched in satisfaction as both men took huge bites. 'That's better. I daresay they forgot to feed you?' Jenny gushed, playing the well-meaning but slightly dippy cook to perfection, then poured herself her own mug of tea.

By now, neither constable was aware of the incongruity of her doing such a thing. Her opening gambit had successfully induced a feeling of 'them and us' just as she'd intended. 'You lot must have been so busy the last few hours. I know we all have—in the kitchen, I mean. Well, you have to carry on, don't you? Even when tragedy strikes, ordinary people like us just have to get on with things,' she rumbled on cosily.

'That's true,' the older constable said, licking his lips free of jam. 'My partner will be wondering where I am. I should have come off duty hours ago.'

'Me too,' his companion agreed. 'But my girlfriend knows I'm not in an ordinary job. No office clerk hours for us, eh, Pete?'

The older one shook his head, and eyed the plate of scones. Jenny promptly bent down and sliced into another, this time adding apricot jam. These young lads were all alike. Strawberry mad. They didn't seem to realize that other fruits were just as tasty.

'Well, when something as terrible as this happens they can't expect you to work normal hours, can they?' she asked approvingly. 'And it's so awful, isn't it? Not that I knew the victim much, you understand,' she continued chattily. 'I was only here to cook for the party,' she carried on, allowing distress to put a wobble in her voice. 'But his poor parents!' She let the silence hang there for a moment, then tut-tutted and shook her head. 'How could anybody predict that some wicked person would put poison in the champagne?'

The older lad shook his head. 'There's some evil people about, Miss Starling,' he said sadly, and Jenny nodded gloomily.

'I don't doubt it, especially after last night. That poor boy, dying in front of all those people. You know, I just can't, for the life of me, think how it was done. I mean, with all those people around, you'd think somebody must have seen something, wouldn't you?' she asked guilelessly.

'You would,' the youngster agreed. 'Especially with the needle and all.'

Jenny sighed deeply and nodded. 'I know. It's terrible. Still, at least your Inspector Mollineaux knows what he's about.' She spoke quickly but calmly. She mustn't let them realize the mistake they'd made. Spooking them now would make them clam up faster than a reprimand from Sergeant Mollern.

But it was very interesting to learn about the needle.

'That's true. Nothing much escapes Inspector Mollineaux,' the older one agreed.

Jenny was just about to ask something innocuous when the door opened and Mollern himself stepped into the room. His eyes went from the young constables to Miss Starling then to the plate of scones, then back to Miss Starling. He looked, she was offended to see, very suspicious.

'Just bringing your lads some food, Sergeant,' she said cheerfully. 'Fresh-baked scones. Would you like some?'

'No thank you, Miss Starling.' He opened the door wider and stood by it, waiting pointedly. Jenny gave him a sweet look as she passed and tried not to notice when the door slammed shut—hard—behind her.

In the ballroom, Mollern walked slowly over, noticing that the lads had begun to shuffle their feet. At the table he looked down at the scones. They were crammed with sultanas and steamed slightly. His mouth watered. He glanced once more at the constables, his face grave. 'I do hope you haven't been discussing the case with the cook?'

'No, Sergeant,' they chorused in unison.

'Good. Don't let's forget that Justin Greer was poisoned. And in poisoning cases we nearly always look to the cook first,' he lied, and had the pleasure of watching them go green around the gills. Their eyes flitted to the scones. The younger one swallowed hard. 'Right then. You two get off home. Be back at eleven o'clock tonight, mind. Inspector Mollineaux wants a police presence in the house round the clock. Just in case somebody else gets poisoned.'

He watched the two scuttle away, a happy grin on his face. Immediately after the door was shut, he quickly turned to the scones and ladled out some apricot jam. He sunk his teeth in with a sigh of bliss. They were the best scones he'd ever tasted.

JENNY WAS CROSSING the hall, the slammed door still ringing in her ears, when the main door flew open in a flurry of wind and rain. The ominous black clouds had at last let loose a downpour that had caught Daphne Williams unprepared as she'd been returning to the house with a few items she'd bought in the village. She put her bag down and slipped off her cardigan to give it a good shake, her usually elegant chignon looking bedraggled and wet.

It was this that made Jenny stop in mid-stride. Not because she was surprised that the housekeeper's panache should suffer in the rain, just like everyone else's, but rather the actual, physical sight of the wet, fair hair itself. With an icy shock, she knew she'd seen it before.

Hair of exactly that silvery gold shade. Hair that wet. A scant second later, as she remembered exactly where, the cold feeling intensified even more to form a solid block, somewhere in the middle of her spine.

At that moment Daphne noticed her, and gave her a rather weak smile. 'Hello, Miss Starling. I wouldn't go out if I were you.' She indicated her wet skirt and blouse with a wry, self-conscious grimace.

Jenny smiled, but knew that her face must look stiff

and unnatural. 'Yes. I think I'll have to postpone my daily walk.'

Daphne retrieved her bag and made as dignified a dripping exit as possible. Jenny watched her go, her eyes thoughtful and worried.

The last time she'd seen sodden hair of that colour, it had been on the body of Jimmy Speight as he'd been dragged from the pond. Jimmy Speight, whose family had moved here four years ago. Around the same time that Daphne had started work for the Greers.

Jimmy Speight was adopted, according to local gossip.

And Daphne had gone out of her way to make friends with the Speights, which had puzzled even Martha.

Back in the kitchen, Jenny poured some flour in a bowl and added a good dollop of butter to it. She was preparing rhubarb crumble, but her mind was on other things.

She didn't see the cat slink through the door, hug the shadows by the wall and stealthily slide under her table.

She knew she'd have to tell Mollineaux her theory about Daphne, although she was not looking forward to it. For if Jimmy Speight was Daphne's biological son, it would put her squarely in the middle of everything that was going on.

Now she could understand why Daphne had been acting so oddly lately. And sympathize. For the day Jenny had arrived here, Daphne had just learned that her son was dead. And, even worse, she had been denied the simple and natural need to grieve. For how could she grieve without telling the whole world why?

Jenny sighed deeply. Surely she could have had nothing to do with the murder of Justin, could she? Unless she had reason to suspect that Justin had killed her son.

Jenny sighed again, even more deeply, and turned her

thoughts to what she'd learned from those nice young policemen. A needle—surely they meant a hypodermic?

Jenny began to vigorously rub the flour, sugar and butter together. How did a hypodermic needle fit into all this? Could Justin have been injected directly with neat paraquat? Surely not. Somebody would have seen. Besides, she couldn't see Justin standing still while somebody jabbed him with a needle. Unless the crush at the party was so intense someone had been able to jog against him, inject him, then move away. But surely, surely, *somebody* would have noticed.

Unless he'd been injected upstairs in his bedroom, by Tom Banks.

Oh, right, Jenny thought exasperatedly, and Justin never thought to mention it to anybody, but had rejoined the party, laughed, drank and eaten for half an hour, then fallen dead after the toast.

Very likely.

But if Justin hadn't been injected directly (and surely the coroner would have found the mark), then how did the needle fit in?

Just then she felt a swift injection in her ankle and she shot back, her heart leaping into overdrive. For a fraction of a second she thought that death had come to claim her, and that the murderer had just given her a fatal injection of paraquat.

Then a grey streak shot from under the table, bounded onto the dresser, knocked off a cream jug and shot out the window.

Jenny watched the cat go, and almost laughed. 'Wonderful timing, cat,' she murmured in a voice rich with admiration and profound relief. 'Wonderful timing.'

Then her smile fled. She said again, very quietly and

thoughtfully, 'Wonderful timing,' and returned to her mixing bowl.

Yes. It really must have been wonderful timing, she thought savagely. However it had been done.

FOURTEEN

MOLLERN PUT DOWN the telephone just as the inspector walked through the door. It appeared that Mollineaux had managed to catch a few hours' sleep, but the evening sun was giving all the overtired policemen still at the crime scene ideas about home, wife and bed.

'The lab, sir.' Mollern indicated the telephone. 'The syringe *did* contain paraquat as we thought.'

Mollineaux nodded, not at all surprised. 'I've just heard from the hospital. Alicia Greer is being released tomorrow.' He looked, however, paradoxically grim at the good news. It was explained a moment later when he added quietly, 'She insists on coming home. Her father, too, won't hear of anything else.'

Mollern sighed. 'We have to get rid of the house guests then. Can't keep them here with Miss Greer about. Especially Watkins.'

So far, Watkins had continuously denied that any argument had taken place on the night of the party. But with Alicia back home to say different, he might not feel so cocky.

Mollineaux slowly sank into a chair and ran a hand over his lips. He looked both thoughtful and tense. Finally he shook his head. 'No. They stay. And so do we. I've arranged with Mark Greer for us to move into one of the bedrooms in the attic. Shared accommodation, I'm afraid, Sergeant. But there it is.'

Mollern shrugged philosophically. 'Just like going

back to my army days, sir.' He didn't add that such an unusual step meant that Mollineaux must be very concerned about the return of Alicia Greer indeed. He didn't need to. He too could feel that things were about to break.

'We'd better have another word with our cook,' Mollineaux continued. 'Get all the gen we can before we start putting the wind up our little gang.'

Mollern smiled. 'I'm looking forward to putting it to that Arbie chap almost as much as I am in lighting a fire under our friend Watkins.'

Mollineaux smiled wearily. He hadn't failed to notice his sergeant's antipathy towards Arbie Goulder. In many ways it was quite understandable. There was something about Goulder that would rub any policeman up the wrong way. Perhaps it was his lack of fear that was so annoying. Perhaps it was his obvious intelligence. Brains (not brawn) were a policeman's chief enemy after all. A clever criminal, sad though it was to contemplate, could very often get away with murder.

'Right. Kitchen,' he said, more to bolster his own flagging energy than to spur on Mollern. Although the junior man had had as little sleep as anyone else, there was something of the tireless dynamo about his squat, powerful frame that Mollineaux had often had to rely on in the past.

'Now that our theory about the needle and what it must mean has checked out,' Mollern said, leading the way, 'what do we do if our suspect list changes?'

Mollineaux closed his eyes briefly. 'Don't even think it, Sergeant,' he chided wearily. 'Don't even think it.'

JENNY LOOKED UP as the two policemen descended the few steps into the kitchen and glanced across at Martha. The cook resolutely turned her back and put every ounce of effort into upgrading her ears. Mollineaux coughed. Martha continued to deal with the ingredients of a rice pudding. Mollineaux coughed again, and not even Martha could ignore it. Reluctantly, she put her ears on stand-down, and turned inquiringly. 'If you wouldn't mind, Mrs Vaughan. We'd like to have a few moments alone with Miss Starling here.'

Martha sniffed, but shot a look of triumph at Jenny as she left.

'Are you about to make her day?' Jenny asked, amused, and when Mollineaux raised a questioning eyebrow, added drolly, 'Are you about to arrest me?'

'Nothing so dramatic,' Mollineaux assured her. 'We just need your help. It's about the afternoon of the party.' Jenny nodded, her alert eyes moving from sergeant to inspector and back again. 'The champagne arrived when exactly?' he asked.

'About ten, I think. A delivery man brought it in.'

Mollern questioned her closely about his appearance and made notes. 'And you directed him to the pantry?' he continued smoothly.

'No. The housekeeper did.'

'Mrs Williams?' Mollineaux said sharply. 'Why did she do that?'

'Alicia told her to, apparently,' Jenny said, wondering why the police were so concerned about the arrival of the champagne all of a sudden. At their continued silence, she felt obliged to explain further. 'Apparently Alicia was afraid that if the wines were put in the cellar, along with the rest of her father's vintages, there might be a mistake made, and some of her father's other, far more expensive wines might be retrieved by mistake. Apparently Mr Greer buys wine more as an investment than to actually drink,' she added, unable to keep the disapproval out of her voice. In her opinion, wine was made for drinking, even if she very rarely imbibed herself.

'I see,' Mollineaux said. He didn't look happy, Jenny thought—not happy at all. 'And after the wine was stored in the pantry,' the policeman continued, so nonchalantly that Jenny instantly knew they'd come to the crux of the matter, 'who else had occasion to go into the pantry?'

So that's it, Jenny thought, the answer coming to her in a flash. The syringe the young policeman had talked about must have contained paraquat. Which meant that the police believed it had been used to inject the champagne with poison through the cork. What else? How very clever. How very, *very* clever, she mused.

'Miss Starling?' Mollineaux prompted sharply, not at all liking the look of comprehension that had flickered briefly across her face.

'Eh? Oh, the pantry. Yes. I can see that's very important,' she murmured, trying to rein in her racing thoughts. 'Well, the first one to go in there was Justin Greer, to look at his birthday cake.'

But that obviously didn't count, Jenny realized, then brought herself up to an abrupt halt. Or did it? Justin had certainly been in the pantry long enough to take out a paraquat-filled hypodermic and shove it into a champagne cork. Had he, in fact, meant to murder someone else and somehow it had all gone terribly wrong? Or had the intended victim perhaps found out and turned the tables (or rather the champagne bottles) on him?

'Miss Starling,' Mollineaux said again, beginning to feel hot under the collar. If he didn't know better he could swear the cook was already ahead of him. But that was impossible.

'What? Oh, sorry. Who else. Hmm, let's see. Mr Greer, Mark Greer that is, came down with Mr Goulder.

Alicia had asked Mr Goulder to bring some of the wine to the ballroom.'

Mollern, who had perked up considerably on hearing Arbie's name, scribbled happily. 'And Mr Goulder was alone in the pantry?' Mollineaux persisted, which made Jenny abruptly frown. She was mad at herself because, of course, she hadn't been paying particular attention. Which meant that she just didn't know.

'I'm not sure,' she admitted reluctantly. 'Mr Greer could have handed out a crate to him. Or he could have gone in after it himself. I just don't know.' She could see the disappointment on their faces and felt guilty. 'Well, it's hardly my fault,' she snapped. 'I was rushed off my feet preparing a six-course meal and party nibbles. How was I to know somebody would be injecting paraquat into the champagne?' she challenged them grimly. 'If I had, I can assure you, I'd have been taking more notice.'

Mollineaux stared at her, his jaw very nearly falling to his knees. 'Injecting paraquat into the champagne?' he repeated. His face darkened. 'And how, pray tell, did you know that, Miss Starling?'

Jenny felt like giving herself a hearty kick on the shins. If she hadn't been wearing such heavy sensible shoes, she might have done just that. 'Er, well, I just happened to, er, overhear something about a hypodermic found somewhere and, naturally, when you came here asking about who had access to the pantry with the champagne in it, I just put two and two together. Tell me, Inspector, where was the needle found exactly?'

'In one of the bins in the ballroom. The one under the champagne table to be exact,' he said grimly. 'Since you seem to know so much already, you may as well know it all.'

Jenny flushed guiltily. 'Yes, well. Now, who else went

into the pantry?' She quickly turned back to the original questioning, hoping she hadn't got either of the two young constables who'd inadvertently spilled the beans into trouble. 'Mr Harding carried out a crate.'

'Keith Harding?' Mollineaux said, thankfully turning his attention elsewhere. 'When was this?'

'The same time as Mr Greer and Arbie.'

Mollern glanced across at his superior and Jenny could tell they were both thinking the same thing. Why might Keith Harding poison the champagne? The answer, of course, was obvious to all three. To kill Justin who so heartily disapproved of him and was intent on making trouble. And who had been on hand to prevent Alicia drinking too much of the champagne herself? Again, Keith Harding.

'Even so,' Jenny said, thinking her thoughts out loud, 'that would have been very risky. He does love her, after all.'

Mollern nodded, not seeming to notice that the cook was echoing his own thoughts almost to the letter. 'I think he's genuinely in love with the girl too,' he said judiciously. 'So would he take such a terrible risk with her life?'

'And again, I'm not sure if Keith actually went into the pantry alone, or if—' Suddenly, she stopped. Both Mollineaux and Mollern glanced at her quickly. 'I suppose,' she said thoughtfully after a moment or two, 'that the champagne must have been injected while it was still in there.' She nodded to the back pantry. 'It couldn't possibly have been done in the ballroom?'

Both policemen shook their heads at once. 'Too crowded. With so many people around, someone would have been bound to notice if a hypodermic was whipped out and stuck into a bottle.'

Jenny sighed. 'Yes. I suppose so. But, in that case, it doesn't make sense,' she said, her voice so chagrined and disappointed and frustrated that both policemen had to fight back a smile. Mollineaux was not about to ask her to explain herself, however. He was well aware that a lot of things about this case didn't make sense. And number one on that list of things that didn't make sense was how the killer could possibly have arranged for the poisoned bottle to be served only to Justin and Alicia Greer and nobody else.

'The wine waiters are all agreed that they began filling the guests' glasses for the toast just before the cake was brought in.' He went over it again out loud, just to make sure he hadn't missed anything. He was confident that if he did, Jenny Starling would soon pounce on it. 'They took the champagne from the table, where the head wine waiter had uncorked it, a chap of unblemished record who didn't know the Greers from Adam. Under all those watchful eyes, they'd circulated with the glasses until every guest had one, and then Alicia Greer gave the signal for the birthday cake. The lights went out, everybody oohed and ahhed over the cake, then the lights came on again. Alicia went to her brother and signalled for their glasses to be filled. Another waiter— no, a waitress this time—was handed two glasses from the head wine waiter, who swears he poured the glasses from a bottle he picked at random, and again with over a hundred eyes watching the waitress took the glasses to the brother and sister. Justin and Alicia drink and…hey presto.'

'What about when the lights went out?' Jenny said.

'No good.' Mollineaux shook his head. 'I've checked with everyone at the party. They all said it went dark— practically pitch-black. Nobody could have seen to pour poison into a champagne glass. Besides which, we already have a hypodermic filled with paraquat. No. It just doesn't make sense. Somebody pre-injected the champagne—or why the needle?—and somehow, *somehow,* arranged that only Justin and Alicia drank from it.'

'Which brings us back to the waitress,' Mollern said, and looked at Miss Starling thoughtfully.

Jenny looked away. 'Yes,' she agreed miserably.

'Yes,' Mollineaux echoed her prim word sardonically. 'Did you, by any wild chance, happen to know who that waitress is, Miss Starling?' Mollineaux asked, so silkily she knew that the game was up.

'Hmm? Oh, yes, I believe she was, no, still is—for the moment anyway—Mr Harding's wife. Estranged wife, I suppose I should say. I take it that you've questioned her?' she added casually.

'Oh, yes,' Mollineaux said grimly. 'We've had one of our top interrogators questioning her for hours now.'

Jenny felt a wave of sympathy for Margie Harding wash over her, and winced. 'And you've run into the same problems as before,' she mused. 'Margie Harding, to my knowledge, never set foot in the pantry. So she couldn't possibly have injected the paraquat beforehand.'

'No,' Mollineaux said heavily. 'She also had nothing to do with the opening of the champagne, or the distribution of it. The head waiter, or one of his more trusted minions, always opened the bottles. They then poured and gave trays of the stuff to the waiters and waitresses to circulate with. Including our Mrs Harding.'

'Still,' Mollern said, 'she did hand over the fatal glasses to Justin and his sister.'

'But she wasn't stood at the champagne table before the toast,' Jenny pointed out quickly, and both men nodded gloomily. 'Also, it was the head waiter who actually poured out the glasses. From a random bottle. And somebody would have seen her if she'd tried to poison just one glass, surely?'

Jenny simply didn't want it to be Margie Harding. Of all the suspects, she was the only one Jenny actively *wanted* to be innocent. Any of the others—Arbie, Trevor Watkins, Babs, even Keith—any of those she could cope with as a murderer.

'Pity, though,' Mollern said. 'She had the motive, and so very nearly the opportunity. And I don't think much of her reasons for being at the party. I don't believe a woman would go to so much trouble just to be near her husband.'

'Then you don't know much about women, Sergeant,' Jenny said crisply, and rose to her feet. 'Cup of tea?' she asked pleasantly. Both men quickly agreed, and the cook took out a large, rounded fruitcake. 'Baked this morning,' she said. 'When Martha wasn't looking,' she added, eyes twinkling. For a while, silence reigned as tea was sipped and cake appreciatively munched.

'So, what next?' Jenny asked, and Mollineaux, after giving her a quick, exasperated look, finally gave in to the inevitable.

'We question Arbie and Keith about the crates,' he confirmed, his voice as discouraged as he must have felt. 'But they'll only deny everything. I don't suppose anyone else could have come down during that morning and afternoon. Babs Walker, perhaps?'

'I doubt it,' Jenny said miserably. 'If they had, I'm sure Martha or Vera would have seen and mentioned it, even if they'd chanced to come down on one of the rare occasions when I wasn't in the kitchen myself.'

'Besides, Babs Walker has no motive,' Mollern said, sighing. 'She lost all her chances of a wealthy marriage when Justin died.'

'Oh, but…' Jenny said, and then stopped.

Mollineaux, reaching for a second piece of cake, stopped in mid-action and looked up, gimlet eyes glinting. 'Oh, but what?'

'Well, Justin had already broken it off with Babs,' Jenny admitted reluctantly. She *hated* being a stool pigeon. 'He told me so just before they went into dinner. He said he was keeping an eye on her in case she caused a scene. Well, in case she took reprisals was more accurately what he hinted at.'

'I wish you'd told us that before,' Mollineaux said, too weary to be really angry, and Mollern suddenly began pushing back his notebook pages with an energy that had both Mollineaux and Jenny staring at him expectantly. Eventually, and with a small grunt of triumph, he stopped and tapped a page with his pencil. 'I thought so. One of the guests said they saw Babs Walker leave the party for a brief spell, somewhere about 11.30 p.m. She went out into the garden for some fresh air apparently. The last he saw of her, according to his statement, she was heading towards the greenhouse.'

Where there was paraquat.

'Really?' Mollineaux's eyes began to gleam.

Jenny's lip's twisted wryly, instantly seeing the flaw. 'And she just happened to have a handy hypodermic needle in her handbag, I suppose?' Both men wilted slightly. 'Unless the needle is a blind,' Jenny mused, only half-serious.

'The classic red herring, you mean? To put us off the track?' Mollern rolled the thought around—with some scepticism, it has to be said—while Mollineaux sighed heavily.

'I wouldn't put it past our killer,' he agreed morosely. 'The more we get into this case, the more intricate it becomes. But that needle narrows it down a little. Don't you agree, Miss Starling?'

Jenny did. She could quite see that if she was right about the business with the hypodermic, then it narrowed it down very considerably indeed.

To just one, in fact.

But it still didn't make sense.

Mollern pushed back his chair and stood up. 'I suppose we'd better see Miss Walker about that turn in the garden.'

'Hmm? Oh, yes,' Jenny murmured, and then gave a clearly visible start as memory gave her a jab in the ribs. 'Oh, there was just one other thing.'

'Yes, Miss Starling?' Mollineaux asked, his voice so calm it made her give him a double-take.

'You know that little talk we had. About my not interfering,' she began carefully, not trusting Mollineaux's calmly inquiring look one little bit.

'Yes, Miss Starling,' he said smoothly, 'I remember it well.'

Jenny swallowed. 'Well, I took it to heart, I assure you,' she said quickly. 'But I assumed that you didn't mean for me not to make a suggestion or two, if a thought occurred to me.'

Mollern glanced at his superior and very nearly smiled at the look on his face.

'Yes, Miss Starling?' Mollineaux said, by a great effort of will actually managing to avoid grinding his teeth. 'And I take it that a thought has actually occurred?'

Jenny took a small step sideways, just out of his arm reach. Well, you never knew. 'Yes. I think you might find that Daphne Williams is Jimmy Speight's real mother.' She got it all out in an undignified rush.

Mollern, who thought he'd been prepared for anything

and was waiting with his notebook at the ready, very nearly dropped his pencil.

'You did know he was adopted, didn't you?' Jenny added quickly, just to break the rather deep quiet that had suddenly fallen over the kitchen. Mollineaux stared at her for a moment, then seemed to pull himself together.

'Yes, Miss Starling. We had managed to gather that much information all by ourselves,' he acknowledged, the sarcasm so finely dealt out that she almost missed it.

She blushed. 'Good. Well, that was all.' She made a vain move in the general direction of the door.

'Just a moment,' Mollineaux said, his voice rising loudly before he brought it back firmly under control. 'Just what makes you think that the housekeeper is Speight's real mother?'

So Jenny told him. When she had finished, and Mollern's ever-busy pencil had finally scratched to a halt, Mollineaux had calmed down in fact as well as in appearance. He was silent for a few moments, and then said quietly, 'It's very slim evidence on which to base a theory, Miss Starling.'

'Oh, yes, I know. That's why I wondered if you could possibly check it out more thoroughly before we... *You*... talk to Daphne.'

'I'll get onto it,' Mollern offered. 'It might be tricky getting names from the adoption agency. They can be very strict about things like that. But a murder investigation cuts a lot of red tape.' And with that gem of wisdom, he took a step backwards, and complete pandemonium broke out.

A sound that would have made a fire-engine siren seem piffling by comparison rocketed around the room and made Mollern jump even further back, going into an instinctive half-crouch. Mollineaux as well shot back and flinched as a grey streak leapt, hissing and spitting, onto the table. The cat, whose tail Mollern had just trodden on, ran maniacally across the table, jumped into the sink, shot out again, paused on the marble-topped workspace for an emergency lick, then shot up to the top of the dresser, landed on the table again, and would have set off on the circuit all over again if Jenny hadn't quickly grabbed it.

'Be careful!' she said crossly to the sergeant, cradling the panting cat close to her impressively padded breast and tucking his twitching and stinging tail firmly under its own furry body to keep it warm. She began stroking the ears back from its head with long, gentle strokes.

Mollern flushed red. 'Sorry,' he said instantly. 'I didn't know it was there,' he added defensively. He looked at the cat guiltily. Mollineaux, on the verge of unrestrained laughter, nodded his head to the doorway and Mollern, still feeling like a first-class bully, slunk off.

Together the policemen left to question Arbie and Babs Walker and then get on to the adoption angle.

Jenny continued to absent-mindedly stroke and comfort the cat, her mind on other things. That needle bothered her. And the conclusions she'd tentatively drawn from it bothered her even more. And she did so hope Margie Harding hadn't had too hard a time of it.

Her thoughts came to an abrupt halt when someone started a lawnmower going in the kitchen. Jenny looked around quickly, but she was most definitely alone. Then, realizing where the sound was coming from, looked down. The cat, eyes closed, was purring contentedly, not to mention awesomely noisily, its fluffy grey cheek pressed against her sternum.

Jenny was so flabbergasted that she stopped stroking. The cat opened his wide orange eyes and stared at

her. He too looked surprised. All at once his ears began
to flatten, and Jenny put the animal down even more
quickly than she'd picked it up. All available claws pro-
tracted, but by then Jenny was already making her way
to the steps.

FIFTEEN

ARBIE LOOKED UP from his gin and tonic and grimaced as the door opened. He'd been about to ask Babs to marry him, and this time he was sure she'd say yes. He'd give her no other option. So he was furious at the interruption.

It was a little early to be drinking, but he hardly cared what the police thought, and so he met Inspector Mollineaux's ironic eyes with a jaunty smile.

'Ahh, here you are, Miss Walker. I was wondering where you'd got to,' Mollineaux said jovially. Babs flushed. She took a large sip of her own gin and tonic and stared at the unlit fireplace. 'I have a few questions, Miss Walker. I'm sure you won't mind?'

'Perhaps she minds very much,' Arbie shot back, his voice lowering dangerously.

'I don't see why,' Mollineaux said mildly. 'You do want to help us find Justin's killer, don't you, Miss Walker?'

'Of course I do,' Babs said quickly, and cast Arbie a 'shut up' look.

Arbie rapidly changed tactics. He shrugged amiably but at the same time hitched his chair just a little closer to Babs. Mollineaux chose to sit opposite her, on a little two-seater sofa. He gave Mollern a blank look, which his sergeant instantly read, and joined him on the sofa. Babs now faced two implacable officers of the law, and she crossed her legs nervously, showing off long, silk-clad limbs to perfection. Neither man so much as glanced at the feminine attractions on show, but Arbie looked at her with hungry eyes before forcing himself to look away again. It was impossible to tell whether he was amused or annoyed.

'Now, Miss Walker. You and Justin Greer were engaged to be married, is that correct?' Mollineaux started off gently.

'That's right.' Her voice came out as a nervous squeak, and she coughed and said again, more forcefully, 'Yes. We were.'

'But didn't Justin break off your engagement just before the party?' Mollineaux asked, looking genuinely puzzled and sounding only mildly curious.

Arbie Goulder instantly stiffened. He saw the danger at once, although Mollineaux didn't believe the object of his desire had done so. Babs looked surprised that the police had found out, and certainly angry and a touch humiliated, if the colour in her cheeks was anything to go by. But she didn't look scared. Not well up on the brains department, Mollineaux thought interestedly.

'Why do you say that?' Arbie challenged, before Babs could speak.

'We have it on good authority,' Mollineaux said, meeting the florist's gaze with equanimity.

'Oh?' Arbie looked downright disbelieving. 'Whose, may I ask?'

'Certainly,' Mollineaux granted. 'Justin Greer himself.'

Babs gasped and put a hand to her mouth. All three men looked at her. 'What sort of cheap crack is that?' Arbie asked angrily, his voice rising at last as the policemen finally succeeded in dragging a genuine reaction from him. 'Greer's dead.'

'Oh, you noticed?' Mollineaux said sardonically, then before Arbie could open his mouth, slipped in quietly,

'Before he died he told someone that he had just, er, dis-engaged himself—as it were—from his fiancée. Is that true, by the way, Miss Walker?' He suddenly turned to Babs, giving her no time to think.

'Well, yes,' she admitted, proving that, overall, it was far less taxing to tell the truth than to invent a lie. Arbie gave her an exasperated look, and Mollern smiled over his notepad.

'How did you feel about this, Miss Walker?' Mol-lineaux asked softly, and put up a hand as, out of the corner of his eye, he saw Arbie's mouth open. 'I can, of course, take Miss Walker to the station to be questioned without interruption,' he pointed out warningly. And as Babs gave another gasp of dismay, Arbie furiously sank back in his chair defeated. Mollern was sure he could actually hear him fuming.

Mollineaux turned again to the beautiful woman opposite him, who re-crossed her legs. He waited.

'Well, naturally I was surprised.' She gave an agonized glance to her one-time lover, obviously seeking reassurance. Arbie, unable to help her, gave Mollineaux a look that could kill.

'Only surprised?' Mollineaux asked, his voice rising in disbelief. 'Weren't you upset?'

Babs flushed. 'Of course I was. Very.'

'Hmm. Upset enough to want to kill him, Miss Walk—er?'

'Don't be ridiculous. How could I kill him?' Babs shot back, getting to the very heart of the matter, perhaps more by luck than judgement. And Mollineaux just stopped himself from sighing out loud. Yes, how indeed? Instead, he changed tack.

'You left the party at about 11.30 for a turn around the garden,' he stated, as a fact. 'Where did you go?'

Babs looked blank. 'I did? Well, to get some fresh air, I suppose.'

'Yes. But where did you go?' Mollineaux persisted, and could see Arbie fairly squirm in his chair. Babs merely shrugged a very pretty shoulder. She opened her wide pansy-brown eyes even further.

'I can't remember. Just around the lawn, I think. Smelled the roses, you know, that kind of thing. Too much party can get you down sometimes. Especially if you're not in the mood for it.'

Well, it had certainly got Justin Greer down, Mollern thought, but didn't hesitate in his shorthand scribbling.

'I see. You obviously like flowers.' Mollineaux glanced sardonically in Arbie's direction before continuing. 'Did you go to the greenhouse? To see if there might be any orchids?'

Babs shook her head. 'No. I would have remembered if I'd done that.'

Mollineaux continued to stare at her thoughtfully. 'I see. Well, thank you, Miss Walker. If you wouldn't mind, I'd like to talk to Mr Goulder now. Alone.'

Babs was very swiftly out of the chair and out of the room. If wild horses wouldn't have dragged Arbie from her side in times of danger, the same wild horses couldn't have kept Babs Walker by *his* side, when it was his turn to face the firing squad.

'Now, Mr Goulder. Wasn't it unusual for you to "do" the flowers for the Greers' party, when not long ago, Justin pinched your girlfriend?'

Arbie smiled, not at all put out. 'Alicia asked me to "do" the flowers, as you so delicately put it.'

'And you didn't object?' Mollineaux asked, letting his voice drip disbelief. 'You didn't mind providing the flowers for your hated rival's birthday party?'

Arbie let the 'hated rival' pass. 'Naturally not. I'm a businessman, Inspector. I don't run my nurseries as a rich man's hobby but as a business. Alicia paid full whack for every daisy and rosebud, I promise you.'

'Yes, I'm sure that's all perfectly understandable,' Mollineaux concurred placidly. 'But you stayed for the party afterward. Why on earth would you want to do that?'

'Alicia invited me,' Arbie said with a shrug.

'That's all? You didn't, perhaps, want to stay in order to see Miss Walker again?'

'Of course I did,' Arbie admitted readily. And said nothing more.

It's like trying to get blood from a stone, Mollineaux thought wrathfully. He has no pride. He readily admits to chasing a woman who had previously given him the elbow, and he doesn't care a jot for the opinion of others. And that made him not only unusual, but dangerous as well. Mollineaux did not like him. But was he a killer?

'You keep paraquat at your nurseries, Mr Goulder?' he asked, deciding a blunt instrument was the only chance he had of battering down the florist's defences.

Arbie blinked. 'I might have some, forgotten about, amongst the old stock, but I doubt it. Why do you ask?' There was such a wealth of suspicion in his voice that Mollineaux felt his heart sink. His instinct told him that nobody could act that well. He glanced at Mollern and saw a similar dismay deep in his own eyes. Arbie Goulder seemed so right for it. He had motive, and, somehow, opportunity. They didn't know yet just how Justin had been poisoned, but everyone at the party had opportunity, if only they could figure out how. Moreover, Arbie was psychologically right for it. Tough. Arrogant. Clever. But did he actually do it?

Mollineaux sighed. 'That's all for now, Mr Goulder.'

'He was poisoned with paraquat, wasn't he?' Arbie said. 'That's why you wanted to know if Babs had gone to the greenhouse. Old Thorne might still have some of the stuff tucked away somewhere. So that's what killed Greer,' Arbie deduced thoughtfully. He didn't sound particularly sympathetic. Nor, alas, did he sound particularly guilty.

Mollineaux rose to his feet, fighting his anger. He glanced at Mollern, who also rose, and together the two policemen left, well aware that Arbie watched them go with mocking eyes. Outside he gave Mollern a speaking look and sighed deeply. He'd never known a case so complicated and so full of unhelpful witnesses and potential suspects.

'Let's get onto the Daphne Williams angle,' he said heavily. 'There, at least, we should be able to make some sort of headway.'

JENNY WOKE UP the next morning and dressed. She had slept badly, tossing and turning and trying to pick holes in her own theory. But no matter how she kept rearranging it, it always came out with the same name. But there was still so much that she didn't understand. Besides, one piece of evidence alone didn't convict a killer.

'Oh, hell,' she murmured to herself and walked to the window, which was, of course, wide open. Even in the depths of winter Jenny slept with her bedroom window wide open. Fresh air was better than medicine, her mother was always saying. And she should know. She practically lived up doomed trees in makeshift tree houses.

Out of the window she saw Trevor Watkins wander over in the direction of the herb beds, and was instantly out the door. Jenny very badly wanted to have a word with the cockney crook.

She followed the vile scent of cigarette smoke across the lawn, past the delightful herb garden to a rock garden on the other side. And there, sitting on a dry-stone wall was Trevor Watkins, glaring rather testily at a noisy robin singing in a nearby plum tree.

'Hangover?' Jenny asked sweetly, and saw the way the man tensed. His feet were flat on the ground, ready to move. His free hand was palm down on the wall, ready to launch himself at any attacker. Jenny would have bet her fee that he had a weapon, probably a knife, on him somewhere. His eyes passed over her swiftly, and he slowly relaxed.

'Hello,' he said pleasantly. 'And yes, as a matter of fact, I did have a bit too much to drink yesterday evening.'

'Our friends the police been giving you a hard time?' she asked, glibly and totally without sympathy.

'They take it in relays,' Watkins agreed, neither missing her sarcasm nor acknowledging it. 'I keep telling them Justin rang me up and invited me to the party, and they keep saying no way. I keep telling them I came down only to have a nice time at a fancy do, and they keep telling me that I killed Greer. I keep saying why on earth would I, and they say that perhaps it was Alicia I was after. They keep asking about the argument I had with her, and I keep saying what argument? As an hour's diversion it's bearable. As an all-day sporting event, it lacks a little something.'

Jenny nodded and took her place a little along the wall from him. 'So why not just tell them that Alicia owed you money and have done with it?' she asked, and saw him pause in the act of lifting the cigarette to his mouth.

Trevor Watkins turned and glanced at her. His face was totally blank. 'Come again?'

Jenny shrugged. 'I heard Justin tease his sister about

her gambling debts. Just over there, in fact.' She nodded her head to her left. 'By the lake. Then I hear around and about that you own a gambling place. I imagine Justin could be just as mischievous as his sister, and invite you to the party. Ergo...'

'Alicia owes me money,' Trevor finished. 'How very clever you are. And how right. Alicia *does* owe me money,' Watkins admitted, for the first time his voice revealing a ruthlessness that must always have been in his character. 'But I doubt that you're as clever as you think,' he added, standing up and grinding the cigarette out under his heel. He stared at her levelly, to see if she'd got the not-so-subtle hint, and Jenny stared unflinchingly back. Trevor grinned. 'You're a game bitch, I'll give you that,' he said, almost cheerfully. 'But don't cross me, there's a love.'

And with that, he was gone.

Jenny watched him go, her heart thumping. She was sure that she had come off the worst in that little exchange, and she wasn't thinking of the threats either. Those she totally disregarded. They were second nature to someone of Trevor's mentality. 'I doubt that you're as clever as you think you are,' he'd said. And Jenny had the dismaying feeling that he was right. She was missing something. Oh, she was on the right track, she was sure of that. And no doubt Trevor Watkins was going to prove to have played a very big part in it all. But what that part was, she had failed to find out.

No doubt she was not as clever as she thought she was.

WHEN SHE FINALLY LEFT the wall, about an hour later, she was just in time to see a car pull into the drive. For the first time she saw Sherri Greer, standing by her husband's side, waiting at the door. She looked pale and hollow-eyed, but a smile trembled on her lips as a figure climbed out of the car and stood looking vaguely around in the bright morning sunlight.

Jenny's eyes roamed straight past Keith Harding and alighted on Alicia Greer, who moved into her mother's outstretched arms with a small sob. Her father completed the circle, closing his arms around his daughter's shaking shoulders as Keith Harding, still the outsider, looked on unnoticed.

Jenny slowly approached, aware that Chase, Daphne Williams and Martha were all clustered in the doorway, not wanting to miss the triumphant return of the young mistress of the house. Jenny stopped silently when she reached Keith Harding's side, and watched. Standing as tall as he, she did not have to look up to notice that his jaw was clenched tight, and that a little muscle ticked away furiously by the side of his mouth. His fists, too, hung at his sides, clenched so tight that his knuckles were white. He looked deeply unhappy.

As if sensing that someone was missing, Alicia turned and smiled at Keith, her eyes glancing across the few inches of space to Jenny.

Her expression changed abruptly. 'What are you doing here?' she asked, her voice pinched and tight, her already pale and ill-looking face going even paler. 'One of the nurses told me about you,' Alicia said accusingly, her voice, weak and exhausted though it was, still clearly echoing across the suddenly thick and motionless air.

Obviously she was still unwell. It was not surprising that she swayed weakly against her father's supporting arms. The poison may have been pumped out of her system, but its effects would obviously make her feel ill for some time to come, Jenny guessed. Not that Alicia seemed to be taking much notice of its effects now. Her eyes were large, bright with burning emotion and fixed on Jenny.

Behind her, the cook saw Mollineaux's silver head appear.

'What are you talking about, dear?' Sherri Greer asked anxiously. Having her daughter return home had rallied her spirits considerably. It had been the only thing that had managed to drag her from her bed. But she wondered now if the hospital hadn't released her too soon.

'That woman,' Alicia said, pointing imperiously at Jenny, 'was arrested for murder once before. I know. A nurse told me. She'd been reading the papers about Justin'—the young voice faltered as tears threatened—'and she remembered Miss Starling's name before. One of her other employers was murdered too!'

This dramatic announcement made Martha gasp in delight. Chase gave a very happy sniff of displeasure. Jenny met Mollineaux's eyes and gave a tiny, almost imperceptible shrug. Well, it had been bound to happen. Her thoughts stopped abruptly as by her side Keith Harding swung around to face her, his eyes murderous. Jenny took a very hasty and utterly instinctive step back.

'You lay a hand on her,' Keith hissed, his face wild, 'and I'll kill you. Do you hear?' And since he was shouting fit to be heard in Alaska, Jenny had no trouble at all in hearing him.

She sighed in relief as, out of nowhere, Mollern—good, squat, very *solid* Mollern—appeared at her right shoulder and laid a restraining arm on Keith Harding, who didn't even seem to feel it. He was too busy staring at the cook in animalistic rage. And in that moment, Jenny had no doubt at all that Keith was capable of murder. Hers.

'I can assure you, sir, that Miss Greer is in no danger,'

Mollern began soothingly. 'Both myself and Inspector Mollineaux are staying on at the house. And Miss Starling, I can assure you, has never murdered anyone.'

Keith Harding continued to stare at Jenny, hate and loathing and fear emanating him from him like a noxious cloud.

'That's as may be,' Keith gritted, his voice cold and hard. 'But I'm staying too. I'm moving into the room next to Alicia's and anyone, *anyone*,' he reiterated, leaning closer to Jenny menacingly, 'who comes near her is going to answer to me.'

As he turned and headed towards Alicia, Jenny couldn't help but notice that for once, and at last, Mark and Sherri Greer were openly approving of him. Alicia, however, wasn't quite through yet. 'And there's another thing,' she said spitefully. 'Where did she get that watch she wears?'

Jenny, taken by surprise, instinctively raised her watch and looked at the obviously expensive gold and diamond timepiece. Everyone else looked at it too. Mollineaux raised a questioning eyebrow.

Jenny shrugged. 'It was a gift,' she said flatly, definitely in no mood to explain herself, or her father's extravagance.

Alicia snorted. 'More likely you stole it,' she accused.

Mollineaux coughed warningly. Taking the hint, and together as one family, the Greers and Keith Harding turned and walked into the house, Alicia between them, the most precious object in all their lives. Keith shot her a final, hate-filled warning look over his shoulder.

Mollineaux joined Jenny out on the gravel, looking relieved that the nasty scene was over. 'You can't blame him,' he said softly, glancing at the now closed door. 'He almost lost her.'

'No,' Jenny said, robustly beginning to rally. The whole episode had shaken her more than she'd care to admit. 'I don't blame him at all,' she assured him stoutly.

The two policemen exchanged relieved glances. They both felt a renewal of respect for the impressive cook as, in unspoken accord, they also began to head for the house. 'And I meant what I said,' Mollern added reassuringly. 'Alicia Greer will be well protected.'

But Jenny was hardly listening. Somehow, she needed solid proof before she could voice her theories out loud.

'By the way,' Mollineaux said, as neutrally as possible, 'that tip you gave us about the housekeeper turned out to be right on the button. We finally got confirmation this morning. Daphne Carter, as she was then, gave her son up for adoption seventeen years ago, almost to the day.'

'Oh? Good,' Jenny said, and then wondered. What was so good about it? It meant poor Daphne was now in for a grilling, and just when she was at her lowest ebb.

Mollineaux coughed. 'We will, of course, have to question her again,' he remarked, and glanced across at Mollern, who was studiously inspecting his shoes. 'We thought it might be best if she had someone with her. Another woman, I mean.'

Jenny glanced quickly at him, just managing to keep the horrified look from her face. 'Me, you mean?' she asked bluntly.

'Well, it either has to be you or Mrs Greer. And considering the delicate nature of our enquiries…' He trailed off, having no need to go any further.

'No.' Jenny sighed. 'And if it turns out to be irrelevant, there'll be no reason at all to tell the Greers about Jimmy Speight's true parentage. Right?' she asked, her chin rising in challenge, and was satisfied when Mollineaux agreed with her.

If she was going to have to fight Daphne's corner, she'd make sure she did it properly.

SIXTEEN

THEY FOUND DAPHNE WILLIAMS in the library, catching up on the household expenses. Mollern carefully closed the door behind him and checked that the windows were closed. The housekeeper glanced apprehensively at the policemen, curiously at Jenny, and then, quite suddenly, as if aware of what was to come, became very calm.

'Inspector Mollineaux,' she acknowledged quietly.

He coughed. 'Mrs Williams, I'm afraid we have a few questions that we have to put to you. I've asked Miss Starling to be present to…er…'

'For moral support, Daphne,' Jenny said firmly and went to sit beside the housekeeper. 'In a few days I shall be gone and I expect you'll never see me again. Often we can turn to strangers for help when our friends are the last people we'd want to see.'

Daphne smiled, but her calm blue gaze went quickly back to Mollineaux. 'Ask away, Inspector. I shall be quite truthful and as concise as I can be, I assure you.'

'Thank you, Mrs Williams. I'll try to be as brief as possible.' Mollineaux walked to the empty fireplace and turned. 'You were the natural mother of Jimmy Speight, were you not?'

If he expected consternation, he was disappointed.

'Yes, I was,' Daphne agreed quietly and without any sign of surprise that they should know this.

'And you followed the Speights down here to be near your son?'

'Yes, I did. I learned, quite by accident, who had adopted my son, and, well, I became curious. And once I'd seen him, I had to keep on seeing him. Not to tell him who I really was, of course,' she added quickly. 'No. I made my decision seventeen years ago and I could see that he was very happy with his adopted family. I had no intention of causing either Bernie or Jean or Jimmy any trouble.'

'That's why you made friends with Jean Speight,' Jenny said softly. 'Just so you'd have the excuse to be around Jimmy from time to time?'

Daphne glanced at her, and gave a wry sort of smile. 'Exactly. And then I was able to get him a job here. It was me who recommended him to Thorne and Mr Greer. So I could see a bit more of him. It was enough,' she added quietly.

Mollineaux sighed. 'And on the morning that your son died, did you see him arrive?'

'No. He came early that morning, because of the football. I was going to go into the village and watch him play. I'd already arranged to have the afternoon off.' Her voice began to crack, just slightly. Jenny took her hand and squeezed it. After a startled pause, Daphne squeezed back.

'So you don't know what his movements were likely to have been?'

'I expect the first thing he did was make himself a cup of tea, Inspector. As all the staff do.'

'So everyone has access to the kitchens when Martha Vaughan is not around?' Mollineaux asked.

'No, Inspector.' Daphne smiled. 'They keep a little gas stove and kettle in the little shed, by the greenhouse. Teabags and some sugar too, but not milk. It goes off too quickly in the summertime. They prefer to have their own hidey-hole.'

'I see,' Mollineaux said, and glanced at Mollern. The police had found no evidence of tea-making facilities in the shed, but that was not surprising. That wily old gardener had probably cleared it out as soon as the police had arrived. 'I see. Mrs Williams…'

'It's not really Mrs Williams,' Daphne said, with another wry smile. 'It's always been Carter. I never married, but when I started seeking housekeeping jobs it was easier to play the widow. You understand?'

Mollineaux did, but was not about to be sidetracked. 'I'll stick with Mrs Williams then. Mrs Williams, had you heard about the argument Justin Greer had with your son just prior to his death?'

'Yes,' Daphne said quietly. 'Jean had told me that Jimmy wanted to be a reporter. He wrote a lot of pieces for various magazines and papers. Quite a few were accepted,' she added proudly. 'I knew that he was insatiably curious about life and people, but also that he could get into trouble because of it. Not everyone understood him as I did.'

'And what did you think of Justin giving him a dressing-down?' Mollineaux asked neutrally.

Jenny felt herself tense, but Daphne seemed unaware that she was heading for dangerous ground. 'Well, I didn't like it, of course, but I understood it. And Justin was quite within his rights to resent Jimmy poking around in his private things.'

'So you did nothing about it?' Mollineaux prompted, and Daphne frowned.

'Of course not. Why would I?'

'Mrs Williams, do you think that your son's accident

really *was* an accident?' he asked softly, and saw her stiffen in shock.

'Of course I do,' Daphne said, and then paled as the realization hit her. 'You think someone *killed* Jimmy?' she whispered, aghast.

'In view of what happened the other night, I think it's a possibility,' he said, as gently as he could. 'Do you have any idea who might want either your son or Justin and Alicia Greer dead, Mrs Williams?'

But Daphne seemed hardly to be listening. Finally she shook her head. 'No,' she whispered. 'No, I don't.'

Mollineaux glanced at Jenny, who gave a very slight, almost imperceptible shrug. 'Well, I think that's all for now, Mrs Williams. We will, of course, keep this conversation strictly confidential,' he added. But as the housekeeper rose and walked on stiff legs to the door, he doubted whether she understood or appreciated his discretion.

Once the door closed behind her, the tension eased.

'I believed her,' Mollern said at last. 'About thinking her son died accidentally, I mean.'

Jenny stared at the empty fireplace, thinking furiously. 'If Jimmy Speight was having tea in the shed,' she eventually spoke her thoughts out loud, 'then he'd have had a clear view of the greenhouse.'

'And anyone who'd gone into it to steal some paraquat.' Mollern, quick as lightning, picked up the thread.

'Which means either a stranger,' Mollineaux continued, 'or someone from the village he knew.'

'Why a stranger?' Jenny asked, so quietly that it was almost a whisper.

Mollineaux shrugged. 'I can't see either Sherri or Mark Greer poisoning their own children. Justin is dead and Alicia nearly died. That leaves the staff. I can't see timid little Vera nor Martha Vaughan wanting to do away with Justin or Alicia.' His lips twisted wryly. 'And I refuse point blank to say that the butler did it. No. It had to be someone else. And Jimmy Speight saw who, and had to be silenced.'

Mollern scratched his head. 'Arbie Goulder wouldn't need to steal paraquat, having plenty of poisonous stuff at his own nursery. And Babs hadn't even arrived by then, nor had Watkins. I don't get it. The more we find out, the less clear this case becomes,' he said plaintively.

But Jenny didn't agree. It was becoming clearer by the moment.

'Well, thank you for your help with Mrs Williams,' Mollineaux said to Jenny. 'I know your presence helped us all through a difficult interview,' he added, in obvious dismissal.

Jenny smiled, took the hint, and left.

HAVING LEFT THE LIBRARY, however, Jenny didn't want to go to the kitchen to face Martha's self-righteousness after the morning's fracas. Instead she wandered about her room for a bit, generally feeling sorry for herself. Restless and unable to settle, she grabbed her bag and headed for the door, relieved to see that the hall was deserted. Outside, however, Mollineaux and Mollern had re-emerged and were standing on the porch, discussing tactics.

No doubt they'd settled Alicia down and asked their preliminary questions. She wondered what they'd found out, but knew better than to ask. 'Hello again. All finished?' she asked instead, bright and cheery and showing no signs of her previous strain.

'Yes,' Mollineaux agreed, as unforthcoming as she'd expected.

'Off somewhere?' she tried again.

'We thought we'd left Tom Banks to stew long enough,' Mollineaux commented mildly, not fooled by her delicate questioning, but not dissatisfied either. He was beginning to realize that Jenny Starling could be very useful, if you handled her right. 'No doubt, by now, he thinks he's missed the police net. It's about time we pointed out he hasn't. As a motive, his is as strong as any,' he added, unnecessarily.

'Hmm,' Jenny said thoughtfully. 'When you get there, ask him about the paper knife he stole from the library.'

'What?' It was Mollern who asked the startled question and Jenny sighed and dutifully related the events of the night of the party and her interruption of Tom Banks pursuing some, to say the least, enigmatic activities.

Mollineaux's face had grown more and more grim with every word she uttered. 'You should have told us all this before,' he snapped when she'd finished, and she had the grace to look a little abashed. However, she quickly rallied.

'Well, Inspector, if Justin had been found stabbed with a rather pretty, oriental-type paper knife, I no doubt would have done,' she parried neatly, and this time it was Mollineaux's turn to look discomfited. To cover it, he gave her a killing look and left the porch at a leisurely pace, heading towards their police car, parked out of sight on one of the long bends in the drive.

Jenny followed his lead without even thinking about it, Mollern bringing up the rear.

'Yes. We will definitely bring the paper knife up,' Mollineaux conceded. 'Not that I can see how the two incidents connect.' He paused and rubbed his chin wearily. 'I just don't see how the poisoning was done,' he said helplessly, his voice full of defeat. 'However it works out, I can't help but believe that the murderer, to get the poison to Justin and Alicia Greer, must have taken some incredible risks, and most of all with the other party's lives. It makes me shiver to even think it, but perhaps the killer didn't *care* if others died as well. Perhaps it was only luck, or divine providence, that steered the poisoned champagne so that it hit its intended target right away.'

For a long while the three people stood in silence, each contemplating that hideous thought. Eventually Mollineaux shook his head again. 'To take such a risk is beyond belief.'

Jenny, her eyes narrowed and her thoughts far away, slowly nodded. 'Yes,' she agreed thoughtfully. 'It was such a *desperate* risk to take. Quite, quite reckless in fact.'

Both the policemen looked at her quickly, struck by an identical thought. Namely, that Jenny Starling wasn't thinking along the same lines that they were. She seemed, in fact, to be thinking about something else entirely. And not just thinking, but *knowing*.

Tom Banks looked up from his paper as three short sharp raps came on the door. His wife looked up from the houseplant she was pruning and frowned, but made no attempt to answer it. With a sigh, Tom rose and went to the door and found himself face to face with officialdom.

'Mr Banks?' Mollineaux didn't wait for confirmation. 'I'm Inspector Mollineaux, and this is Sergeant Mollern. May we come in for a few moments? We're making routine inquiries about the murder of Justin Greer.'

'Oh, yes, of course. Come in.' He veered off to the left. 'Let's use the little front room, shall we?' he murmured. 'It gets the sun this time of year.'

Comfortably seated in an old but well-made armchair, Mollineaux nodded to his sergeant, who, less comfortably perched on the edge of a very low sofa, retrieved his note-book and pen. Tom Banks, standing nervously in front of the unlit fireplace, didn't seem to notice the policeman's telling gesture.

'Now, Mr Banks. You were invited to Mr Greer's party, more or less at the last minute, weren't you?' Mollineaux began nice and easy.

'That's right. I daresay Alicia never thought of it. Mark invited me.'

'That was nice of him,' Mollineaux agreed blandly, then added silkily, 'It was by way of a retirement fare-well, wasn't it?'

Tom Banks flushed. 'Yes.'

'You're fifty-five, aren't you, Mr Banks?'

'Yes.'

'A bit early to retire, isn't it?'

Tom began to fidget. He reached into his trouser pocket and withdrew a pipe, then stared at it, realizing he had nothing to light it with. 'Yes,' he finally agreed. 'When Mark's son took over the firm he started like a new broom. Mark thought a twenty-year-old whizz-kid was good for business,' he added grimly. 'And since he'd made enough personal money to enjoy an early retire-ment, well, that was that.'

Mollineaux tut-tutted sympathetically.

'Greer Textiles used to be a happy firm to work for.' Tom, obviously embittered, had the bit well and truly be-tween his teeth now. 'The workforce was well motivated and contented. Mark really knew how to run a company. But Justin, well, he only cared about making himself his own fortune. And it didn't seem to matter to him what he had to do to get it either.' He seemed to run out of steam momentarily, and Mollineaux watched him carefully.

'You didn't like Justin Greer, did you, Mr Banks?'

'No, I didn't,' Tom admitted readily enough, then suddenly looked up from his pipe, as if only now scenting danger. 'But I didn't kill him, if that's what you're thinking.'

'Do you do much gardening, Mr Banks?' Mollineaux changed the subject, not commenting one way or another on his declaration of innocence.

Tom blinked, totally wrong-footed. 'Huh? Er, no, I don't. That's Fran's province. She's in the sitting room now, as a matter of fact, tending to the houseplants. She loves to potter about in the garden. A result of spending all her time at home alone, I suppose,' he acknowledged, as if, for the first time in all their long years of marriage, wondering how his wife must have spent her time during all the hours he'd been at the office.

His statement had the unerring ring of truth in it, and Mollineaux and Mollern exchanged glances. Damn. No use asking *him* about paraquat then.

'I see. Tell me, Mr Banks, what were you doing rifling in the Greers' library on the night of the murder, and what, exactly, did you want with a paper knife? Come to that, what were you doing in Mr Justin Greer's bedroom? You were seen on both occasions,' Mollineaux added quickly, just to nip in the bud any blustering denials.

But Tom Banks didn't seem all that interested in denials. He shrugged his shoulders and put his pipe back into his pocket. 'It was bound to come out, I suppose,' he acknowledged with a heavy sigh. 'I was looking for evidence, Inspector. That's what I was doing in the library and in his bedroom.'

Both policemen perked up. 'Evidence of what?'

'Bribery and corruption,' Tom said starkly. 'I don't suppose you know much about the textile business, Inspector?' he asked, and Mollineaux had no trouble admitting that he didn't.

'Before Justin took over, Greers was a respectable firm, but not one of the top ones, and it wasn't making anywhere near enough money to suit Justin. Then, all of a sudden, we began landing prestigious orders. A new fancy hotel in London. A marquis of somewhere or other wanting the baronial pile re-fitted out. One or two huge forcign orders that had been rumoured to be heading towards top manufacturers, that kind of thing. Suddenly they were being landed by Greers.'

As the policemen continued to look blank, Tom Banks sighed angrily. 'Well, it's obvious, isn't it? Young Justin had to be giving out backhanders to somebody. He also had to have spies in the other camps to know exactly what offers were being tendered, and so undercut them. And where so much dodgy business was going on, there must have been records. Justin couldn't have kept it all in his head. The scandal if it had all come out! It was too much. I just couldn't stand by and do nothing.'

Tom began to look a little abashed now, and his next confession explained the uneasy look. 'I kept the paper knife, after I couldn't find any evidence in the library, in case I came across a strongbox in his bedroom. I thought I might be able to jemmy the lock.'

'I see,' Mollineaux said, straight-faced. 'And did you find any evidence in his bedroom, sir?'

'No. He must have kept it somewhere else. But not in his office—I'd searched that before leaving the company. Nobody could ever accuse Justin of being stupid, Inspector. He had his father well and truly bamboozled. If Mark had ever found out what he was up to...' Banks trailed off, suddenly looking like a very sad, old man. 'We worked for years together to make that firm a success. But the merchandise we're running off now is just miles and miles of cheap and nasty stuff.' He shuddered visibly. 'Oh, it's profitable all right. It makes the money. Mass market, and all of that. But our reputation as makers of fine carpets and blankets and materials is all but destroyed. And yet we're still pinching a lot of the prestigious contracts away from the top dogs. Although that'll all stop now that Mark's back in control, of course. I only hope he doesn't find out what his son was doing. That's what I'm hoping for now. It's bad enough as it is, with Justin being murdered I mean.'

He stopped abruptly, as if only now realizing that the man he'd been vilifying as a crook and a vandal had been summarily poisoned to death. Again he shook his head. 'But I didn't kill Justin Greer,' he said simply. 'I'm not a murderer.'

Mollineaux rather believed him. He was really rather a pathetic figure. 'Well, I don't see why Mark Greer should get to hear of your midnight escapades,' Mollineaux said, seeing the relief flood across Banks' grey and haggard face. 'No doubt he has enough to cope with as it is. You may be pleased to hear that his daughter has just returned from hospital.'

He watched the man closely, but Banks showed little reaction at all to the news of Alicia's return, except to give a brief smile of relief. 'Well, thank you, Mr Banks, that's all for the moment. You don't have any immediate plans to leave town, do you?'

Banks agreed that he hadn't, and showed them out. He shut the front door with a weary feeling of relief, and returned to the sitting room, prepared for a grilling by Fran. But his wife was nowhere in sight. He went through the open French windows and saw her on the lawn. Better get it over with, he supposed.

As he approached, he saw that she was wearing protective rubber gloves, and was making up a solution of something or other in a large bucket. As her husband walked towards her, Fran Banks poured a carefully measured dose of paraquat into the water.

JENNY HEARD THE overhead bell tinkle and looked up. She was in Meg's Tea Room, a tiny little establishment she'd discovered tucked away overlooking the village green. No doubt it was only open during the tourist season.

The tiny converted cottage had no more than four little tables crammed onto a meagre floor space, but they were covered with pretty red and white check tablecloths, and each housed a vase of freshly cut flowers. From the kitchen, where Jenny had instantly pointed her nose, came the smell of freshly baking scones and on the counter stood a large, china teapot. The teapot and the smell had induced her to stay.

She'd enjoyed the excellent tea and well-cooked scone in solitary splendour, and now she looked up at the sound of the bell, not particularly pleased to have company. Then she saw Margie Harding, looking dead on her feet in the doorway, and quickly changed her mind.

'Hello, Mrs Harding,' Jenny said pleasantly, and saw the woman's eyes widen as she recognized her. She began to make a U-turn, no doubt anxious to escape, when Meg emerged from the kitchen. She appeared to be eighty, if she was a day, but she bustled like a spring lamb, and there was steel in her slender frame.

'Hello, Margie. You look like you could do with a good cup of tea, my girl,' Meg said, more as an order than an observation, and disappeared back into the kitchen to start a new brew.

Surrendering to the inevitable, Margie came fully into

the room, glanced at Jenny, who smiled sympathetically back, and shrugged her thin shoulders. She joined the Junoesque cook at her table, slumping down with a complete lack of energy.

'Those policemen can be very thorough.' Jenny accurately assessed the reason for her inertia. 'If they asked me one question about the cooking I did for that damned party, they asked me a thousand. Honestly,' she grumbled chattily, 'how many times can you reassure a policeman that you always washed your hands after handling meat?'

Margie, for what seemed like the first time in years, felt her lips twitch. 'You think you had it bad...' she said wearily.

'Yes. Well, you were rather suspicious, worming your way into the party like that. I daresay the police thought it all very interesting,' Jenny pointed out reasonably, making it clear, straightaway, that she knew what she knew, and wasn't going to beat about the bush.

Margie gave her a startled look, then, seeing nothing but sympathy in the surprisingly beautiful blue eyes of the woman sat opposite, shrugged wearily. 'I needed to see him. I had to see him. It's as simple as that.'

Jenny sipped her tea. 'I know. But I don't suppose the police thought it was so simple.'

'No. They didn't.'

'And it was really bad luck that you should be the one to serve the champagne for the toast.'

Margie flushed angrily. 'You can say that again. I wish Will had served it. Or Martin. Anyone but me!'

'But you couldn't resist having a closer look at Alicia, I expect. Up close, I mean, hmm?' Jenny prompted softly, and Margie bit her lip and looked away.

After a moment, she looked back again. 'She didn't even recognize me,' she said, not denying the cook's

totally accurate guess, and her voice was low with remembered disbelief. 'All the times we met in the village
before she and Keith, well, you know, but for all those
times we bumped into each other, it just goes to show she
didn't even notice me. I was just another frumpy house-
wife to her—another little nobody. Not the beautiful lady
of the manor. Oh, no.'

Jenny ignored the understandable bitterness. It was
only to be expected. 'But Keith must surely have seen
you. Why didn't he stop you, or at the very least, take the
tray off you?'

'Why should he?' Margie asked, genuinely puzzled.
'He didn't know the wine was poisoned. *I* didn't know it
was poisoned. Though I'm not surprised someone other
than me wanted to kill her,' Margie carried on, her voice
dripping with spite now. 'You should have seen her that
night. Issuing orders like Napoleon, she was. Do this,
do that. Put that there. No, not there, *there*. I don't know
why she got that party co-ordinator in. She was always
interfering. Everything had to be exactly right. The cake
had to be brought in on the stroke of midnight, not a
minute later. The wine had to be opened for such and
such a length of time before serving. It had to be the
right temperature. She was an absolute bitch about it
all,' Margie said, her hands curling into tight fists as she
talked. 'I wouldn't have been at all surprised if the head
wine waiter hadn't done it, because she gave him hell. She
gave us all hell, treating us like slaves rather than cater-
ers. Even the head waiter said he'd never known a hostess so fussy. She hovered over all of us all night, like the
Wicked Witch of the West.'

She seemed to run out of bile at last, and Meg chose
that moment to come out with more tea. If she was surprised to see her two customers sitting together she didn't

show it. She simply set down another pot of tea on the table, glanced at Margie's pale and shaking frame and muttered something about soda bread doing the trick, and headed back to the kitchen.

'You shouldn't let hate sap you of all your energy, you know,' Jenny cautioned her at last. 'You never know when you may need it. Energy, that is, not hate.'

Margie, who'd obviously not taken on board a word of the good advice, absently stirred the spoon around her cup. At last, she looked up, her face pale and tight and oddly defiant. She met the cook's level-eyed gaze without flinching. 'I was sorry when her brother died, you know,' Margie said quietly. 'Not because I liked him—I didn't. But because he died and not her.'

Jenny nodded, not at all shocked by the other woman's statement. 'Yes,' she said enigmatically. 'I know.'

SEVENTEEN

MOLLINEAUX HAD JUST stepped into the hall with Tom Banks' words still rumbling around in his brain. They already knew that rumours had been circulating about Justin Greer's fast business practices, but there was a big difference between aggressive business tactics and *illegal* business tactics. Had Justin been knee-deep in bribery and corruption? And if so, could it be that there was a motive for his murder that they hadn't even thought of yet? A purely business-related motive? The thought worried him.

Who was most mixed up in the company business? Who would want Justin's illegal activities stopped at all costs? Who had the most to lose if Greer Textiles became embroiled in a legal scandal? Tom Banks was retired and in any case had only been an employee. That left the boy's father.

'Inspector? Sir?' The urgent voice of one of the young constables who manned the incident room interrupted his rather unsavoury line of thought. He looked up, a half-annoyed frown on his face. 'Telephone, sir. The lab boys,' the constable said quickly, sensing his superior's displeasure.

Mollineaux hurried forward, Mollern not far behind. The inspector headed straight for the desk, sitting down as he reached for the telephone. A few seconds later he was glad that he had, for the lab boys' news came as a distinct, if not to say nasty, shock. Mollern saw his face go slack in surprise.

'What?' Mollineaux croaked, then quickly cleared his throat. In a more normal tone of voice, he asked, 'Are you sure?' Mollern waited as the silence stretched out, and could feel his nerves doing the same. 'Are you sure you have all the corks?' Mollineaux asked next, and waited, tapping a finger absently against the base of the telephone as he listened. 'I see. Yes, I'm sure you are. All right. Thanks,' he added, not particularly sincerely, and hung up. He looked at his sergeant morosely. 'Well, that blows it. Damned if it doesn't.'

'Sir?'

Mollineaux leaned back in his chair and sighed heavily. 'This case is going to drive me insane,' he said wearily. 'Or to an early retirement, at any rate,' he added more moderately. 'That was the lab. They've checked all the corks under their microscopes, and guess what? Not one of them has a puncture hole of any sort.'

Mollern's jaw dropped. 'What? Not one of them? Then they must have missed one. A cork, I mean. There was a hell of a mess here that night. Empty bottles and party rubbish everywhere.'

Mollineaux shook his head. 'No, they checked. The number of the empties and full bottles tallied exactly with what was ordered for the party, and they definitely have all the corks accounted for. Besides which, the chief techno just gave me a lecture on cork markings. Apparently each cork was marked with a star or another symbol, denoting excellence. The best champers, of course, was kept for the toast. And not one of them had a puncture mark.'

Mollern sighed. 'And we thought we were lucky that

the waiters all had those popper things that get the corks out without the need for a corkscrew.'

Mollineaux sighed. 'That was Mark Greer's idea. He was worried that using a corkscrew might lead to bits of cork falling into the wine.' Mollineaux heaved a massive sigh. 'So what does it actually mean? Did our killer bring a spare cork to the party and pocket the punctured one?'

Mollern perked up instantly. 'Well, he must have done, sir, mustn't he? Otherwise why the needle? Our man really is a crafty one. You have to give him that. He thinks of everything.'

'Yes,' Mollineaux agreed heavily. 'And he's also lucky. He was damned lucky about that paraquat being so potent, or had he carefully planned it that way?'

'Sir?' Mollern asked, lost.

Mollineaux glanced at him, then made a vague gesture with his hand. 'Sorry, you weren't there when I got the facts from the science boys. Apparently paraquat burns the mouth when drunk, which was why it was put into cold champagne. But even more clever than that, it would normally take weeks for paraquat to kill somebody, according to the lab boys. But it seems that the poison used was extracted right from the bottom of an old bottle, where the sediment was most concentrated. Oh, the boffin came out with long, chemical phraseology for it, but with the upshot being that the paraquat that killed Justin was mutated stuff that killed almost immediately. And I was just wondering. Was it important for the killer that Justin died *quickly* or was it just that the killer happened to pick an old bottle, and using the needle meant that the dregs of the bottle were siphoned up by pure chance? See what I mean?'

Mollern did, but like his superior, had no answer to give. This new development also meant that the paraquat had now definitely come from the Greer greenhouse, and not from Arbie Goulder's nurseries.

Mollineaux rubbed his eyes and sighed. 'I don't like all this,' he finally said plaintively. 'Syringes and mysterious corks. We've got suspects coming out of our ears, not to mention Watkins. It's all just too much. I get the feeling that we've been manoeuvred, somehow, Mollern. Toyed with almost. And I don't like it. And I especially don't like Watkins.'

Both policemen fell silent as they savoured the possible delights of incarcerating, at last, the notorious Trevor Watkins.

'That's if he actually did it,' Mollineaux added gloomily. 'As it stands, I still haven't the foggiest idea what went on that night.' That thought seemed to trigger another, for he glanced quickly at his watch. 'Have you seen Miss Starling around?' he asked, hoping his voice sounded neutral.

Mollern shook his head. 'Not since this morning. She was off to the village, I think.' And he looked at his superior with sympathy.

JENNY WAS AT THAT very moment walking the last few steps up the tree-lined avenue and pausing for breath under the last shady lime tree. She looked at the house with disfavour. And The Beeches seemed such a nice pleasant place that first morning she had come here.

Automatically, she turned and headed for her sanctuary, the herb garden. Although Martha had banned her from the kitchen, stating fiercely that they would all be poisoned by one of her shepherd's pies, she could still, at least, walk among the basil and thyme and go over old recipes in her head. Which was always a soothing pastime. But she never, of course, actually made it. She was just passing the roses when a shadow moved and the rustle of parted bushes caused her to spin. Hackles rose up all the way along her spine.

She turned to face not the expected Trevor Watkins but Keith Harding instead. For a moment she simply looked at him, waiting. She was ready to scream, if absolutely necessary, and even use her impressive build to good effect as a last resort. She'd taken a self-defence course a few years ago, the instructor taking one white-faced look at her before putting on extra padding. And it had definitely come in handy from time to time.

But Keith Harding didn't look hysterical. In fact, he looked a little nervous. 'Hello, Miss Starling. I was hoping to catch up with you.'

Jenny relaxed slightly, and smiled politely. 'Oh?'

'Yes. I wanted to say sorry for what I said earlier. I mean, when I brought Alicia home I was… Well, I didn't want her to come back here at all, to be perfectly honest, and I was feeling upset. I wanted her to stay at the hospital, where she'd be safe.'

Jenny nodded. 'I'm sure you did,' she said blandly, but something in her voice made his chin rise, and all appeasement seemed to leave him. For a long while they continued to look at each other like a pair of wary cats. Eventually, Keith let himself relax a little.

'Inspector Mollineaux put us straight. About that last time, I mean—you being mixed up in murder and all that. I know now that you had nothing at all to do with your employer getting killed, and, well, I want to say sorry for…' He trailed off and shrugged helplessly.

'Threatening me?' Jenny suggested mildly.

'Yes.'

'Apology accepted.'

Keith blinked, surprised at her easy acceptance,

then rubbed his sweating hands on his trousers. He was dressed in simple black slacks and a white, V-necked pullover. Alicia's choice, she was sure. He was beginning to look as if he belonged in his environment, and she could almost see his past, working-class life slipping away from him. Soon he would wear tennis whites and learn to play. Probably well too, for he was athletically built. It all seemed so pathetic somehow.

'I saw Margie this morning,' she said bluntly, giving him no warning. 'In the tea shop actually,' she continued casually, and saw him wince.

'How is she?'

'Fine.' She positioned herself so that the sun was behind her and she could see his eyes clearly, before she next spoke. 'The police gave her a hard time.'

He tensed, then nodded. 'I daresay. She was the one who served the champagne toast.'

'Not exactly,' Jenny corrected him. 'She carried the tray. The wine waiter poured the actual drinks.'

'Oh. Yes, of course.'

He really is handsome, Jenny thought, utterly unbiased. She could quite see why Alicia would fall so hard for him. For, unlike many others around here, Jenny didn't for one instant doubt Alicia's sincere passion for her garage mechanic.

'You didn't...' Keith hesitated, then took a deep breath. 'You didn't happen to see the kids too, did you? Were they with her? Did they look all right?'

Jenny thought back to the two old biddies in the village shop, no doubt busily knitting their cardigans for the village 'unfortunates' and forcing Margie to accept their charity. She felt her heart harden. 'No,' she said abruptly. 'She was quite alone.'

Keith looked her straight in the eye. 'You think I'm a

right bastard, don't you, Miss Starling?' he said bleakly. 'But I love my children. I still, in a way, love my wife. I never wanted any of them to get hurt.'

Probably all very true, Jenny silently agreed. 'But they have been,' she said simply, and had the satisfaction of forcing him to drop his eyes. He hung his head to stare at his shoes. New shoes, Jenny noticed. Alicia wouldn't want his old dirty pair muddying the carpets in The Beeches.

His dark hair fell forward across his face, putting his eyes into shadow. 'I know,' he mumbled at last, 'but there's nothing I can do about it.'

Keith lifted his head at last and his face once again was absolutely resolute and Jenny sighed. People, and poets in particular, tended to think of love as noble, self-sacrificing and all-important. They often forgot how destructive it could also be.

'Anyway, I just wanted to say sorry,' he reiterated, no doubt anxious now to be away from her disapproving and uncomfortable presence. Like many before him, Keith was beginning to suspect that this strange, large-but-sexy and deeply enigmatic woman saw a whole lot more than you wanted her to. 'But I meant what I said, about protecting Alicia,' he warned her, and Jenny shrugged.

'I'm sure you did. And I rather suspect Inspector Mollineaux hopes you'll keep a special eye on our unwanted guest, Trevor Watkins.'

Keith's lips twisted. 'That creep I keep seeing around? Who is he, anyway? Mr Greer won't talk about him.'

'I'm not surprised. He owns nightclubs, casinos and, er, does various other things. Definitely crooked, is our Mr Watkins. Poor Sergeant Mollern practically drools whenever he's near. He can't wait to slip on the cuffs.'

Keith's handsome dark brows drew themselves together into a frown. 'But why does Mollineaux want him here? What was he doing at the party anyway?'

'Oh, I'm pretty sure Justin invited him. To play a prank on his sister.'

Keith's eyes darkened. 'What kind of prank?'

Jenny shrugged a masterfully nonchalant shrug. 'Oh, I daresay he just thought it was funny. With Alicia owing him so much money in gambling debts. I suppose…'

'Gambling debts?' Keith said, his voice and face totally stunned. 'Don't talk daft! Alicia doesn't gamble!' He began to look both exasperated and angry. 'Why do people always think the worst of her? Alicia has brains, you know, as well as beauty. She's too damned sensible to do anything so stupid as gamble. Oh, what's the use in talking to you?' Keith finally snapped. 'Everybody wants to the think the worst of her. They're just damned jealous, that's all it is.'

And with that, he turned and ploughed back through the rose bushes, oblivious to the thorns snagging his lovely white V-necked jumper.

Jenny watched him go with troubled eyes. Because, thinking about it now, she really rather believed him. Alicia *was* too smart to gamble. Gambling was a mug's game, and Alicia liked her high life too much to risk just chucking it away on a toss of the dice. In which case, Justin had got it all wrong about his sister.

So where did that leave her? And, more importantly, where did it leave Trevor Watkins?

'THERE SHE IS, SIR,' Mollern said, nodding in the direction of a garden seat that was nestled in a large hedge of box. Mollineaux nodded and set off across the lawn, wondering vaguely how old the box hedge must be. Centuries, he was sure. Didn't box grow really slowly?

Jenny, who had headed for the seat, shade and solitude in order to cogitate on Keith Harding's angry but probably accurate assessment of his love life, glanced up as the policemen drew level with her. Without waiting to be asked, she shifted herself along a bit, allowing them to sit, one either side of her.

'Good'—Mollineaux checked his watch, saw that it was five past twelve, and finished—'afternoon, Miss Starling. Did you enjoy your walk?'

'Yes, thank you. I went to the village and saw Margie Harding.'

Mollineaux nodded. Yet another promising suspect with a strong motive. He sighed. 'Did she have any fresh light to shed on the murder?' he asked, without much hope. He was beginning to think that the Greer case was going to be left on the 'unsolved' pile. Which was never good for a copper's chance of promotion.

Jenny said nothing. She was barely listening. She was sure, in fact she was absolutely *convinced,* that someone, at some time in the past, had said something vitally important, and she just couldn't for the life of her think what it was. No doubt it had been mentioned in passing by someone, and had seemed unimportant at the time. But she had the tantalizing feeling that it held the clue that would bring the whole intriguing puzzle into one sharply focused picture at last. But what was it? Who had said it? When?

Mollineaux, still waiting for an answer to his question, looked at her and instantly recognized someone who was deep in thought. He looked across to his sergeant, who waited placidly. 'We've had some rather interesting news from the labs. About the corks,' he said, burning the last of his bridges. If his chief ever found out he'd confided vital information to a suspect, he'd be finished.

Jenny knew it was no use trying to force a memory. She would simply have to wait until her subconscious chose to spit it out—whatever *it* was. She sighed deeply and leaned back against the slated wooden planks.

'The corks?' she echoed, trying to force her mind onto a different track, and eventually nodded. 'Oh, yes. The corks. I daresay they told you that none of them had a puncture mark,' she guessed offhandedly.

Mollern nearly fell off the end of the seat. Mollineaux simply stared at her. 'You knew that none of the corks would have been tampered with?' he asked at last, his voice a disbelieving squeak.

Jenny, still half lost in another world of thought, nodded vaguely. 'That's right. When I found out the syringe had been discovered in the bin under the wine table, I suspected that your theory was wrong—about somebody sneaking into the kitchen and injecting the paraquat into the champagne when it was still in the pantry, I mean.'

Suddenly, as if aware that the atmosphere had turned decidedly chilly, Jenny half-turned on the seat, and laid a consoling hand on Mollineaux's sleeve. 'Not that it wasn't a wonderful theory, of course,' she said, and could have added that the killer also expected the police to latch onto it. However (call her psychic), she didn't think Mollineaux was in the mood to know he'd been second-guessed by the murderer.

'Thank you,' Mollineaux said, through gritted teeth. 'So it was a good theory, but false. You, I'm sure, know how it actually *was* done?' he added, having little choice but to believe it. 'You wouldn't happen to know who the killer is as well, would you?' he added sarcastically, and Jenny, who was once again trying to capture that elusive memory, stirred.

'Hmm? What? Oh, yes,' she said, matter-of-factly. 'I've known who killed Justin for some time now. And how it was done. No, what really worries me,' she carried on, oblivious to the fact that two sets of jaws had practically hit the lawn either side of her, 'is *why it was done*. It has me absolutely baffled.' And she shook her head in frustration.

She paused, but still the memory that tantalized her refused to come. 'Strange, isn't it?' she mused, turning to Mollineaux again. 'Usually the motive is always the first thing you…figure…out…' Her words slowed and then trailed off as she became aware of his thunderous face.

She looked at Mollern and saw a similar rage in his own suet-like features. Hastily, she turned back to Mollineaux. 'But I thought that you *knew* as well,' she said, genuinely surprised. 'I mean, you've had access to all the evidence as well. And questioned all the suspects.'

Aware that she was being less than tactful, she stopped talking. 'Oh, dear,' she said. They really were still in the dark.

'Miss Starling,' Mollineaux took a deep, long-suffering breath and turned on her, feeling like a modern martyr.

'Yes, Inspector,' she said meekly.

'You will tell me, clearly and precisely and in detail, exactly how you suspect the murder was done, and by whom. Is that clear?'

'Yes, Inspector?' she said meekly.

'Right now!' he roared, making her jump.

So Jenny told him. Sheesh. He really was a grouse!

EIGHTEEN

JENNY CAME DOWN to breakfast the next morning feeling tense and on edge. She knew that Mollineaux and Mollern would return, either with the proof she expected or—just as conceivably—not. In which case she was wrong about everything, and would have to start all over again.

But she didn't think she *was* wrong.

The dining room was full and noisy, but as she pushed open the door and walked in, everyone fell silent. It did nothing at all to help her nerves. Then Mark smiled at her, and said pleasantly, 'Good morning, Jenny. Bacon?'

Jenny never said no to bacon.

At the far end of the table, Babs Walker leaned closer to Arbie and said something quietly into his ear. Arbie smiled. Next to her mother, Alicia watched Jenny with a rather petulant interest, but she soon found the spectacle of the hired cook helping herself to scrambled eggs, kidneys, bacon and fried tomatoes less than stimulating, and quickly turned to Keith. At the far end, with nobody sat next to him at all, was Trevor Watkins. He watched the cook with blank, unnerving eyes.

Jenny took a seat next to Mark, glad that Mollincaux had put him right about her real role in the murder of her previous employer. She turned to Sherri and said apologetically, 'I really would prefer to eat in the kitchen, but I'm afraid that Martha…' She trailed off helplessly, and shrugged.

Sherri smiled understandingly, and Jenny noticed with some relief that a little colour had returned to her face. But her hands, as she raised her teacup to her lips, still had an infinitesimal tremble.

Jenny poured herself a cup of tea and glanced across at Babs, who looked radiant in a dark-chocolate-coloured silk blouse and cream skirt. The ensemble showed off her blond hair and pansy-dark eyes to perfection. Her hand, Jenny noticed, was curled around Arbie's sleeve.

Arbie himself was the life and soul of the breakfast table. He chatted happily with Mark, who was obviously grateful for his presence, and together the two men cordially dissected the current political scene and the cricket scores.

Babs, from time to time, cast interested eyes in Trevor's direction. No doubt she'd learned who and what he was, and like a lot of silly women, was intrigued by the handsome 'bad boy' of the bunch. Not that Jenny was all that worried. Babs was far too mercenary to make a play for Watkins. It could only be a matter of time before he was the guest of one of Her Majesty's Prisons, and that would not suit Babs at all.

Jenny wondered what Margie Harding was doing at that moment. She wondered too how she would react when Mollineaux returned with his warrants. News would travel fast in a village the size of Rousham Green. She glanced quickly at Keith Harding, her eyes moving away the instant they turned in her direction. It was almost over. She could feel as much. And would she ever be glad to leave The Beeches behind.

Then she felt guilty as she thought of the devastation she'd be leaving in her wake. She glanced again at Sherri and wished she didn't look so frail. Then Jenny turned a rather different gaze onto Mark, who was arguing ami-

ably with Arbie about England's chances against Austra-
lia at Lord's. Jenny shook her head slightly and sighed.

The breakfast party broke up surprisingly quickly.
Babs and Arbie rose together, Arbie murmuring some-
thing about reading the papers in the lounge. Keith and
Alicia simply left, telling nobody where they were going.
And Jenny, not wishing to be left with Trevor Watkins
for any longer than need be, quickly followed suit.

Outside it was another warm day. The birds were singing, and as she stood indecisively on the porch, she saw a
blue tit with a beak full of insects head for a broken drain-
pipe near the kitchen drains, and disappear. A moment
later, with the food safely delivered to ever-hungry
chicks, it flew off again in a whirr of lemon, blue and
white feathers.

How idyllic it all seemed. And yet there was murder
here, betrayal and death. An ugliness that wasn't visible
but could, nevertheless, be felt. And a moment later, the
returning car of Mollineaux and Mollern turned up the
drive and pulled to a halt under the shady beeches.

Jenny didn't want to meet them. She wanted to go to
her herb garden and come out only after it was all over.
But she couldn't. She'd made a silent promise to Justin
that she would see his murderer punished.

With yet another sigh, she straightened her shoulders,
took a quick look around and, confident that nobody was
about, set off across the gravel. Mollineaux and Mollern,
she noticed, waited at the car for her, making no move to
meet her halfway. They too wanted to be out of earshot
of the house. Even before she reached them, she could
see in their faces that they'd been successful.

'You were right,' Mollineaux confirmed quietly as
soon as she joined them under the beech tree. Above
her, a slight breeze whispered in the leaves.

'It was where I thought it was?' she demanded, and Mollineaux nodded.

'It took us some time to find it. But yes, between us we tracked it down.'

Jenny nodded. 'And the man is willing to testify who he sold the needle to?' she asked, wanting to be sure of where they all stood.

Mollineaux nodded. 'No doubt of it. He made a positive identification from the photograph.'

Jenny sighed. 'Damn. Oh, damn. It's going to mean a life sentence, isn't it?' she asked wearily.

'Probably,' Mollineaux agreed. For a long while the party of three stood in the shade, listening to the beech and lime trees whisper around them.

'So,' Jenny said, making a determined effort to be practical, 'we have some physical proof, at least. You agree with me on how it was done?'

Mollineaux nodded. 'Now that you've explained it, we can't see how it could have been done any other way,' he agreed ruefully.

'Yes, but will a jury see it that way?' Jenny wondered. 'I'm still not happy about it all. If only I knew *why!* The picture just isn't complete yet.'

She didn't fail to notice the look that passed between the two policemen, and she lifted an eyebrow at Mollineaux.

'You've hit the hammer right on the nail head, Miss Starling,' he agreed. 'Without motive, we're missing a huge chunk in our case. And when we run it past our chief and the lawyers…' He shrugged expressively.

Jenny sighed heavily. 'Yes. I see your point.'

'It's not that we disagree with you,' Mollineaux hastened to add. 'Or that we're giving up. But we must have that motive.'

Jenny again nodded. 'The really irritating thing is, I'm sure that somebody, at some time, has already pointed it out to me, but I just can't quite get a hold of it. Oh, it makes me feel so stupid!'

Mollern allowed himself a smile. 'I can assure you, Miss Starling, you're definitely not that!'

Jenny gave a ladylike grunt of disbelief. 'So, what do we do now?' she asked Mollineaux, who spread his hands.

'Now that Mollern and I know where to concentrate our efforts, we'll do some serious digging. Who knows, perhaps we might actually earn our pay and come up with some answers for ourselves,' he added, just a shade bitterly. And together, the two policemen returned to the house, Jenny watching them go with troubled eyes.

AN HOUR OR SO LATER, it was as if Jenny had stepped into a twilight zone, courtesy of a strong sense of déjà vu.

After watching the slump-shouldered policemen disappear into the hall, she had turned straightaway for her herb garden to do some serious thinking. On the whole, it hadn't helped. Knowing who and how didn't equal knowing why. And she was so deep in thought that they were almost on top of her before she realized it.

From the gap in the hedge, the young, passionate voices catapulted her back in time to that first moment she'd heard them together.

'I'll be glad when all these policemen leave,' Alicia's voice, petulant but defiant, wafted on the rose-scented breeze and had Jenny's head snapping up.

'I won't,' Keith's voice came back. 'I feel safe with them around. If anything happened to you, I think I really would die.'

'Oh, Keith!'

There was a long, tender moment of silence, and Jenny had no difficulty at all in guessing what was happening just a few yards away on the other side of the green hedge. Quickly she stirred herself and stepped into the corner, withdrawing into the shadows and trying to shake off the cold shiver of déjà vu currently playing with her spine.

'Wasn't it funny, that fat cook turning out to be some sort of amateur sleuth?' Keith asked, and Jenny saw the hedge bulge. She could just picture him leaning against it, his handsome face creased in a smile, his smouldering eyes fixed on his love.

'Oh, don't remind me,' Alicia groaned. 'She must have watched too many of those Agatha Christie serials on television. I'll be so glad when everything's back to normal. It's all been so horrid. I just want peace again.'

'Peace?' Keith teased. 'I thought we were going to get married?'

'Won't that be peaceful, then?' Alicia purred a challenge, and Keith laughed.

'Hardly. Besides, we're going to have children, aren't we? Lots of tots.'

And what of Margie's children? Jenny couldn't help but wonder. It was all very well starting a new family to assuage the guilt and longing for offspring that obviously still plagued Keith Harding, but what of his first family?

'Well, I don't know about lots,' Alicia's voice laughed back. 'One or two, perhaps. I don't want a huge family, petal mine. That's so lower class.'

Keith laughed, but there was not much humour in it. 'I am lower class, Al,' he pointed out grimly. 'I like to watch football on a Saturday afternoon. I don't go in for all this so-called sophistication of your lot—all this playing around with booze and drugs. Playing your silly little upper-class games and then expecting your rich daddies to bail you out when it's time to face the consequences. I like eating sausage and mash, and being a man in my own home.'

'Well! A proper caveman, aren't you?' Alicia teased, but Jenny could detect just a touch of strain in that sweet and teasing voice. 'Come on, my big brave Neanderthal. Let's go to the summerhouse.'

'What? Now?' Keith sounded surprised, but allowed himself to be led away, and Jenny emerged from the shadows and stood in the bright sunlight.

At the back of her mind she felt a nibble. The nibble became a sting and then, in a flash, she heard again the passing remark that had been torturing her all night. And suddenly she knew.

For a while she simply stood still, running it all through her mind. And then she nodded.

MOLLINEAUX LOOKED UP as the door was opened without so much as a knock. The reprimand that was on his lips died when he saw that it was not some offending constable after all. He needed only one look at Jenny's face to feel his heart jump.

'You know, don't you?' he said simply, and Mollern, turning at the sound of his superior's voice, was just in time to see the cook nod.

'Yes. I do. And I want you to make out another arrest warrant.'

'Another one? You mean there was an accomplice?' Mollineaux was surprised.

Jenny lowered herself into the chair facing him and smiled. 'You're going to enjoy this, Inspector,' she promised. 'The warrant is for Trevor Watkins.'

Mollern wanted to whoop for joy, but instead he

reached for his notebook and began to scribble furiously as Jenny spoke in a quiet, tired voice. 'You can charge him with blackmail, for a start.'

Carefully and succinctly, she told the police the 'why'. When she'd finished, Mollineaux was silent for a long time. 'We'll have a hard time getting him to confess,' he said at last. 'Watkins is a tough nut. He won't crack.'

'Find the clinic then,' Jenny said bluntly, too tired now it was all over to even think about being tactful. 'Now you know what you're looking for, it shouldn't be hard.'

Mollineaux nodded. 'I agree. With the testimony of the doctor concerned, Watkins will have no choice but to really "help us with our inquiries".'

'Especially if you point out that a case could be made against him for accessory to murder,' Jenny pointed out.

Mollineaux frowned. 'From what you've told me, I'm not sure that it could.'

Jenny smiled. 'If it wasn't for Watkins, Inspector, Justin Greer would still be alive today. If you looked at it all in a certain way.'

Mollern smiled. He could look at it that way all right. But he doubted a jury would. Still, blackmail was a start.

'Right.' Mollineaux slapped his thighs with his hands and rose quickly. 'Back to London, Jack,' he said to Mollern, for the first time using the sergeant's first name. 'We've got work to do. And when we've found the doctor, we'll haul Watkins in.'

Mollern grinned. 'Yes, sir,' he said happily.

THEY CAME FOR WATKINS remarkably soon. Jenny had expected them to be gone for the day, but at 4.30 that afternoon they came back and very politely asked Trevor Watkins, who'd been playing patience with an infinitely bored expression on his face, to accompany them to the station. He very quickly stopped looking bored.

Only Jenny and Babs Walker, who both happened to be passing through the hall, saw them leave. Mollineaux gave Jenny a brief nod in passing, but didn't speak.

When she turned around, Babs Walker was staring at her intently. She looked like nothing more than a frightened little girl who was well out of her depth. Jenny smiled. 'Would you take a little advice, Miss Walker?'

Babs nodded wordlessly.

'Go home,' she said flatly. 'Go back to your mum and dad in their council house and find a job—' She stopped, seeing at once she was wasting her breath. Babs was already backing away and shaking her head. On the landing, above her, Arbie watched and smiled as Babs joined him, and together they disappeared into one of the bedrooms.

Jenny shrugged and turned for the kitchen. Some people just couldn't be helped. And Martha or no, she needed to bake something.

Anything.

IT WAS NEARLY SEVEN O'CLOCK when the police returned. Martha spared a few seconds out of her self-imposed task of watching every move Jenny made in order to look out of the window.

When she did, the old cook sighed deeply. 'Here they are again. They're coming and going like fiddlers' elbows today,' she commented, and Jenny, who'd just taken her fruitcake out of the oven, felt the room grow cold.

'Hello,' Martha said, her voice dropping an octave. 'There's a whole gaggle of 'em this time. Who's the fancy one in all that braid, Mr Chase?' she asked, and the butler quickly joined her by the window, not wanting to miss out on anything.

Jenny reached for a knife and with the utmost concentration, began to prise her cake from the tin. Nevertheless, she heard every word that was said.

Chase straightened. He knew top brass when he saw it. He moved quickly in order to answer the door on time, and as Jenny transferred her steaming cake onto the cooling tray, she heard their voices in the hall. Martha quickly shot up the stairs, anxious to earwig. Jenny gave her cake a morose look.

'You couldn't have taken another ten minutes to cook, could you?' she asked it balefully. Reluctantly, she too left the kitchen and trudged wearily up the few steps and out into the hall. There, the first person she saw was Mollineaux. He was stood next to his chief, and caught the cook's eye. Jenny leaned against the open kitchen door and waited, a feeling of dread settling over her.

But it had had to be done, of course.

Chase, sensing something momentous was about to happen, quickly disappeared into the drawing room and emerged a few moments later with Mark and Sherri Greer.

'Mr Greer,' Mollineaux said, his voice heavy with the weight of authority. 'This is Detective Chief Superintendent Wainwright.'

The chief, used to power, nodded at the prominent businessman, just as a door opened above. Babs Walker and Arbie emerged onto the landing and peered down at the scene. Nervously, Babs grabbed her companion's sleeve and hung on, tight.

Just then, a sudden tinkle of light laughter cut across the scene, the sound so unexpected and so shockingly inappropriate that nearly everybody winced. Out of the dining room came Alicia Greer and Keith Harding, both dressed for dinner. Alicia was wearing a mint-green dress that floated around her like angel wings. Keith looked awesomely handsome in a black, tailored evening jacket. They both stopped dead at the scene awaiting them.

The atmosphere became so oppressive that Jenny saw Martha put a hand to her throat, as if she had difficulty breathing, and Jenny knew how she felt.

Mollineaux took a step towards the beautiful couple standing together. As he moved, he withdrew a long, white, stiff-papered document from his jacket pocket.

'I have a warrant for your arrest,' he said, his voice loud and portentous, his eyes fixed on their target.

Keith Harding took a step back, as if he'd been physically punched. He opened his mouth. 'What…?' But he had no opportunity to say anything more, for Mollineaux was upon them. He reached out and something silver flashed in his hands, and everybody stared. It was a pair of handcuffs.

'Alicia Justine Greer, I arrest you for the murder of your brother, Justin Mark Greer, on the night of May the—'

'No!' The strangled, howling scream came not from the lady herself, but from Keith, who launched himself at Mollineaux, knocking the man away. Mollern was there like a flash, his bullish strength easily manhandling the thrashing and hysterical younger man away. 'Take it easy, son,' he said soothingly, but nobody believed Keith actually heard him.

He was staring at Mollineaux who, now free, quickly slipped the cuffs onto Alicia's white, shaking hands. Alicia, Jenny noticed, wasn't even looking at the policeman arresting her. Instead she watched Keith struggling helplessly against Mollern's steely grip, her eyes dazed and disbelieving. Mutely, she shook her head.

Keith, at last, grew still. He stared into her large, tear-filled blue eyes, and Jenny saw the knowledge finally hit him. He seemed to crumple. The hall was deathly silent.

Finally, Mark Greer's voice croaked out of him. He said only one word.

'Alicia?'

But Alicia didn't answer. There was nothing, really, that Alicia could say.

NINETEEN

JENNY WALKED SLOWLY down the stairs, her suitcase in hand. The hall was quiet and empty, with no echo of the dramatic scene that had been played out only a few hours before. Now it dozed in the early evening mellowness. The grandfather clock ticked ponderously, the only sound to be heard.

Alicia had been taken away, and Keith had gone with her, as had her parents. Jenny could imagine Chase and Martha in the kitchen, sitting in numb silence, sipping tea and trying not to meet each other's eyes. Jenny had no idea where Daphne was, and made her way to the door feeling a little bit like a thief stealing away in the middle of night.

She opened the large doors and stood for a few moments, looking around. Then she sighed, straightened her back and closed the door firmly behind her. Most definitely time to leave.

But as she took her first step away from The Beeches and towards her van, a car pulled up the drive and swept around the curve, pulling to a halt in front of her. Jenny watched as Mollineaux and Mollern wearily climbed out.

'Inspector,' Jenny said, stowing away her case into the van. 'I hope you have no objection to my leaving now?'

Mollineaux shook his silvered head and smiled. 'None at all, Miss Starling.'

'How are Mark and Sherri?' she asked quietly.

'They're bearing up as best they can. They don't believe she did it, of course. And they're bringing in some fancy lawyers.'

Jenny nodded. 'Of course.'

'She won't get away with it though.' Mollineaux sounded confident. 'That's why the chief is doing all the processing now. He wants his face in the papers. He wouldn't be so keen to be involved unless he knew we had a good enough case for a conviction. No, she'll be indicted for killing her brother all right. But we aren't so sure about our chances of convicting her for Jimmy Speight's murder,' he admitted grimly. 'That's why we made no mention of it when we arrested her. It'll be a matter for the CPS to decide whether or not the prosecutor goes for a double-murder trial.'

'She did kill him though,' Jenny said quietly. 'I'm sure of it. Poor Jimmy couldn't have resisted spying on her when he saw her come down to the greenhouse so early in the morning. It was well known that Alicia wasn't an early riser.'

'And with his "journalistic" instincts aroused, he'd have crept along to see what she was up to,' Mollineaux agreed, almost picturing in his mind how it must have happened. 'And wondered why she'd injected a hypodermic with paraquat.'

'And Alicia saw him spying. Which meant she'd have had no other choice but to kill him,' Jenny agreed. 'Because when her brother died of paraquat poisoning a day later, well, little Jimmy Speight would have been able to point the finger right at her.'

Mollineaux nodded. 'I imagine it was a simple matter for her to lure him onto the bridge. For a woman of her looks and abilities, she could easily have come up with some excuse.'

'And, of course, although poor Jimmy must have been

curious, he wouldn't have had any reason, then, to be in mortal fear of his life. Besides, men never do think they have to fear women, do they?' Jenny swept on sadly. 'But Alicia could have "accidentally" broken off the branch, laughed about her clumsiness, and then whacked him over the head with it before he even knew what was happening.'

'I agree that's how it almost certainly happened,' Mollineaux agreed. 'But whether it'll come out at the trial or not…' He shrugged helplessly.

Jenny nodded, not wanting to dwell on it. 'Well, I'd better be off, I suppose.' She opened the door to her van and Mollineaux looked at her with a mixture of amusement and frustration.

'Damn it, Miss Starling. Just how did you *know* Alicia was our killer? I mean, what made you think of it all? Work it all out, I mean?'

Jenny shrugged helplessly. 'Well, it was more or less obvious right from the start that it had to be Alicia,' she said, then hesitated as she heard Mollern give a rather disbelieving snort.

Knowing this could take some time, Jenny tried to marshal her thoughts into some sort of reasonable order. 'Right from the beginning, I had to ask myself, *who* was the most likely person to have orchestrated the poisoning? Who had the most chances to arrange it all? And the only person who came to mind was either Alicia or the party co-ordinator. But why would a party co-ordinator want to poison her customers?'

She glanced at the two men. 'Think about it,' she urged them quickly. 'Who hired me in the first place? Alicia. And why, specifically, would she want me to cater the party?' Jenny shrugged. 'I think it could only have been because she'd read about me in the papers all those months ago, and knew I'd been mixed up in murder.'

'So you thought she wanted you there for a sort of warped moral support?' Mollineaux asked, puzzled, and Jenny snorted.

'Hardly! She wanted me there to be a prime suspect. A cook with a reputation for murdering people! What better distraction could there be for her? Whilst people were looking askance at me, who would think of looking at her? But of course, I wasn't the only one she had set up. She invited Arbie Goulder for exactly the same reason. He had a glaring motive for wanting Justin dead. And that was another thing that made me suspect her,' she continued. 'It just didn't add up with Alicia's almost manic desire to make the party perfect for her brother.'

Mollern grunted. 'That's what gives me the creeps. Her pretending to throw the best birthday party ever, just so she could kill him.'

Jenny frowned. 'I rather think, you know,' she said quietly, 'that Alicia really *did* want the party to be the best ever. I think she went to so much trouble to make it the happiest day of his life, just because she *was* going to kill him. In her own twisted way, Sergeant, I think she actually loved her brother. And she wanted his last day to be perfect.'

This time, Mollineaux shivered at the thought. 'You think she's mad, then?'

But Jenny quickly shook her head. 'Oh, no, Inspector, not mad. Just utterly selfish. She loved her brother, but with him dead, she knew the company would have to come to her one day. Of course she'd have sold it right away, with a big portion going to Trevor Watkins to keep him silent. But that was as far as her magnanimity went.

Justin was doomed, I think, from the moment she met Keith Harding.'

For a while they were all silent, until Mollern shifted restlessly. 'I still don't see why you were so sure.'

'Oh, there were lots of other little things as well,' Jenny said quickly.

'Such as?' Mollineaux asked, anxious to know. He'd just watched this woman solve a most baffling case, and he badly wanted to know how she'd done it.

'Well, for a start, there was the way she avoided going into the kitchen on the morning of the party,' the big cook said, and seeing their blank gazes, went on to explain, 'When the champagne was delivered, she knew that eventually, if all went according to her plan, anyone who had entered that kitchen would be a suspect. That's why she deliberately sent Arbie down, to give him the supposed opportunity to poison the champagne. At the same time, she had to make absolutely certain that everybody knew that she had *not* gone down, thereby putting her in the clear.' Jenny paused for breath and thought back. 'Yes, that was very clever. I asked her twice, you see, to come into the kitchen—to look at the cake and so on—and both times she practically ran in the opposite direction. That's why she was so angry when she learned that Keith had volunteered to help with the wine, because it would later point the finger of suspicion at him, who also had a motive for wanting Justin out of the way. Something she had never intended to happen.'

Mollineaux nodded. So simple—now that it was pointed out to him. 'Anything else?' he asked, and Jenny nodded.

'The way she ran the party,' the cook continued. 'She went way over what was to be expected of a conscientious hostess and hardly necessary, since her father was paying the party co-ordinator an exorbitant amount, just to make sure that everything ran smoothly. The wine waiter, Georges, and all the rest of the staff told us that very first night when you interviewed us all together, that it was Alicia herself who'd timed the arrival of the birthday cake. Later, we found out it was Alicia who insisted that the wines be uncorked five minutes before pouring. And, of course, it was Alicia who insisted that the wine and champagne be put in the kitchen in the first place. Why, I wondered, did she object to them going into the wine cellar? Good catering staff could tell wine that had been racked for years from crates that were newly arrived.'

Jenny shook her head. 'No. All along, it was Alicia who had the best opportunity to organize the crime. And then there were the less obvious clues, such as her personality.'

Neither policeman felt comfortable when it came to dealing with the psychological aspects of cases. But they listened attentively, nonetheless.

'Right from the start, it was obvious how much Alicia loved money and the easy life,' Jenny pointed out, prosaically enough. 'It was also obvious that, for some reason or other, she never seemed to have much money herself. She had to scrounge off her own brother to buy herself a new dress for the party, for instance. She cadged her jewels off her mother, and even tried to persuade Sherri to hand over to her the gems on a permanent basis. She'd got her father to buy a house for herself and Keith Harding once they were married, and since she could so obviously wind her father around her little finger, it was obvious that Mark gave her a very generous allowance as well. So I had to ask myself—where did all her money go? She'd even sold her fancy car and brought a very modest little runaround, and that must have gone very much against the grain for someone like her.'

Jenny smiled a little grimly. 'At first, I believed Justin when he said that she'd lost it all gambling. But Keith Harding himself pointed out that Alicia was much too clever for that.'

Jenny cleared her throat, wishing she'd thought to have a long, cool drink before leaving. All this talking was making her throat dry.

'Alicia was certainly clever all right,' she soldiered on gamely. 'But she was also inherently lazy. So why, I had to ask myself, did this idle, selfish, rich little girl want her brother's party to be so perfect that she felt compelled to do so much work herself? It just didn't fit in with Alicia's selfish personality. And that was another arrow that pointed straight at her.'

For a while she remained silent, letting the policemen assimilate her thinking. At last, Mollineaux nodded, silently admitting that she had a point. Policemen tended to go for the certainties—motive, opportunity and evidence. Now he could admit that he should also have taken personality into consideration. Once again, now that it was pointed out to him, it all seemed so obvious.

'So you had a good general idea it was Alicia,' Mollineaux said. 'But suspicion is one thing. How did you get from there to producing the evidence for us? That hypodermic, for instance. We found the love-nest hotel Alicia and Keith shared by showing their photos around and using a little discretion. And from there we found the big new chemist shop. Oh, yes, I know.'

Mollineaux raised a hand as Jenny was about to speak. 'I know that you overheard Alicia and her mother talking about this big chemist shop she went to. And I can see—just—how you came to believe that she must have bought the hypodermic needle there.'

Mollineaux, too, was forced to pause for breath, and he shook his head helplessly. 'But I still don't understand how you worked out the actual mechanics of how the murder was done.'

'Ahh, that,' Jenny said thoughtfully. 'Oh, that was because of the needle, Inspector.'

'But you knew it hadn't been injected into the corks,' Mollineaux said, sounding just a little exasperated now.

'Oh, it wasn't what it was used *for,* Inspector,' Jenny explained gently, 'but where it was *found* that made it all so clear.' Then, seeing only two sets of blank eyes looking back at her, she sighed. 'Don't you see? The moment I heard that a hypodermic needle that had contained paraquat had been found in a bin in the ballroom, I immediately asked myself a very simple question. Why?'

'Why?' It was Mollern who echoed her, his large moon-shaped face totally baffled.

'Exactly,' Jenny said. 'Why? Say the killer had injected the champagne through the cork, as we were meant to think. *As Alicia intended us all to think.* Why would the killer then take the needle into the ballroom and throw it into the bin? If the poisoning had been done in the afternoon before the party had started, the killer would have had ample time to get rid of it, wouldn't he? He could have buried it in the garden, or thrown it in the lake—it would never have been found then. Or simply have taken it home with him and put it in the bin. But no. The killer had all these opportunities to get rid of the evidence, and what does he do? He puts it in the bin in the ballroom under the champagne table, where the police were bound to find it.'

'I get it,' Mollern said, realization dawning. 'Alicia wanted it found.'

Jenny smiled gently. 'Well, not exactly, Sergeant. I think she left it in the bin mainly because *she had no other choice*. She actually injected the poison into the champagne at the party, not through the cork earlier, as you thought. And, of course, once she'd done that, she had no other choice but to get rid of the needle, the vital evidence, as soon as possible. Which meant then and there, in the ballroom. Because, you see, of all the people there, *only Alicia Greer never had the opportunity to get rid of it anywhere else!* People surrounded her all the time. And then she was taken to hospital afterwards, where the police or a nurse would have been bound to find the needle had she slipped it into her handbag.' Jenny looked from one to the other of them. 'Don't you see? Of all the people in that ballroom, she alone was the only one who would have had no opportunity to get rid of the needle after the deed was done. Thus it was found in the bin. As soon as I knew that, I was sure it was Alicia.'

Mollern sighed gently. 'That's really breathtaking, Miss Starling. Almost as breathtaking as when you told us how she did it. The actual poisoning, I mean.'

'Oh, that.' Jenny dismissed that piece of deduction with a wave of her hand. 'But you see, only Alicia could have done it that way. You see, the wine waiters told us that Alicia gave the signal for all the guests' glasses to be filled for the toast. And it was Alicia who had the cake brought in when only she herself and Justin were the last to be served. And she was stood right by the wine table, ready and in position when the lights went out, to poison the champagne. And, luckily for her, all the main suspects were also close by. Arbie, Trevor Watkins, even Margie Harding, although Alicia knew nothing about her at the

time. The actual poisoning was simple. All the guests had
their glasses full, so there was no danger of any of them
getting a dose of the poisoned bottle by mistake. The cake
came in on her signal, and the lights went out. Everyone
remarked how dark it was, and nobody's eyesight had
time to adjust from the bright glare to the sudden loss
of light. That included Alicia's own eyesight of course,
hence the needle. She'd had the wine waiters open the
champagne bottle for herself and Justin a few minutes
in advance, so it was already open and waiting. In the
darkness she couldn't possibly have poured in the paraquat from a little vial, for she was as blind as the others,
and it would have been too messy and hit-and-miss. But
with a hypodermic it was easy. All she had to do was feel
for the opening of the bottle with her fingers, carefully
insert the needle tip inside the neck of the bottle, push
the plunger, toss the hypodermic into the bin—a bin, in-
cidentally, which she'd had placed there—and Bob's your
uncle. The lights come back on, and there's the poisoned
bottle of champagne, all innocent and waiting. And no
chance of getting a full set of fingerprints either, from
off just the rim of the bottle.'

Jenny took a deep breath. 'The wine waiter said he
chose the bottle at random, and no doubt he thought he
had. But picture the scene—the host and hostess need
their glasses filled. Standing on the table, no doubt a little
bit in front of all the others, was this newly opened and
very expensive bottle of champagne. Of course he picked
that one.'

The two men, enthralled by her narrative, allowed
themselves to relax. 'So poor Margie Harding, being in
the wrong place at the wrong time, received the poisoned
drinks from the wine waiter and gave them to Justin and
Alicia in all innocence,' Mollineaux finished.

Jenny nodded then noticed Mollern frown. 'Something wrong, Sergeant?'

Mollern scratched just below his left ear and sighed. 'I just can't get over the way Alicia Greer took a swallow of that drink, Miss Starling. Knowing that it was poisoned, I mean,' he said at last, and Jenny nodded.

'Yes, I know. It was such a desperate risk to take,' she agreed, which made Mollineaux glanced at her quickly. So *that's* what she meant, he thought with a smile, remembering the time they'd talked about the risks the killer had taken. He and Mollern were talking about the risk they thought the murderer must have taken to poison the wine. Only Jenny Starling was thinking about the risk Alicia had taken in taking a sip of the champagne she knew to contain paraquat.

'I daresay she only took a tiny sip,' Mollineaux said.

'Yes,' Jenny agreed. 'Still, I wouldn't have done it.' She shuddered. 'But what really had me worried was the why of it all. Why did she kill her brother? She was short of money, yes, but she was getting by. She could always squeeze what she wanted from either of her parents or Justin himself for that matter. They all indulged her. Cars, houses, jewels. No, there had to be a definite reason *why* Justin had to die. And I just couldn't see what it was.'

'But you finally figured it out,' Mollern said quickly.

'Hmm. Eventually,' she agreed ruefully. 'And it was Keith who told me, though I'm sure he didn't mean to. When he pointed out so confidently that Alicia didn't gamble, I had to think of another reason. And I was sure it still involved Trevor Watkins. That argument they had at the party was surely significant. As was the way Watkins came so meekly to stay at the house. I knew he would never have put himself in the middle of a murder investigation unless he was looking out for his own interests. But what were they? And then I heard Keith talking about having children, and I realized just how old-fashioned he really was. If you ignored his single aberration of falling in love with Alicia, what did you have left? A hardworking, simple man, who loved his wife and kids. And Alicia, who loved him devotedly, knew him better than anyone, of course.'

'I still don't see...' Mollineaux began and Jenny smiled.

'Neither did I, till I remembered something Martha had said. Yes, Martha, of all people.' Jenny allowed herself a slight smile at the irony of it. 'When she was talking to Vera about Trevor Watkins's reputation, she mentioned the fact that he organized discreet abortions. Nowadays you need the consent of two doctors to have an abortion, and they're mostly granted on the grounds of the woman's mental health. But I'm sure if you ask around you'll find that the Greers' family doctor is the kind of man who disapproves of abortion, the kind who'd make it as hard as possible for his patients to go down that route. And Alicia would know how easily a rumour could start, especially in a small community like this. So she'd have to go to someone who could arrange it all very quietly. Two tame doctors who'd agree to it, and a clinic far, far away, was what she needed, and the deed was done. And so, suddenly, it all made sense. Keith Harding was hardly likely to have been Alicia's first lover. Even in this day and age, birth control isn't a hundred per cent effective all the time. Her mother and father, though appalled, would forgive her if Trevor Watkins had told them that their precious daughter had had an abortion, and Alicia and Watkins both knew it. But when Alicia fell in love with Keith, who had kids of his own, well, then it all changed.

Alicia knew Keith would find the thought of abortion totally unacceptable. He might not be able to forgive her
an abortion, and she simply wasn't willing to take that
chance.'

'And so Watkins began to blackmail her,' Mollineaux
finished. 'No doubt he realized right away who must have
murdered Justin and why. With Justin dead, she was the
main heir.'

'Exactly,' Jenny said. 'I always knew that man was
aware of much more than he was letting on.'

'I can see why Alicia couldn't risk Keith finding out
about the abortion,' Mollineaux agreed, rubbing his chin
thoughtfully. 'But why not kill Watkins, instead of her
own brother? It would have saved her from having to
pay off blackmail for the rest of her life. And if, as you
think, she really did love her brother after all, howbeit in
a twisted sort of way, why not kill Watkins instead?'

Jenny sighed. 'I'm sure she would much have preferred
to, Inspector, but how could she have managed it?' She
shrugged graphically. 'Watkins is a crook, with an animal's canniness. No doubt he was also surrounded by
minders down in London. How could she kill him and get
away with it? Buy a gun? From where, and how to shoot
him without getting caught? She could hardly attack him
with a knife in a dark alley. No. She needed an environment where she could stack the odds in her favour. After
all, getting caught and spending her life locked away
from Keith was definitely not in her plans. She couldn't
arrange to kill Watkins. But her brother, Justin, right here
on her home ground, and with all the time in the world
to think out a plan, and be in a position to arrange it all,
that was different. That was doable.'

Mollern, who'd listened to all this with growing horror,

said gruffly, 'So Justin Greer died just because he *could* be murdered?'

Jenny heaved a heavy sigh and nodded. 'That's about the size of it, Sergeant. Alicia must have her darling Keith, and she must have money. With Justin gone, she believed she would have both.'

'And so she might,' Mollineaux said grimly, 'if not for you. And to think, that day she came home from hospital, I actually wondered if she might be in some danger.' Mollineaux smiled. 'I just don't know how to thank you, Miss Starling,' he said softly, and held out his hand.

'Please, call me Jenny,' she said cheerfully.

Mollineaux nodded and glanced at her van. 'So, where are you off to now?'

Jenny shrugged. 'I've no idea. But I expect I'll find somewhere to lay my head,' she said airily.

'You mean you don't even know where you're going next?' Mollern asked, sounding appalled at the thought.

'Not at the moment,' she agreed. 'I'll stop at the first good hotel that comes along. There's bound to be a job for a good cook somewhere. There aren't that many of us about, you know,' she informed them seriously.

Saying a final goodbye, the two policemen walked over to their car, got in and drove away. She gave them a wave as they went and was just about to get into her van when she paused, spying a grey form perched on the wall with its back to her. Very stealthily tip-toeing up, she used her height to peer over the stone wall. As she suspected, there was a nice soft lawn on the other side. Very quickly she planted a hand firmly on the cat's unsuspecting back, and gave a firm but gentle push.

The cat gave a muffled 'meumphhh' (not having either

the time or the breath to let out a good bellowing miaow) and disappeared over the wall.

Jenny Starling smiled, climbed into her van and drove off into the evening sunshine.

* * * * *

REQUEST YOUR FREE BOOKS!

2 FREE NOVELS
PLUS 2 FREE GIFTS!

WORLDWIDE LIBRARY®
Your Partner in Crime

YES! Please send me 2 FREE novels from the Worldwide Library® series and my 2 FREE gifts (gifts are worth about $10). After receiving them if I don't wish to receive any more books, I can return the shipping statement marked "cancel." If I don't cancel, I will receive 4 brand-new novels every month and be billed just $5.24 per book in the U.S. or $6.24 per book in Canada. That's a saving of at least 34% off the cover price. It's quite a bargain! Shipping and handling is just 50¢ per book in the U.S. and 75¢ per book in Canada.* I understand that accepting the 2 free books and gifts places me under no obligation to buy anything. I can always return a shipment and cancel at any time. Even if I never buy another book, the two free books and gifts are mine to keep forever.

414/424 WDN FEJ3

Name _____ (PLEASE PRINT) _____

Address _____ Apt. # _____

City _____ State/Prov. _____ Zip/Postal Code _____

Signature (if under 18, a parent or guardian must sign) _____

Mail to the **Reader Service:**
IN U.S.A.: P.O. Box 1867, Buffalo, NY 14240-1867
IN CANADA: P.O. Box 609, Fort Erie, Ontario L2A 5X3

Not valid for current subscribers to the Worldwide Library series.

Want to try two free books from another line?
Call 1-800-873-8635 or visit www.ReaderService.com.

* Terms and prices subject to change without notice. Prices do not include applicable taxes. Sales tax applicable in N.Y. Canadian residents will be charged applicable taxes. Offer not valid in Quebec. This offer is limited to one order per household. All orders subject to credit approval. Credit or debit balances in a customer's account(s) may be offset by any other outstanding balance owed by or to the customer. Please allow 4 to 6 weeks for delivery. Offer available while quantities last.

Your Privacy—The Reader Service is committed to protecting your privacy. Our Privacy Policy is available online at www.ReaderService.com or upon request from the Reader Service.

We make a portion of our mailing list available to reputable third parties that offer products we believe may interest you. If you prefer that we not exchange your name with third parties, or if you wish to clarify or modify your communication preferences, please visit us at www.ReaderService.com/consumerchoice or write to us at Reader Service Preference Service, P.O. Box 9062, Buffalo, NY 14269. Include your complete name and address.

WWLI1B